Wedding Belles

Also by Beth Albright

THE SASSY BELLES

Watch for the next book in The Sassy Belles series
SLEIGH BELLES
Coming soon from Harlequin MIRA

BETH ALBRIGHT

Wedding Belles

HARLEQUIN® MIRA®

Recycling programs
for this product may
not exist in your area.

ISBN-13: 978-0-7783-1529-2

WEDDING BELLES

For questions and comments about the quality of this book, please contact us at
CustomerService@Harlequin.com.

Printed in U.S.A.

First printing: August 2013
10 9 8 7 6 5 4 3 2 1

For my beautiful, precious Susan: an angel who walks among us. You are an inspiration for us all.

For Brooks and Ted, my universe.

1

I still can't believe Myra Jean, the trailer park psychic, was right about everything! We wouldn't have even talked to the psychic in the first place if Vivi hadn't insisted on a reading as her wedding present. I mean, really, who asks for a visit with the town clairvoyant as a serious wedding gift from her matron of honor? And matron of honor would be me: Blake O'Hara Heart, attorney and lifelong best friend of the bride.

It all blew up after Vivi hung up from the "sample reading" phone call with Myra Jean. We were sitting in Vivi's kitchen at the oversized oak table that took up most of the room. She lived on a gorgeous plantation that had been in her family for generations. It was hot as hell in the middle of a Tuscaloosa summer. The air outside felt as if a dog were breathing on your face. *Sweltering* is too mild a word to describe the Deep South in early August. Still, nothing was hotter than Vivi's temper at the moment—and with a redhead, that's usually a dangerous thing.

"What the hell does Myra Jean mean, there's another woman?" Vivi slammed her hand on the table, fixin' to pitch a bridal hissy fit, which is actually in a category between hissy fit and conniption fit. Much worse than a plain ol' hissy, but not all day long like a conniption.

I watched Vivi jump up and start pacing. The sample reading had only been five minutes long, but Miss Myra Jean had given Vivi an earful, and it was enough to get her fuming. She blew a bright red curl from her eyes in frustration. Vivi Ann McFadden has been at war with her mop of red, wiry hair since childhood, always pushing it from her face or fighting with relentless tangles. But it looked striking against her year-round sheet-white skin. And she had sparkling emerald-green eyes, which she consistently paired with the reddest lips. I always thought she was just beautiful. She and I were best friends and true Sassy Belles. We'd made our little club called The Sassy Belles way back in junior high. We even had a motto: *Be sassy, classy and a tad smart-assy.* We'd done a pretty good job upholding that motto ever since, and considered ourselves Sassy Belle sisters in every way—except in the looks department. I'm taller by an inch—all of five foot four—brunette and busty and tan. My eyes are blue-green just like my grandmother's. But I love Vivi like she's my own flesh and blood. And I hated to see her upset like this, especially with her big day on the way.

In less than two months, Vivi was getting married to the love of her life, the Alabama Crimson Tide's star football announcer and my brother-in-law, Lewis Heart. She was due to have a full, proper psychic reading at her bridal-baby-bash shower later this month—yes, it was a combo shower since the bride would be nearly seven months pregnant at her wedding. She had thought it would be fun for everyone to have a reading as part of the shower festivities, but if this was Vivi's reaction to the sample, I knew we were in trouble.

Vivi stopped pacing long enough to get two glasses down from the cabinet and slam them on the counter. "I can't wait till my shower to see what else that woman has to say."

"Honey," I said, "she's all booked up till then."

"Well, she's just gonna have to unbook somebody." Vivi yanked open the refrigerator, whipped some ice into the glasses, then sloshed some tea on top. Some of the tea even made it into the glass. "I won't sleep a wink till I know what the hell she's talking about."

Vivi tore off a couple of mint sprigs from her plant in the kitchen window like she was ripping off Lewis's limbs. "He wouldn't do this to me," she said, slam-dunking the sprigs into our glasses. And I had to agree, after all these two lovebirds had been through, it was hard to imagine Lewis being unfaithful. I hadn't always been his biggest cheerleader, though. When he and my husband, Harry, had their falling-out years ago, I took Harry's side immediately. I'd spent years viewing Lewis through Harry's eyes, but I'd learned recently what a mistake that had been. It took a long time for me to realize just how jaded Harry was, but now that we'd separated, I'd finally begun to think for myself again. And that's when I began to see what a good man Lewis really was.

"This other woman... Maybe it's the baby," I said, trying to throw something out there that would settle Vivi down. "You've been saying all along that you just know it's gonna be a girl. Maybe Miss Myra Jean is talking about *that* other woman—your baby girl."

"A woman and a baby are two different things." Vivi sat at the table and crumpled up a cloth napkin before finally exhaling. "Oh, you're probably right. It's gotta be the baby. What other female would my Lewis have in his life besides me..."

Vivi's voice trailed off and she looked out the huge kitchen window above the sink. She didn't look completely convinced, and, in my heart, I wasn't so sure I was right. I was just hoping Vivi could get past this news from the reading. Otherwise, that's where her mind would be till she got her answer—and right now I needed her mind on better things.

See, in the Deep South, women can wring your neck, hug your neck and bless your heart all in the same day. So I was hopeful we'd be moving away from the whole "wring your neck" mood pretty quickly. At least if she'd just say, "that ol' Myra Jean—bless her heart," then I'd know she was moving past this. I tried to change the subject.

"You know these psychics, Vivi," I said. "They always word things in the most mysterious ways—and most of it's just a bunch of malarkey anyway. Besides, we've got so much else to think about right now. I have a conference with some new clients later this afternoon, but first I'm off to meet up with the Fru Fru Affair boys to plan your shower. It's gonna be quite the shindig. They're just full of ideas and are so looking forward to doing your wedding, too." I was trying to get Vivi's mind on something other than the psychic, but I've known her for twenty-five years and she was not about to let this little bombshell go.

"But, Blake, Miss Myra said there *is* another woman involved. *Is.* That means current, like *now*. I'm going crazy." Vivi took a sip of tea, then got up to grab the phone. "I'm gonna call Lewis and ask what he thinks. I'm sure he can explain all this."

Oh, Lord, please don't let him answer. I crossed my fingers under the table. My prayer was answered. Lewis didn't pick up. Vivi left a message and sat back down, ready to chew on the subject some more.

"I love you, Vivi, but I have to run. Don't worry," I said. I knew that was like telling the Pope not to be Catholic.

I kissed her cheek. "Everything's gonna be fine. I promise. Lewis loves you like he's never loved anyone. You know that. I'm sure it's just the baby. And *is* would be the word the psychic used 'cause that baby *is* on the way. She's alive and kicking. I felt her myself."

"Don't forget you're meetin' me at the courthouse later to witness us getting our wedding license. Oh, Blake, I'm so excited I can hardly stand it."

"I'll be there, sweetie, wouldn't miss that for the world." The wedding was only a couple of months away, but it already looked like it might be the longest two months of my life.

I grabbed my purse and headed out the front door to my car, waving to Arthur, the gardener and Vivi's longtime friend. He waved back with a smile. Arthur had lived with Vivi's family on the planation since Vivi was a child. They'd always been close, but now that her father had passed away and her mother was living out at Splendor Acres retirement home, Arthur was the closest thing Vivi had to family out at the plantation. Over the summer, Arthur had been building a barbecue business on the side property, getting it ready for the Alabama Crimson Tide kickoff game on the first of September. That would be here before we knew it.

I drove down the gravel drive to the plantation gates and headed to my grandmother Meridee's house, thinking all the while about Miss Myra Jean's comments.

Heaven help us, they just couldn't be true. Sure, Lewis did have a reputation as a ladies' man. After all, he was tall and masculine, with wavy dark hair and adorable dimples, and his blue eyes were just too gorgeous to belong to a man. Women love his confidence and flirty personality, but it was clear to all of us that he really loved Vivi.

But between managing the wedding planning and an emotionally high-strung pregnant bride, I was beginning to feel like a ringmaster overseeing a three-ring circus gone wild. And now, because of Vivi's meltdown, I was probably going to be late to meet with the event planning dream team.

Coco and Jean-Pierre, who we'd hired to plan the wedding and shower, were meeting with me at Meridee's about Vivi's upcoming bridal-baby-bash. They owned an event planning and catering business called A Fru Fru Affair, and their choice of a company name pretty much summed up their fun flamboyant personalities.

In high school, they were known as Craig and John-Paul, but in the process of launching their business, they decided they needed something with a little more style. Now almost no one called them by their given names except for my grandmother Meridee and my mother, Kitty, who had both known the boys since they were children.

Coco and Jean-Pierre always disagreed about taste and style, but somehow, in the end, they would pull off the most amazing events. Some of their ideas were totally off the wall. Like the time they wanted the groom to skydive into the ceremony...but his aim was a tad off and he ended up in the Warrior River. Another time they threw a Tarzan-themed wedding and the bride was supposed to swing in on a vine. She hit the minister by mistake. Vivi's dream was much simpler— and a whole lot safer. She only wanted to be a princess, and it was my job to make sure they didn't have her ride down the aisle bareback.

A pregnant woman should *not* be on a horse.

Yet even with this meeting to keep me occupied, I had to admit, I couldn't stop thinking about this other woman the psychic mentioned. I had known Miss Myra Jean most of my life and, strange as it may seem, she was usually right...in her own special way.

Well, I told myself for the hundredth time, *Vivi is getting her wedding license in just a few hours and then the other woman, whoever she is, won't matter.* I kept repeating that, but somehow I wasn't totally convinced.

I arrived before Coco and Jean-Pierre, entering the kitchen where Meridee was standing in her apron at the stove, humming "Summertime." I felt that instant sedative that always kicks in the second I enter Meridee's house and see her busy making something delicious to eat. Being here always settled my nerves, no matter what was going on.

"Hey, Nanny." (*Hey* is the way we greet each other down South. I can't remember anybody ever saying *Hi*. And *hey* is almost always followed by a hug, unless you're a man.) I leaned in and hugged her hello. She smiled and kissed my cheek just as the Fru Frus rang the doorbell.

"Hey, baby girl," Coco called, then shot me an air kiss as he stepped inside. He took in my red pencil skirt, sleeveless navy blouse and white pearls. "You are rockin' the patriotic look big-time today."

He hugged me, then stepped back. "Are you wearing MAC Red Ruby Woo lipstick?"

Stunned, I nodded my head.

"I knew it. That is the best 1940s red I have ever seen."

Jean-Pierre walked in right behind Coco. "Oh, precious, that red, white and blue outfit is so *summer,* so *July,* so *America,* so...future senator's wife."

Cringing a bit, I hugged Jean-Pierre, too. Harry's run for senator was exactly the reason we'd kept our separation a secret. Despite our differences, I still wanted to support Harry through this major turning point in his career. And I knew how difficult it would be for him to present himself as Senate material with nasty divorce gossip spreading all over town. We'd decided not to announce anything about our split until after the election. And that meant suffering quietly through awkward moments like this one.

He inhaled deeply. "Miss Dior perfume. Heavenly," he said all singsongy.

He hugged Meridee next. "Oh, my, and you are wearing Charles of the Ritz. I am inspired by you already."

They were a sight for sure, both of them tall and skinny and immaculately dressed. Coco had long sandy hair and beautiful ocean-blue eyes. He had an angular jaw and a wide, warm megawatt smile. He was so tan. He loved wearing bright-colored skinny jeans and striped short-sleeved shirts. He usually wore a long knotted scarf around his neck and a beret on his head. He just loved his namesake, Coco Chanel. And French was his style in a nutshell.

Jean-Pierre was a little more understated. He had long spiky dark hair and green eyes. His clothes were usually less flashy, but still fashionable. Today he wore skinny black jeans and a dark dress shirt with the sleeves rolled up, his arms full of books and planning agendas. He looked more studious in his black thick-rimmed glasses. He was sarcastic and dry, while Coco was more quick and funny and much louder.

Coco scanned the room, looking beyond the doorway, as well. "Is this the venue for the big double event? We can work with this, sugar! So much space."

"We can even use the big yard outside," Jean-Pierre said.

My grandmother laughed. "Oh, gosh, honey, not outside unless you want big ol' mosquito bites all over our momma-bride. That yard is a feeding ground this time of year!"

"She sure would be a sight," Coco said. "I hear welts are the new black."

Jean-Pierre smiled. "Very funny. Indoors it is. What are we talking about for space?"

"Mostly the living room, kitchen and dining room," I said. "Meridee has given us the go-ahead to decorate anything we want. We should talk about the shower theme, though. I want it to be really fun."

"Honey, there's no way it won't be a blast," Coco reassured me. "I've already come up with an invitation idea. Picture this…" He gestured as if reading from a theater marquee. "The Bride We Are Lovin' Has a Bun in the Oven. Don't y'all just love that?" Coco was so proud of himself.

Meridee stood in the living room doorway, her eyes bugging out of her head.

"Oh, my, we'll have to talk about that a bit later," I said, trying to be nice. "That theme might need a few revisions."

"Can we run down and see the basement?" Jean-Pierre said. "We wanna party all over this house."

We all headed downstairs. This had been my playground every rainy day of my childhood, back when the Ouija board was at the height of its popularity. It was a tad musty down there, but it still had the old pool table, TV set and a big octagon-shaped wooden card table. Bookcases lined the wall to the left as you entered the main room. The basement held a lot of memories for me, but I don't think the boys were too impressed.

"Oh, dear, that smell might be an issue," Jean-Pierre said, his nose crinkled with distaste.

"Sometimes it gets damp down here," I explained.

"Well, since the theme isn't Mildew Madness, I think we need to stay upstairs," Jean-Pierre said, shaking his head and leading the way back to the main floor.

Meridee directed us into the kitchen. She had fixed coffee and iced tea and put out some mini coffee cakes she'd just pulled out of the oven. "Watch out. These are hot. Have a seat and help yourself. Don't be shy."

"Oh, Miss Meridee, you shouldn't have gone to so much trouble," Jean-Pierre said, taking a seat next to Coco at the yellow laminate table. "But, honey, I am so glad you did."

"My word, everything sure does smell delish." Coco took a bite of the coffee cake. "Mmm, wonderful. Thanks for letting us use your lovely home for this very unique event."

"My pleasure, y'all. Miss Vivi is like a granddaughter to me. She grew up in this house almost as much as did my Blake. I will do whatever y'all need." Meridee poured herself a fresh cup of coffee and walked over to the sink to wash the coffee cake pans.

"Okay, down to business," I said. "I want this event to feel extra special to Vivi, like she is a princess for the day."

Jean-Pierre grabbed his notebook. "Okay, a princess bride and baby momma combo. Got it. We can have a lot of fun with all the games and activities this way." He jotted down a few notes, then peered over his glasses. "Anything else you want to throw into the mix?"

Meridee spoke up from the sink. "I thought y'all were goin' down to see Miss Myra Jean for Vivi's shower."

"Oh, Nanny, I haven't had a chance to tell them about the

psychic yet." I would have used a little more tact, seeing as
they were the ones planning the shower.

"A psychic?" Jean-Pierre asked slowly.

I cringed. They were a classy company. They even had
swans planned for the wedding. Swans! I wasn't sure where a
psychic would fit in with an affair planned by guys who considered swans and string quartets essential to an event's success.

"Yes," Meridee went on. "My dear old friend Myra Jean
does readings and talks to spirits. We're gonna take all the girls
down to see her. Isn't that gonna be fun?"

"Seriously?" Jean-Pierre was already frazzled. He stood up
and walked around the table. "Does this visit to the tarot card
lady or whatever she is really need to be part of the shower?
I just don't know if it will fit in with—"

"It surely does," Meridee insisted. "And Myra Jean only uses
tarot cards sometimes. Besides, Vivi is the one who decided
it would be fun for everyone at her shower to have a reading.
She believes in Miss Myra's gifts."

Yes, Vivi did believe what Myra said, and I just hoped that
her shower day predictions didn't trigger a homicide attempt
on the hubby/daddy-to-be.

Jean-Pierre glanced at me, a bit exasperated. "Can't you do
anything to stop this?"

"Not likely," I said. "The readings are her wedding gift
from me."

His mouth dropped open in horror, as if I'd shattered his
former belief in my exquisite taste.

"Don't look at me like that," I protested. "Vivi asked for
this and I just want my best friend to be happy. That is my
job, after all. I *am* her matron of honor."

"Okay, then," Jean-Pierre said, throwing up his hands.
"We'll put group mystic reading on the list. The day *is* all
about Vivi, after all."

"Oh, I just love the whole idea!" Coco stood up and began moving around excitedly. "I always wanted to have a reading myself. It sounds like a teetotal hoot and a half." He leaned over to a grumpy Jean-Pierre and linked one arm with his. "Hand me my ruby slippers, honey, we're off to see the wizard!"

I smiled at his enthusiasm, relieved to have at least one of them on board with the idea. I was just hoping the "other woman" the psychic spoke of didn't turn out to be the Wicked Witch of the West.

3

That afternoon I met Vivi at the courthouse, and Lewis was waiting there on the sidewalk with his soon-to-be bride.

"I am so excited I can't even think," she said. "Can you believe Lewis and I are going to get our marriage license?" She was exuberant.

"Hey, Blake, thanks for coming and being a witness to history," Lewis said as he gave me a hug.

"Wouldn't miss this for the world," I said, smiling at them.

"Hey, baby," Vivi said, turning to face Lewis. "Did you know that the psychic this morning said there was another woman in this little domestic portrait we're painting?" Vivi threw it out there just like that. Completely out of nowhere, without giving either of us a warning. I should've expected something like this. She'd been so upset this morning, and she was probably stewing on it all day long while I was with the planners. Looking at her now, I could tell she couldn't take the worrying anymore. She needed to get this out of the way as soon as possible. Of course, Lewis was stunned.

"What?" he said, confused at the sudden turn in the conversation. "Another woman? Hell, ain't nobody but you, Red. Nobody for me but you." He gave her a reassuring smile.

"Aww, sugar." The relief in Vivi's face was obvious. "I love you. But that psychic did give me a scare. She's usually right about the things she sees, but I couldn't believe it when she suggested you'd been cheatin'. Blake says she's probably picking up vibes from the baby. *She's* the other woman," Vivi said as she patted her stomach. She gazed up at Lewis and smiled. "I mean, I just know it's a she."

"I'm sure that's it. And besides, I've already told you I've never trusted those psychics. They just make things up to keep you comin' back for more." Lewis helped Vivi up the courthouse steps and into the lobby of the beautiful old building.

"Here I go. Oh, Blake, I can't stand it, I'm so excited, I'm gonna burst."

"Honey, let's hope not." If this was how she felt picking up the license, we'd likely need to give her medication on her wedding day. We went inside and followed the signs down to the marriage license office.

As we walked through the door, Lewis stopped and held Vivi in front of him. "I love you, Red. Today's our day," he said with a grin. "We're gonna be official. I am so happy, baby." He leaned down and planted quite a kiss on her.

She blushed right up to her red-haired roots, then smoothed her dress over her five-month baby bump and laughed. "I'm so nervous. I changed clothes six times."

"Well, you look gorgeous. Let's do this." Lewis was just as excited as she was.

We approached the lady at the counter. She looked to be around fifty-five, with straight brown hair cut in a severe bob.

She scanned Vivi's burgeoning belly. "Oh, honey, I'm sorry, you must have the wrong room. This is the office to apply for a wedding license."

"And what the hell makes you think I'm in the wrong room?" Vivi snapped, but her eyes were smiling. She loved toying with people.

The lady looked down at Vivi's tummy. "Well, I just, um…"

"Yes, I am pregnant *and* I am wearin' white at the wedding, too." Vivi was loving this. "Now can I apply for my marriage license, please?"

"To each his own. You can work out those details with your minister," the woman said with disinterest. "Y'all got your information ready to go?"

"It's all right here." Vivi handed over her paperwork.

"And how about you, sir?"

Lewis was grinning like I had never seen him before. His face was flushed with joy as he lay down his documents. "Never been more ready than I am today."

The lady studied the information and typed all the appropriate answers into the computer on the counter. After a few moments of awkward silence, she frowned at the screen and then cleared her throat.

"Well, sir, I'm not so sure about that. I think you may have been a little more ready about thirteen years ago," the woman said, clicking a few more keys. She looked up at him. "The great state of Alabama frowns on bigamy, and you, sir, are already married. By the way, aren't you our play-by-play announcer? Roll Tide." She smiled.

"Wait. Already what? Did you just say my fiancé is already married?" Vivi repeated in shock.

"There is no damn way!" Lewis was livid, his face turning a blotchy red.

"This is a mistake," Vivi said, her voice rising. "I have

known him for every one of those thirteen years and he has never been married!" She was about to pitch a full-out conniption fit right here in the courthouse.

"Ma'am, I have never been engaged, much less married," Lewis insisted. "A person would know that, I think."

"Well, sir. This is your birth certificate. This is your social security number. It matches all the information you just gave me, right down to the signature. This wedding certificate belongs to you, alrighty." She printed out a copy and handed it over to let Vivi and Lewis read it for themselves. "As you can see, Mr. Lewis Heart married Miss Tressa Mae Hartman in April of 1999. I have no record of a dissolution of marriage."

Vivi turned white as a ghost and leaned into me. I held her up and walked her over to the bench just outside the room. I was fanning her with some pamphlet I had picked up, and she looked about ready to faint.

Lewis followed us, holding the evidence in his hand, his mouth still dropped open. "There is just no way in this world, no way," he said again. "This can't be real. I know it can't."

"Get me some water, quick," I said. "Vivi's gonna pass out."

"Where's the water? Where?" Lewis went into panic mode.

Great, I thought. *Now they're both flippin' out.*

"Oh, I see it." He ran down the little hallway in his slick dress shoes, heading for the watercooler, when he wiped out completely and landed on his back. I could hear the breath leaving his body from twenty feet away.

Vivi was crying and muttering, "No, no, no." She didn't even see him fall.

"Lewis, oh, my God, are you okay?" I asked.

"Fine," he groaned, stumbling to his feet. "I'll get that water now." He made his way hurriedly toward the watercooler down the hall, his dress shoes still slipping on the newly waxed vinyl floor of the Tuscaloosa courthouse.

He grabbed some pointy paper cups, filled two of them and ran back to us, sloshing water all over his chest and slip-sliding as he came. He was a mess.

"Here you go, baby." He gave Vivi one cup. She was still hyperventilating.

"Lewis Heart, please tell me this is a mistake," she begged.

"I swear, I can explain."

"Explain? Oh, my good God in heaven!"

Vivi jumped up, turning beet-red, looking like she was ready to wring his neck. She faced him down with her hands on her hips. "You mean to tell me this is *true?* You're married for real? Oh, for Christ's sake, Lewis, why haven't you ever told me?"

She dropped back down on the bench, then leaned over onto me and began sobbing. "Why, Lewis? Oh, my God, why? We don't have time for you to get a divorce before our wedding. It's all over. I won't have my wedding day, and I'm gonna have to birth this baby as an unwed mother."

"Oh, honey," he said, getting down on one knee in front of her. "Let me tell you all about it."

"Yes," I said, "I, for one, am interested in the whole sordid story." I scowled down at him. My mind was racing. All this time I'd truly believed he was devoted to Vivi, but this news had thrown us for a loop. And this was my best friend we were talking about. There was no way I was gonna let this ass get off easy for hurting my Vivi.

Lewis clutched Vivi's hands. "Okay, here goes. I sorta remember this."

He had to be kidding. *Sorta?*

"Lewis, you gotta do better than that," I said. Vivi's head still lay on my chest, and my arms were wrapped around her protectively.

"I was, like, twenty-one, and we had this thing at my fraternity," he began.

"This *thing?*" Vivi asked, finally sitting up.

"Well, we were all a bit drunk and someone teased somebody else that he was too chickenshit to get married. Things kind of went on from there, until the brothers at the frat decided to perform a fake wedding ceremony with our chaplain. So this dancer chick, Tressa was her name—"

"Yes, we heard," I interrupted.

"Well, Tressa offered to be the bride and give a lap dance to the lucky groom."

"Seriously?" Vivi snapped. "You took her up on that?"

"I was a kid! And I was drunk. I'm not saying it's the best decision I ever made, but you know how I was back then. The wild one, the daredevil. We all had a bet that no one would go through with it, and I finally volunteered."

"Always some sort of horny man bet. I hate that. We never behaved that way in college." Vivi folded her arms and huffed. The truth was, we'd gotten in our own sort of trouble back then, but I wasn't about to remind her now.

"Well," Lewis went on, "I figured this guy was pretending to be a chaplain and fake-married us, or so I thought. He had us sign some joke certificate they'd drawn up and everyone toasted us. Then, she gave me my...uh...dance, and I left. I never saw her again." Lewis was up pacing and shaking his head. "I thought it was all a big joke, but I guess the chaplain turned the papers in. He must have been a real preacher—and what he was doing at that party I will never understand. My God, I just can't believe..." He sank down on the bench next to Vivi and covered his face with his hands.

"But that means... Well, this Tressa probably has no idea y'all are married, either," I said, putting my lawyer hat on. "I do know one thing, though," I added, looking at Vivi. "She's not staying married."

The two of them sat there in shock, trying to process the mud slide that had just knocked us off our feet.

"We have to find this woman," I insisted.

"And what are we gonna do when we find her?" Vivi asked. "Show up and tell her, 'Hey, you've been secretly married to the love of my life for thirteen years and, sorry, but we sorta need an annulment today. Just sign on the dotted line. Okay?' Something tells me that won't go over very well."

I cringed, since that was basically my plan. "Look, I'll see what I can find out about her, and then I'll get back in touch with y'all. Go on to your meeting, Lewis, and we will call you later."

"Vivi, you gotta believe me," begged Lewis. "I love you! I don't even remember what this girl looks like. It was so long ago, and it was a frat party, and I was twenty-one and stupid. Believe me, Red, I love only you."

"I know you do, Lewis." Vivi sighed. "I know it. Blake will help us. Right, Blake?"

Uh, yeah, I thought, nodding and smiling. *Just tack it on to the list after "Plan the perfect double shower" and "Tackle the wedding of Vivi's dreams." No big deal.*

But I knew that Vivi needed me and I wasn't about to let her down. And I think it's safe to say that Miss Myra Jean has a gift, for we most certainly had found the other woman.

4

Vivi and I flew back to her house, not even caring about the speed limit. We had a serious appointment with Google on my laptop.

We went inside, and Vivi got the going-to-war food of cookies and iced tea, while I ran up and grabbed my computer. After a couple of hours of snooping, I located one Tressa Mae Hartman in Birmingham, Alabama. Her age matched the woman we were looking for, and when we clicked on images after entering her name, we both nearly fell out of our chairs.

The picture that popped up on my screen was of a woman in her early thirties, brassy reddish-blond hair, frosted lips and a pound of eye shadow in shiny blue. Her pink cheeks made her look like the Little Drummer Boy, and she was wearing a bedazzled string bikini in camouflage...with a beeper from about 1990 attached to her hip. She was pointing at the camera like her finger was a pistol.

Vivi and I were physically unable to close our mouths. For several seconds.

I broke through my shocked stupor first. "Wow, I sure as hell thought Lewis had better taste than that, bless her heart."

Vivi shook her head. "I'd say she's had a nip and tuck and then some."

"I didn't even know implants came in those sizes," I mused. "Surely they're not real. How does she even stay upright?"

"Somehow, I don't think upright is her favorite position," Vivi groused.

"Now, Vivi, come on…" I chided, but I couldn't hold back the fit of giggles that burst out of me. Once we'd managed to get our breaths back, Vivi turned back to the screen.

"It says here she's a bar singer. And who names her kid after a shampoo, anyway?"

"I do believe there's a bar singer in Birmingham who's fixin' to get the surprise of her life," I said. "We're gonna have us a road trip."

My cell phone rang. It was Sonny Bartholomew, Tuscaloosa's chief homicide investigator, my old high-school sweetheart and now full-time man of my dreams. As with the news of my separation, I'd been trying my best to keep my deepening relationship with Sonny under wraps while Harry was running for Senate, because, well, news of the candidate's wife embroiled in a smokin'-hot love affair with the chief of Homicide doesn't really help the campaign.

But the minute that election was over, my life would begin again.

"Hey, handsome," I said. "I hope you're having a better day than we are."

"Well, it's a hard day for a cop, too. We're at the boat, and we've turned up some pretty substantial evidence on the Walter Aaron case."

"Oh, my God, Sonny, I forgot to tell you. I have a meeting with them in just a few minutes!"

"What's going on?" he asked.

"Well, it's a bit much to go into over the phone. If you're going to be at the river for a while, I could meet you after the Aarons leave."

"Okay, beautiful, I'll be here." He hung up.

I loved how Sonny treated me. I know he couldn't go into a lot of detail on an ongoing case, but, as much as it was allowed, he was willing to mix business with pleasure. He was able to work with me on some things, but he never demanded all the credit for something that I discovered. He always let me shine, too. So completely different from Harry.

"Vivi, sweetie, I gotta run out to the river for this case I'm working on. You and Lewis are still okay as far as time to file for the wedding license goes. We will get this girl to sign the annulment papers, and everything will be all right. I promise. We'll go up to Birmingham as soon as we can. Just hang on tight. I'll call you later." It was already late in the day and I still had my real job to get to.

I arrived at my office and parked in the back, as usual. Heat rose up in shimmering waves from the pavement. I hated to leave the cold air-conditioning of my car even for the few seconds it would take to walk inside.

"Hey, Wanda Jo. I'm here," I said to our secretary as I entered.

Harry and I own our little practice together. I had always dreamed of having a husband who could be my partner on every level. Harry was that, and more, when we first opened our office. Now, years later, we barely qualified as reluctant roommates who occasionally inhabited the same space.

"Y'all talk to the mystic this mornin'?" Wanda Jo asked as she brought in my Diet Coke.

"The psychic? Yes, and Vivi is beside herself." I took a swig of my ice-cold drink.

"Oh, no, what did Myra Jean say? Is it bad news?" Wanda Jo stopped in front of my desk and looked at me.

"She said when it comes to Vivi's marriage, there is another woman involved."

"Oh, my Lord have mercy." Wanda Jo sighed and sat herself down in one of my consultation chairs. "You know, I hate to say it, but Lewis was wild in his younger days. He's changed, though, I thought, and he loves that Vivi so much."

"I know. I told Vivi maybe she was having a girl and *that* was what Myra Jean meant."

"Did she buy it?"

"Of course not. And guess what? We just went to the courthouse to get their wedding license and it turns out that Lewis is still married!"

Wanda Jo jumped from the chair. "Oh, my God, what do you mean *still*? That boy ain't never been married far as I know."

"Well, yeah, as far as he knew, too—until he remembered a college prank where he married a stripper as part of a joke."

"Oh, Blake, that poor Vivi. What are y'all gonna do now?"

"Well, I'm gonna pay her a little visit as soon as I can."

"Vivi is so lucky to have you." Wanda Jo smiled at me.

"We'll get this fixed and then we're gonna have us a wedding to beat all weddings," I said, smiling back at her, hoping I was right.

"Okay, then. I'll let you know when the Aarons get here, and then I'm gonna put on the police scanner and listen for news of any new dead bodies."

I looked at her in confusion. "Dead bodies?"

"Well," Wanda Jo said with a smirk, "if Lewis can't get this marriage annulled, it really might be him this time."

5

Wayne and Wynona Aaron arrived right on time. Wanda Jo got everyone drinks and we headed into the conference room. The Aarons' third sibling, Walter, had been killed in a barge accident two months ago and his body parts had washed up on the banks of the Black Warrior River. My cop, Sonny, always believed Walter was *helped* off that barge, but the barge company was trying to say he jumped. Sonny and his assistant homicide investigator, Bonita, were on the case like CSI, looking for clues about Walter's death on the sequestered boat.

"Hey, y'all, so glad you could make it in today," I said to them as I took my seat at the table across from them.

The older brother, Wayne Aaron, was a skinny man of average height with dark hair. His face was sad and earnest. "Thanks so much for taking our case, Ms. Heart. We tried to fight this on our own, but we got nowhere fast."

The sister, Wynona, was the middle of the three children.

She was quiet and rounder than her brothers. "We're simple people. Not used to all this fuss, and we only want this settled as quickly as possible."

I was trying to make sure I did just that, but I had a feeling this case was about to get really messy. "It's not going to be easy. The barge company will not admit to any negligence, and since Walter had a perfect safety record, it's become a battle to prove what happened. The insurance company will not pay out in cases of suicide."

"Ms. Heart," Wynona said, "there is no way my brother would ever take his own life. Even though we were somewhat estranged, we knew he was the happiest he has ever been. He was in love and talking about getting married."

And there it was. The detail that could be the end of the Aarons' case. "Do you know if he ever did get married?"

"Not that we know of. Why?"

"Because, if Walter did marry, and he changed his will, then the bride might be his new beneficiary. If he died before they officially tied the knot, then you two would inherit."

"Oh, I don't like the sound of this," Wynona said. "People might get the wrong idea."

"That's true," I agreed. "The fact that your parents are dead and your uncle recently left Walter a huge inheritance already has the insurance company questioning suicide for his cause of death, though that's still their preference. The possibility that Walter was pushed is being investigated by the police now. This new information about Walter maybe having a wife will give the insurance company even more reason to stall."

"They can't think we were involved," Wayne protested. "We've already been cleared for the night of Walter's death. Sure, things got a bit complicated between us since our uncle left the money to Walter, but, as we told the police, we haven't been in touch with him, except by phone, for several months before he died."

The open-and-shut inheritance case I had envisioned with the Aarons was quickly disappearing into the horizon. "We need to find out about this woman Walter might have married. See if there are pictures. A name. Something we can check into to clarify the situation."

Wayne sighed. "I don't remember him saying much about her other than he had only known her a couple of months. If he did marry that girl, it would have been the spur-of-the-moment. A real whirlwind thing."

"Well, even so, there's got to be a record somewhere."

"We haven't really gone through Walter's effects," Wynona chimed in. "Just kind of packed 'em up and shoved 'em in a storeroom. The thought of looking through all that stuff was too upsetting. There might be something in there, though."

I perked up. "Well, that's a great place to start. Go and see what you can find."

"He sounded so in love," Wynona added wistfully. "Why would his wife want to kill him if they just got married?"

"Money can motivate people to do desperate things," I said. "Then again, we have absolutely no proof that she's had anything to do with Walter's death at all. Do either of you know if Walter had any enemies on the boat?"

"No," Wayne said, getting upset. "Everyone loved him at work. He had been working that barge for over ten years. Walter did *not* jump, but I refuse to believe anyone killed him. I swear that barge company overlooked a safety measure and now they just don't wanna pay. They are looking for every excuse under the sun to get outta settlin' his insurance policy."

"I hope you're right, Wayne, but regardless, we still have a possible new beneficiary floating around out there. That issue has to be resolved," I said. "For our next meeting, I will need any insurance papers you can find. Information on his death benefits and all the policies he had with the barge company or anyone else. Whatever you can't find among his personal effects, I will subpoena. We will get to the bottom of this, I promise."

I stood up and reached out to shake their hands.

"Thank you so much, Ms. Heart," Wynona said as she shook my hand. "We couldn't fight those folks on our own anymore, and things look like they're getting a lot more complicated."

I agreed. "Let's meet in a few days. Call me when you have gathered your brother's paperwork and we will set up a time. Meanwhile, I'll see if I can find out anything from the police. I have some pretty good connections down there at the station, and they will assuredly want to talk to you about this mysterious woman."

I walked the Aarons out to the front lobby and said goodbye. I told Wanda Jo I had to get down to the river.

I was sure hoping Sonny didn't have another body part to show me. I was still recovering from the last one.

6

I made my way down to the dock, perspiration rolling down my chest. Women in the Deep South don't sweat. We perspire. But let me tell you, we *perspire* a lot. One hundred and two degrees, with one hundred percent humidity—that's the Deep South in August.

The cement walkway stopped just short of the barge, leading me onto a rocky path bathed in red dirt. Sonny and Bonita were hunkered down on the deck of the tugboat that was pushing the barge.

"Hey, Blake, glad you could get here. I heard you have some information regarding the Aaron case," said Bonita, the gorgeous, plus-sized, African-American spitfire Sonny hired last spring. She had a degree in Criminal Justice from Tuskegee Institute where her parents were both professors. She was smart and highly opinionated and I knew from the start I liked her style.

She looked amazing in a cream-colored suit trimmed in

black and big, dangly earrings. No one else would dress like this searching for evidence except Bonita. But she's a former pageant winner herself, and it was just her style. Her makeup was done to perfection, and not melting like mine was, even in this unbearable heat. *Note to self: find out how she does it.*

"Yes, I just saw the Aarons. They are the sweetest people. They just want to get to the bottom of this."

I glanced up at Sonny. He was looking at me with a silent grin in his eyes. Hiding our feelings was always more difficult in person.

"Well, the Aarons may have to wait a little longer to settle this case," Bonita said. "We still have a lot of investigating to do."

"Can I come aboard? I'll tell you about the new little wrinkle in this case."

I joined them on the tugboat, but had to stay well back from the cordoned-off area. Once there, I related the Aarons' refusal to believe Walter was suicidal. That in fact, he had sounded happy when they spoke to him and was contemplating marrying a girl he'd recently met.

Sonny's gaze narrowed. "Did they say when they talked to him?"

"Shortly before his death."

"Well, this certainly complicates things," Bonita said, hands on her ample hips. "We're going to have to interview the Aarons again. Do they know anything about the woman?"

"No," I said, "but we have another meeting coming up and they're gonna bring whatever they find after going through Walter's effects."

"Bonita and I are going to be in on that little search," Sonny added.

"Why? Did you find something?"

"Can't go into specifics."

As we walked toward the front end of the boat, I saw the crime scene tape.

I looked around nervously. A tugboat pushed a barge up the river. That much I knew. Was that where they thought Walter fell off, in between the boat and the barge?

I stopped, staring at the area where the two boats hitched together.

I took in the gouges in the wood and the scrapes and scratches in the paint, which didn't look to me as though they'd come from the normal tug and push of the equipment. Dark spots dribbled down the side. My heart sank.

"Do you see something?" Sonny asked, already knowing I did, although he hadn't shown me anything.

"It looks like there was a struggle of some sort in this area," I said haltingly, noting exactly how far along the front and side of the boat the crime scene tape extended. "A big struggle, like somebody didn't want to go overboard, but maybe someone else had a different idea."

Bonita just stared at me, remaining silent.

I turned to Sonny. "The coroner's report said there was bruising on Walter's forearms and shoulders."

Sonny looked grim, but unsurprised. He'd obviously seen that report long before me.

"What do I tell the Aaron family, Sonny?" I asked. "I need to update them so they know why the barge company won't settle."

"Sorry, Blake. This investigation is ongoing," Sonny said. "We'll need to talk to the Aarons again and go through all of Walter's effects ourselves. I'll call his siblings when I leave here and set up a time."

"Who do you think did this? The new wife?" I asked. "Walter's been working here for over ten years and was apparently well liked."

Bonita raised her eyebrows and shot Sonny a meaning-ful glance. "Looks like we got us a tugboat captain to talk to again. That story doesn't quite mesh with my notes about Walter's last day."

"The poor Aarons," I said. "They'll be so upset."

"Well, the poor Aarons better not leave town," Bonita added. "I suspect everybody until proven not guilty."

This time, my eyebrows raised at the investigative team in front of me. "Okay, then." It was definitely time for a sub-ject change—they were clearly in business mode, and I didn't want to be defending my clients to either of them right now. "You coming by Vivi's for dinner tomorrow night after the station's dedication ceremony, Bonita?"

"Yes, ma'am, I wouldn't miss it for the world."

"Why don't you come, too, Sonny? It's gonna be great. Ar-thur and Vivi are cooking together." I smiled at him.

"I'll walk you back to your car," Sonny offered. "You can give me the details."

"I'm gonna stay here and take a few more pictures. I'll see you up there in the parking lot in a few minutes," Bonita said, then walked back toward the front of the boat with her camera.

Sonny and I headed back up the hill. Once out of view, he slipped his arm around my waist. "What else is going on, Blake? You said you were having quite a day. Anything I can help you with?"

I told him all about Lewis and the Tressa Mae situation. And how Vivi was just coming undone over the whole thing.

"Well, it shouldn't be too hard to track her down," Sonny said. "Sounds like you have a good start."

"Yes, Vivi and I found someone that matches her name in Birmingham. I'm gonna try to get up there by the end of the week," I said as we reached my car.

"I'll help, if you need me," he said. He bent closer.

I knew he wanted to kiss me, but we were in public, and I was still the senatorial candidate's wife. I wished I had never agreed to play that role. I hated all this secrecy.

"Will you be at the big ground breaking tomorrow?" I asked. "I'll be there to support Vivi and Lewis."

Lewis was holding a media day at the Brooks Mansion, a huge, historic landmark in the center of town where he'd set up his new radio station, and it seemed everyone was going. The restoration of the mansion was starting so the station would be ready for the big Crimson Tide kickoff game the first weekend in September.

"I'll be there for sure." Sonny grinned at me. "I'm not gonna pass up a chance to be with you, for no matter how short a time."

"And of course there's tonight," I teased, reminding Sonny of our plans later.

"I wish you could just spend the night every night," he said.

I gave him a wink. "See you later, Officer." I opened my car door, then slid in over the warm leather seats. I slipped my legs in, brushing my bare skin against his pants. He inhaled sharply, and I peered up at him and smiled my best bad-girl smile.

He laughed, shook his head and shut my door. I was perspiring again, but the heat I was feeling had nothing to do with the hot summer's day. The plan to spend the night at Sonny's excited us both.

I was trying desperately to hang on to whatever tiny part of the good girl that was left in me, but the bad girl was winning the battle, and I was slowly but surely losing all control of her.

7

It was just after 9:00 p.m. when I arrived in front of Sonny's house. I sat looking at the front door, amber light glowing on the huge front porch, contemplating the changes that were taking place by this one, seemingly innocent act.

I'm just going for dinner, I told myself. But I knew me all too well. It was late, we would have a drink, and his arms would be warm and delicious. I'd been so lonely for so long that my heart ached just at the thought of him holding me.

Today had been hectic and stressful with the shower plans underway, and the Aaron case developing, not to mention the new search for Tressa. I just wanted to relax and make the world go away.

But I had never been inside Sonny's home. Was I making a mistake even being here? My palms were sweaty and my heart began to race. *What am I doing? I'm technically still married, at least until the paperwork is official. Good girls don't do things like this.*

Another errant thought popped in my head: *Good girls go to heaven. Bad girls go everywhere.* Was I a bad girl now?

Sonny appeared on the porch. *Oh, my,* I thought. I would happily learn to be a bad girl for him.

I smiled helplessly at him, his silhouette big and yummy. He looked like a young Tom Selleck, without the mustache. I was a goner. The sight of him made me want to run to him, melt into his arms where it was safe and satisfying. I got out and shut my car door and walked around to the steps.

He whistled, and a chill ran up my spine. I felt the bad girl coming on. And I liked it.

"Hey, beautiful, you're a sight for sore eyes." Sonny reached out and swept me against him, then kissed me passionately.

"Mmm—it's good to see you, too," I managed between kisses. "But we are on the porch," I hinted. "I can't wait to see the inside of your house."

He kept kissing me. "Oh, it's nothing much. I built it myself." He gripped me around the waist and pulled me even closer. "I like to work with my hands."

I giggled lightly, caressing his fingertips as they touched me. "You do have amazing hands."

"Well, sweetheart, I'm even better when I have something beautiful to work with," he said, brushing his fingers up and down my arm.

I got instantaneous chill bumps. It was after nine o'clock, but I was sure my evening was just getting started. I looked up into his glistening brown eyes.

He was looking right through me with that sexy grin on his face. I sighed. I had never felt loved liked this. With Harry, it wasn't ever this deep, this real. I needed this feeling like a drug. How could I ever have walked away from him?

Standing on the porch of Sonny's home, I was reminded of a summer's night many moons ago when we lay in the back of his old red pickup truck and watched the night sky. It was crystal clear and lightning bugs twinkled over his backyard. We counted shooting stars and gazed at Orion.

Sonny was a lifelong Boy Scout. He was in his element outdoors. I always felt so safe with him. That was the first night he told me he loved me. We were sixteen, but Sonny had a depth to him that made him different from the other boys I knew. I remember being with him on a soggy night on a little dirt road just west of town when we were in our senior year of high school. He saw a baby deer tangled in some old rope in a ditch. The fawn had injured himself trying to wriggle free when Sonny pulled up and got out. He went over to the baby and freed him while I sat in the car and watched. He did this like it was all in a day's work to him. Like it was nothing. A good scout is never without his pocketknife. He cut the rope and the little deer scampered away.

Now, years later, I stood on the porch scanning his amber-lit home under the pine trees. It looked like something out of a movie.

"Welcome to my humble abode," he said, leaning over to me. "I hope you will find the accommodations quite cozy."

"I'm sure I will, Officer," I said, flirting with him.

He kept up the playfulness. "Please, let me know if I can make your stay any more comfortable. Your satisfaction is my top priority." He winked at me and lifted that left eyebrow. He was absolutely the sexiest when he did that.

"Don't look at me like that," I said softly, batting my long lashes and letting him know to *please, please* keep looking at me like he could devour me with one bite. He could do anything he wanted to do to me, all night long, if he kept it up. He knew it, too. I bit my bottom lip, then rolled my tongue over my lips.

"Don't *you* look at *me* like that," he shot back.

I had him. He kissed me softly, then more deeply, his tongue tasting my mouth, then my neck. The chemistry was ridiculous with him. I felt his large hand cup my breast and his mouth slide down inside my silk collar to the flesh of my chest. "We should go in, don't you think?" I asked, breathing heavily against his neck. I knew anyone could be lurking out there, and I wanted to make sure we were seen only when and how we wanted to be seen.

"I could take you right here, right now," he said.

"I know, but I wanna see your place," I said. "Besides, we're getting way too, um, relaxed, out here."

"If you insist," he said, still kissing my neck.

Sonny opened his front door for me and allowed me in first. *Such a prince,* I thought. Harry had stopped opening my door the minute we got back from our honeymoon. But this wasn't a show from Sonny. This was ingrained behavior. He was a Southern gentleman. He had opened doors for me even in high school.

I followed him inside and he shut the door behind me.

Immediately, I was struck by the warmth of his home. Someone's house says so much about who they are. His home enveloped me just like he did. I knew I was in trouble. Leaving would be very hard for sure.

His living room was awash in the glow of walls the color of milky mocha and trimmed in shiny white, extra-wide baseboards and crown molding. Shelves floor to ceiling flanked the doorways and were crammed with books, both hardback and soft, all mixed in together.

Some soft, vulnerable place inside me twisted, then released. I was really here.

I walked slowly, looking along the shelves, grazing my fingertips across the crowded unorganized collection. I wanted to explore every nook and cranny of his place.

"I'll be right back," Sonny said. "Make yourself comfy."
He headed off to the kitchen.

I was fixin' to have a seat, but my uncontrollable curiosity
took over and I headed toward his bedroom, which was just
to the left of the kitchen door. I thought I'd only take a peek.

His room was dark with a cream-colored duvet and crimson blankets. His dark red mahogany dresser had a silver-
framed picture of his German shepherd, Bryant, named after
Bama's legendary football coach, Bear Bryant. The coach died
after retiring in 1982, and most of the town closed up for almost three days. It was one of those unreal events when you
stopped in your tracks the minute you heard the news. Everyone in Tuscaloosa knows where they were the afternoon
the Bear died. It was just like Sonny to try to keep a good
man's memory alive.

Bookshelves lined these dark cream walls like in the other
room. But postcards and old photos of hiking trips and scout-
ing knives littered the cubbies. A bay window seat looking
out over the front porch was overflowing with mismatched
pillows. In the corner stood his trombone, balancing on its
case. I was certain that's how he developed those talented lips.

An antique tulip sconce light was just outside the bathroom
door, beckoning me inside. His closet was just to the right of
the door and I found myself touching all of his things, feeling as though I was glimpsing a whole new side of Sonny—
the real man underneath the slick detective's suit. I inhaled
deeply, and the scent of him filled me. His work shirts were
well pressed from the cleaners, his ties hung around the neck
of one hanger.

I paused a minute, then loosened the buttons on one of
his shirts, my heart racing at my bravery. Well, he *did* say to
make myself comfy...

I unzipped my skirt and it fell to the wood floor. I took off my blouse and pulled one of his old cop shirts off the hanger and slipped it on, leaving it unbuttoned halfway down. He hadn't wore one of these uniform shirts since he'd become the chief investigator.

Bare feet and bare legs, I walked back out into the living room just as Sonny appeared in the doorway from the kitchen with two Baileys Irish Creams in highball glasses. He'd untucked his shirt and looked rather relaxed…until he caught a glimpse of me. He set the glasses down on the side table and walked toward me. He was slow and deliberate. He never took his eyes off me, sauntering across the floor.

He fingered the collar of the shirt I had on. "I do believe I prefer this new outfit to the previous one." He smiled like a cat fixin' to eat the canary. "It seems a little more, uh— accessible."

"First, you have to catch me." I ran from him into his bedroom, and he reached down, grabbing the glasses, and chased me. I jumped on his bed, scooching up the duvet and settling into his mound of down pillows.

He set the glasses on the dresser next to the picture of Bryant, crawled onto the bed and straddled me before taking off his white shirt. He was a big, gorgeous man, with a broad chest and strong muscular arms—every inch the sexy cop fantasy.

He stretched out on top of me. "I do believe I've caught you. What's my prize?"

I laughed, loving the feel of his weight on me. "Accessibility. As much as you want."

Sonny gave me a wicked grin. "Sugar, that's an awful lot." He began kissing me all over my neck and chest, in between the buttons of his old uniform shirt.

"You still have your clothes on."

"Yes, ma'am." He slid his pants off.

I heard them drop, belt and all, to the wood floor. I wrapped my bare legs around him and pulled him into me. I loved knowing I was in his bed, even if part of me couldn't believe I was here and was totally shocked at my brazen behavior. The rest of me just reveled in it.

I was putting a pinky toe outside my predictable box, and amazingly enough, I was feeling like I was home.

8

I stared up at Sonny's ceiling and let out a satisfied sigh.

It might sound silly, but I like to think of myself as a free spirit. Okay, I know I'm not like Vivi. Few are. But I will take on an adventure here and there. Let's say I'm a free spirit with a five-year plan. I'm old-fashioned. I'm the girl who loves to have my hand kissed on meeting a new gentleman. And I have always believed I was born in the wrong decade. That was one of the things that first bonded Vivi and me. We loved anything from the turn of the century through the 1940s. When we played dress-up as children in my grandmother Meridee's basement, we loved to put on her dresses and listen to her old standards, like Cole Porter or Gershwin, before adding several long strings of pearls to our costumes. Then we'd dance. This love of all things vintage is what inspired Vivi's wedding planning, and the entire reception was set to have a ragtime theme.

Yes, I was old-fashioned, but I now had proof I was also a

girl who could live on the fly. I could be unexpected. I was lying in bed, not in my own house…and not even by myself. And I was wearing a policeman's uniform! Well, I *had been* wearing it. The shirt's current whereabouts remained unknown, but it was definitely my new favorite article of clothing.

I lay snuggled up next to Sonny, completely satisfied and utterly mussed, my appetite roaring.

"I'm starved," I said. "Let's have dessert."

"I just had dessert," Sonny said. "But I think I know just the thing for you, baby. You still love pound cake?" He remembered from our junior-high days.

"You know it," I said, not knowing what he was planning. It was 2:00 a.m. and I mean, really, was he gonna bake a pound cake right this second?

That would be a *yes*.

Sonny sauntered into the kitchen, fastening his pants as he walked.

The kitchen was small but well-appointed with marble counters and dark oak cabinets to go with the craftsman style of the rest of the house.

There was a farmhouse apron-front sink in porcelain-white with a sprayer nozzle faucet. The oversized island held an array of cookbooks on the shelves underneath and had an additional sink for vegetables. Was Sonny a chef? Sure looked like it with that setup. I found that really sexy.

Sonny had prepared a dinner for me but we never got around to it. He wrapped up the steaks he had thawed and slid them back into the fridge. Then, he covered the potatoes and green beans and put them next to the steaks.

"I'm so sorry I messed up your dinner plans," I said.

"Are you kidding? That was the best dinner I've had in years. It was delicious," he said, and winked at me.

Sonny wiped the countertops down, then opened the stainless-steel fridge and pulled out several sticks of butter and a carton of eggs.

"Don't tell me you can make pound cake from scratch, too, on top of your many other talents." I sauntered around the kitchen, teasing him now that I was back in his shirt and barefooted.

"I can if you let me concentrate."

Outside, it was raining a steady drizzle, and the massive kitchen window was streaked with the sudden condensation. Sonny had the cake in the oven in minutes. He had thrown in a can of 7-Up instead of milk. Meridee made it that way, too.

"Okay, Officer," he said to me, "we got about an hour with nothing to do. Need to make an arrest?"

Sonny put his wrists together and held them in front of me as if to say, *Cuff me.*

"Yes, sir. I do need to make an arrest. I've heard you've been a very bad boy."

He lifted me up onto the cool marble of the island and pressed me against him. "I intend to be a lot worse," he whispered.

He moved against me as I sat on the countertop, my legs wrapped around him tightly. Heat surged through my body as he kissed me. He slipped his arms around my waist and pulled me up into him, passionately kissing my neck, causing chills to join the heat.

The showers outside grew heavy, hitting the window harder until it sounded like it was coming down in torrents, adding a little music and rhythm to our passion. Sonny carried me to the couch, my legs still wrapped around his waist, and we made love with the sounds of the storm all around us. Afterward, Sonny looked down at me and smiled.

"I do love you, Blake. So much."

"I love you, too, baby."

"I think I'm hooked," he said, kissing my nose.

"I know I am."

"Let's go have a drink on the porch."

I knew he wanted to talk. And I liked that.

We stopped by the hallway closet for blankets and went outside to the porch swing. Sonny wrapped us tightly together in cozy cotton quilts I was sure his grandmother must've made. It made the cuddling even better.

"I've had fun with you tonight, baby," Sonny said, snuggling closer. "I enjoy being with you more than I can say. I always have. When I'm with you, I feel like I can come up for air, you know?" He let out a sigh. "You just make me happy, that's all."

I was melting in a cool rainstorm. I gazed up at him.

Sonny was being serious and that was a rare occurrence. He was a playful person. He found the fun and funny in almost every situation. But in this moment, his deeper side was coming out. I relaxed into him, feeling the wonder of what was happening between us.

He kissed my forehead and pushed my mussed hair from my face, his fingertips caressing my cheeks. With a gentle touch, he lifted my mouth to his and kissed me softly. His lips were warm in the wet chill of the rainy night.

"Sonny," I said, pulling away and looking at him, "I want to stay here with you."

"Of course. I sure didn't plan on having you home in this," he said, referring to the downpour.

I bit my lip, hesitating. "No, I mean I want to stay here, like…move in with you."

He was terrifyingly silent.

I died inside. *Oh, good, Blake, here you go, jumping the gun with your incessant planning and thinking ahead.* Embarrassed, I tried to get up. I couldn't believe I'd just blurted that out! Here we were having a beautiful night together, and now I'd ruined it by proposing the next step in our relationship that, by his stunned silence, I was sure Sonny wasn't ready for.

But before I could make it inside, he grabbed my hand and pulled me back down beside him. He cradled his hands around my face. "Oh, baby, I would love that. I thought you weren't ready. That's the only reason I haven't asked. I don't want to push you, but I can't imagine anything more special than finally waking up with you beside me after all these years." Sonny was genuinely excited at this prospect, and nothing could have made me happier.

At that moment, I knew in my heart I would never go back to live in the house with Harry again. He had moved out the first few nights after the big breakup, but he'd recently moved back for the duration of the campaign. We had separate rooms and avoided all extraneous contact with each other, so the living arrangements were totally for show. Even still, it was a difficult setup. Though our divorce wasn't final, living with Harry felt sort of like a betrayal of Sonny. Here was this man who was giving me the most honest, true and deepest love I'd ever known, and I was forcing us to keep it a dirty secret while I played house with my soon-to-be ex.

Vivi now had her own full life with Lewis and Arthur at the plantation, so I couldn't just barge in on her home. But I never wanted to live alone. I wasn't even sure I could, and everything inside me let me know that living with Sonny was where I wanted to be.

I was so out of my comfort zone, but I knew it was what I wanted. "It will have to be after the campaign because I promised, but being with you feels so right. What do you think?"

"You seriously need to ask?" He was grinning as he pulled me into him. "To be able to go to sleep with you in my bed and wake up every mornin' with you next to me has been a fantasy of mine for longer than I can remember. I'm here and ready, whenever you are." He kissed me. "Actually, I'm not so sure about the sleepin' part, but I know you'll be in bed with me."

A damn of emotion broke inside and it was all I could do to hide my tears of joy. I would remember this moment forever. The soaking rain, the night air, the front porch swing and resting in Sonny's embrace. Nothing had ever felt so right.

9

I woke up at Sonny's happy and rested. He had already left for the day and in his spot next to me was a note and a magnolia blossom.

Good morning, beautiful. Thank you for making my dreams come true. I finally woke up next to my angel.
I love you, S.

I wobbled to the shower with a smile on my face.

It was already a scorcher by ten o'clock, but I wouldn't have missed this day for anything. Lewis and Vivi would be in full socializing swing as the ground breaking and renovations at the station got underway. The mayor and Kitty and all of the media would be there, including Dallas Dubois—brazen reporter, ruthless attention-seeker and, of course, my ex-stepsister.

I ran over to Vivi's to pick her up for the event and we rode over to the mansion together, dreading the soaring temperatures outside the air-conditioned car.

The heat was hardly bearable as I set my red sling-backs onto the dirt road near the side of the dilapidated Brooks Mansion. The historic old house had been placed on Alabama's Places in Peril list for a reason. It needed saving. Lewis was our town's official knight in shining armor for doing just that.

Too bad he couldn't do something about the weather. My makeup was already melting and I had only been out of the car for two seconds.

Vivi was so excited as she struggled to get out of the passenger seat, looking anything but graceful in her navy blue sleeveless maternity pantsuit, her baby belly leading the way. She spread her legs in an unladylike squat and just heaved herself out.

I watched her, smiling, and shut my door. Although I wasn't looking forward to that part of being pregnant, for the first time in my life I started to wonder what it would be like to carry the baby of the man you loved.

Harry had never inspired such thoughts. Probably because my having his baby would have taken the spotlight off him, except if he needed us to make his campaign poster look better. But I wondered what it would be like with Sonny.

Vivi waddled over to my side of the car. "Did you see Lewis standing over there, shaking hands with everybody? He makes anything sexy. I gave him that crimson tie today, and he smiled so big, his dimples were deep enough to swim in."

"Lewis looks fantastic," I agreed. "And you, little momma, have never been more beautiful."

I gave Vivi a hug, careful not to mess her updo, not sure that even Aqua Net was up to today's soaring temperatures. I squeezed her hand for reassurance, and then we walked toward the gazebo where Lewis was standing with the mayor.

"Lewis surely is in his element today," I noted.

"He has come such a long way, Blake. I love him so much my heart's filled to bursting. I'm thrilled to be standing next to him, watching as all his dreams come true."

"Can I use that?" Dallas appeared right behind us, following us like a snake in the grass. She was a long-legged bottle-blonde, wearing a hot-pink Calvin Klein skirt, sleeveless low-cut blouse and six-inch white stilettos that dug like pointy little daggers into the red dirt.

"Oh, my good God, Dallas, put a sock in it already!" Vivi, being pregnant in August in the Deep South, had even less patience than usual. "I wasn't talking to you or your microphone, and no, you may not use that."

The looks Dallas shot Vivi were a lot like pointy little daggers, too. She did not like being put off. The trouble with Dallas was that, even when she meant well, she came off pushy, demanding and downright rude. She had a lot to learn about class and manners, and she often didn't care who she had to step on to get a good story. The career woman in me respected her obvious dedication and passion, but she needed to learn there were better—and kinder—ways to make your way to the top.

"Vivi isn't feeling well right now," I interjected. "Can you give her a minute or two? I'll let you know when she can give you a blurb for your story."

"Blake, it's not a *blurb*," Dallas said, taking offense. It was impossible to have a civil conversation with this woman.

"I don't care what it is," Vivi snapped. "You're not getting it now. I am going over to see my Lewis. It's his day, after all. If and when I am ever ready to talk to you, I will let you know. Thank you for backing off."

Dallas fumed. "Fine. I'll be right over there." She gestured to her photographer, setting up the shot just outside the tents.

Local newspaper reporters were also setting up their equipment, along with a couple of other news radio stations.

"Don't hold your breath," Vivi muttered as she picked up the pace and walked in a hasty beeline toward her fiancé. I raced after her, my heels spiking into the ground. Why are we all wearing high heels in red dirt?

"That woman gets on my last nerve," Vivi growled. "She is, without a doubt, the most brazen person I have ever known. She was actually eavesdropping on us while we walked. We could have been sayin' anything and she would have gotten it on tape. Low, low, low. She is just pure ol' dee low."

"I know," I commiserated. "She is lurking everywhere these days. But that's all the more reason to stay on her good side."

I thought of last night, kissing Sonny on the porch, then making love in his big bed, while the stars shone in the window. What would she do with that kind of juicy tidbit? I shuddered. One of the last times I'd seen her, she'd been on my patio, giving my husband, Harry, a taste of her right breast—all in the name of getting information and some high-profile publicity. I had chased her out of my backyard like a homicidal maniac, and though we'd been playing nice, I was afraid she was out for revenge.

She wasn't the type of woman who was a *girlfriend*. Even when she'd been my stepsister, years ago, she'd never had any close friends. My mother married her father when Dallas was only fourteen and I was sixteen. We were friends for about a day and then Dallas started her competition with me—for everyone's attention. She backstabbed me at school and worked double time to steal my clothes and my boyfriends.

Kitty, my mother, and her father divorced about ten years later, but Dallas and I have never given up the battle. I've always wanted to see the good in her—and Meridee, for one, has always insisted it's in there—but we've never been able to move past our teenage rivalries no matter how hard I've tried. And Vivi, it was clear, had given up trying.

In the crowd, I saw my man standing there with Bonita. My heart skipped. I wanted to run to him, but not with all the cameras around, and definitely not with Miss Dallas Dubois there. As long as I kept my cool, I knew I could talk to him without much attention since he was there with Bonita. Plus, we were now working on a case together. So we could at least have a conversation without Dallas thinking she had a story.

I caught his attention and waved at him and Bonita. They waved back as Vivi and I headed for Lewis and the mayor, Charlie Wynn. He was a former captain in the navy. He looked like Jeff Bridges, always had a cigar in his mouth and threw the best tailgating parties on the quad I had ever seen.

Everyone liked him—especially my mother, who'd started dating him a few weeks ago. So far, it seemed like a good match, though Kitty seemed to think most men matched her well enough. She had been married four times, last I counted, and if she had her way, the mayor would be number five.

Vivi and I made our way over to the men.

"Hey, you two," I said, reaching out to hug Lewis first, then the mayor. "What an exciting day for you and all of Tuscaloosa."

Lewis looked radiant. "Blake, so glad you could make it. Yes, it's gonna be a big ol' day. A new beginning. Opening my own station has been a dream of mine for a long time. This place is my baby, and today is kinda like a birth, you know?"

Mayor Charlie reached over and hugged Vivi. "Seems like there's a lotta that goin' around these days."

"Speaking of new beginnings," Vivi said, "with this heat today, I may have my 'new beginning' before I'm ready. I'm gonna have one of those iced teas they're serving for the media before I melt away."

We all followed Vivi to the media tent. We grabbed a couple of iced teas and then went to check out the grounds, which had been cleaned up considerably since Lewis took over the Brooks Mansion, though there was still a lot to do. Dr. Brooks himself had built the house in 1837 and it sat almost in the geographical center of Tuscaloosa.

The Brooks Mansion was an unusual mix of architecture, Italianate and Greek revival. Most of the property around it had been sold off over the years in an attempt to keep the house intact. The building looked a bit shaky, but the good, solid bones were there.

All that was left outside was the gazebo and the huge oak and magnolia trees shading the side yard. The stone sidewalk was still overgrown with weeds and the front porch was starting to fall in, but the beveled glass around the front door glistened in the hot summer sun, bending the light and creating rainbow prisms streaming down the old steps. The mansion's magic was still there. It had potential and Lewis saw that. He and the old house were kindred spirits.

The dedication would happen momentarily, and people were drifting toward the seats and claiming spots in the nearly two-hundred-year-old rotunda. The four of us made our way to the front and took our seats.

Lewis slipped his arm around Vivi's back and pulled her into him. I was filled with such joy for Vivi. They looked good together. Happy. Just genuinely happy. They had found what we all are really looking for—true love—the real thing. Vivi's belief in Lewis, and her love for him, was all encompassing. She was proud of her man.

I looked at Vivi and she was just covered in *Bellerina dust*. A little invention from our Sassy Belle club days, *Bellerina dust* simply means us belles may look like pretty little powder puffs on the outside, but deep down that secret dust transforms us into bulldozers, able to be strong for our friends and families when they need us. Yes, underneath all that lipstick and Aqua Net, in her heart—where it matters, a Sassy Belle can handle anything. And we always have each other's backs. *Always*. Today, Vivi was the perfect example of that for sure.

"Goodness, Lewis, this is amazing," I said. "I am so proud for you."

He grinned. He knew I meant it.

"I couldn't be happier with the way things have gone," he said, squeezing Vivi.

She kissed his cheek. "I always knew my Lewis was somethin' else."

"That's the understatement of the year, Miss Vivi," Mayor Charlie spoke up. "Lewis has done so much good in such a short amount of time, bringin' this town's attention to the importance of preservin' one of its most beautiful antebellum mansions and makin' plans for a great sports radio station. I'm fixin' to see if I can adopt him myself. Ever'body oughtta have a Lewis Heart or two in their family."

"Thank you, Mayor, I just wanted to do right by the town I love so much and make this woman proud to call me hers," Lewis said, looking at Vivi.

"Okay, it's time for the dedication," Mayor Charlie said. "Let's get this show on the road, shall we?" He winked at Lewis and patted Vivi on the arm.

With determined, proud smiles, Lewis and the mayor made their way to the front steps of the Brooks Mansion, where a small entourage of local media had gathered. Dallas was there with her posse, plus some of the Birmingham TV stations and a few radio reporters. This was just the dedication, not the grand opening, but it would still make the evening news.

The mayor approached the crowd of reporters with his

trademark swagger. He stepped up on the bottom step and faced the media, grinning.

"Ladies and gentlemen, thank y'all so much for comin' out today as we put to bed, once and for all, the fate of this grand old place. She has been on the Alabama Places in Peril list for so long, I can't remember her any other way. Many options for her uncertain future have made headlines over the years. Threats to mow her down, rebuild her, replace her and build something else on these hallowed grounds have been the subject of years and years of debate and countless court battles. But I am here today proud to tell you all that this ol' lady is tough like the stuff she comes from. She's part of the very roots of this great town of Tuscaloosa, and she ain't goin' nowhere. My good friend has saved her from a near certain demise as a future shopping center." He gestured toward Lewis. "Lewis, may I say from all of us here in Tuscaloosa, you have made us very proud."

The mayor turned back to the crowd. "I give you the new owner of the Brooks Mansion, the CEO of the new radio station, WCTR, and the voice of your national champions, the Alabama Crimson Tide, Mr. Lewis Heart."

The crowd erupted. Cheers and shouts of "Roll Tide," the mantra for the Alabama Crimson Tide, were heard as others whistled. Vivi bounced and clapped, bursting with pride as Lewis approached the mic.

"Good afternoon, y'all. Enjoying this nice cool weather today?" Lewis was his usual charming, sarcastic self. The crowd laughed as Lewis grinned.

"I am happy to see so many of you on this sweltering day. It means the world to me to be able to save this fantastic piece of Tuscaloosa history and to make my dream come true right inside these doors—my own radio station broadcasting Crimson Tide sports twenty-four hours a day. Once we open in three short weeks, everyone is welcome to come inside for a visit. We'll schedule tours, and maybe even have lunch on the grounds, to fully celebrate this magnificent thread in the fabric of the grand legacy of Tuscaloosa. I couldn't be happier to give this mansion right back to the city that fought so hard to save her over the years."

Lewis looked right over to me and winked. He included me in that fight and was proud of my part in the mansion's preservation. I was overcome by this sweet gesture. I was fully aware, in that second, that he and I would always be on the same page. I was beginning to think Lewis and I had more in common than I had thought. We both loved Vivi and we both loved Tuscaloosa like no place else on earth. Maybe both of us had to get out from under Harry in order to shine.

"Well, my dream has finally come full circle," Lewis continued. "The restoration of Brooks Mansion will begin at a rapid pace to be ready in time for the kickoff game. In fact, the pace will be unprecedented, with construction going on around the clock, along with a record number of people working on this project.

"Plans for the grand opening in three weeks are underway. The party will be right here and it will be a thing to remember. Look around you now 'cause, as my great-aunt used to say, 'Y'all ain't seen nothin' yet.' Thanks again for coming, and Roll Tide!"

Everyone was clapping and hollering.

"Isn't he amazing?" Vivi whispered, joyful tears brimming in her eyes.

Lewis waved to the crowd, then reached his hand toward Vivi. A smile replaced her tears as she walked up toward the mic to be next to him. She waved to the people gathered, too, and everyone cheered. I swear they looked like the new first couple of Tuscaloosa.

I looked around the crowd of supporters and noticed Harry standing off to the side. I was sure he was jealous. I mean, Lewis was once the black sheep of the family, but he was quickly stepping into Harry's spot on the throne. If I knew my old Harry, he wouldn't take this turn of the tables for long. But just what he would do to get back in the spotlight, I didn't know.

10

Harry Heart would not miss a media event for anything, and this dedication of the mansion was certainly no exception. Now that the speeches were over, he made his way over to the crowd of reporters to steal himself some camera time. He couldn't help himself. The media might have gathered for Lewis today, but Harry couldn't just let his brother have the spotlight. No, Harry Heart would go to hell and back to get on camera. He and Dallas shared that trait.

Dan "The Man," Harry's campaign manager, was right by Harry's side, talking to reporters and making sure Harry said all the right things. He caught my attention and nodded his head toward Harry, standing in the middle of a small cluster of cameras, signaling that I was failing in my duties as a future senator's wife. I knew I'd be stuck playing this role for a few more excruciating months, but I'd made a promise and I intended to keep it. I kissed Vivi on the cheek and whispered that I'd be right back. After shooting Sonny a look of apology, I reluctantly made my way over to Harry and Dan and took my requisite spot next to my husband, the candidate.

I had been an actress years ago, so now I acted happy and enthused. I hoped Sonny would understand. I had agreed to this farce, in large part, to protect him. People wouldn't look kindly on the man who broke up the future senator's marriage. The truth was, though he wasn't exactly a model husband, he was exactly right for the role of senator. Our relationship issues aside, I trusted him to take care of the city that I love.

Harry was in full soapbox mode, sermonizing with quick one-liners and forced laughter. Cameras rolled and reporters threw him simple questions. I stood at his side, as obligated, smiling and looking approvingly at him—glancing every so often at Sonny, while inside I felt sick.

"Oh, yes, I am eager and ready for this challenge," Harry said, wearing his starched white shirtsleeves rolled up to make himself look more like a man of the people. "I look forward to making your voices heard in our nation's capital."

He smiled his perfect megawatt smile, and it struck me as bittersweet that we were now so far apart. I had truly loved him once, and I'd been attracted to him from the moment I saw him. Even now, I could feel the shadow of the old familiar tug. He was still preppy gorgeous as he continued to wave and shake hands, but good looks and a few shared interests weren't enough for me anymore. I wanted the fairy tale. The happily ever after. It's hard when you're painfully lonely, especially in the arms of the one you're supposed to love.

"Fellow constituents," Harry went on, "I know, with your help, we can make a difference in Washington and enhance the future for all in this great state of Alabama."

Harry gestured to me. "Please say hello to my wife, attorney Blake O'Hara Heart. She will be an asset for you, as well."

What? I couldn't believe he could lie like that, knowing full well I would not be going to Washington with him. It struck me then how very different we were.

He pulled me forward and I waved as Harry continued to speak of our marriage and me. He was in full senator mode, not caring about anyone or anything but winning.

Sonny stood next to Bonita a few yards away, his hands in his pockets as he watched me, listening to Harry's false laughter and small talk.

I hated this and with what I was feeling now, I was afraid I wouldn't last in this role all the way to November. Sonny was precious to me. He fed my soul and it drove me crazy to hurt him. He was feeling it, too. I saw it in his eyes, even as he sent me a little grin. November felt like a lifetime away.

I went back to listening to Harry, then froze when I saw Dallas approach.

"So, Harry, tell me," Dallas said with a slick smile. "If you win the senatorial election, will your devoted wife, Blake, be joining you in Washington?"

My heart just stopped. I did *not* like that woman. Have I said that already? Well, there, I said it again. Harry smiled nervously at me. Out of the corner of my eye, I saw Sonny stiffen, wanting to protect me, yet unable to jump to my rescue. I felt butterflies—no, make that bats—take flight in the pit of my stomach.

Dallas's smile grew broader as the seconds passed by in awkward silence. "Well, come on, you two. It's really not a trick question." She shoved the microphone closer.

Harry seemed exasperated, too. "I am sure when the time comes, my wife will make that decision. I look for her to be by my side, like she always has been."

Dan gave him a nod of approval. Dallas just smirked.

"Really?" She turned the mic toward me. "Anything you'd like to add to your husband's comment, Blake? I mean, you have your law practice here and, of course, your family and *special friends.*" Dallas batted her lashes. "I'm sure they'd be so tough to leave behind."

Her look said she knew I was spending time with Sonny, and she'd do anything for a juicy scoop. I didn't know how she'd found out about us, but I did know there'd be no more smooching on the porch. This shark was circling for the kill.

"I will always support Harry," I said strongly, utilizing every bit of acting talent I could muster. "Thank you for your interest in my welfare."

She stepped closer. "One more question—"

I shot a quick glance at Dan, and he immediately stepped over to interrupt Dallas.

"Thank you, Miss Dubois, fellow news media and future constituents. That will be all the questions for now as Mr. Heart has another engagement to attend."

Dallas smirked again and sent me a warning look as if to say, *You got away this time, but soon heads will roll.*

I shuddered.

Smiling to hide my nerves, I kissed Harry on the cheek for show and walked back toward Bonita and Sonny. My cop never took his eyes off me as I approached. I wanted to cry on his shoulder. I wanted him to fold me in his arms and cuddle me to him. I wanted to grab his hand and run far away from all this madness.

But, of course, I couldn't do any of those things.

Dallas and half the state of Alabama were watching *me.*

"Hey, you two," I greeted both Sonny and Bonita. "Glad y'all could make it."

I leaned in and hugged Bonita, then Sonny, measuring my every move as I felt Dallas's eyes searing like lasers into my back.

"Hey, beautiful," Sonny whispered to me.

Just hearing those words made me relax all over. He wasn't
the least bit upset. Relief allowed me to finally inhale a full
breath. Sonny understood what I had to do, and he wasn't
gonna stand in my way.

I smiled gratefully.

Bonita greeted someone passing by, and Sonny bent closer
to whisper, "I could eat you alive right this second."

"Why, sir, if you're hungry, there are refreshments available with the caterers. I'm rather starving myself." I smiled
and squeezed his hand before quickly letting go.

"I'm 'bout to pure ol' dee die out here in this heat. I'm
headin' over for some lemonade," Bonita said, dabbing her
neck with a tissue from her purse.

Vivi walked toward us. I saw Kitty and Meridee over her
shoulder with the mayor and Lewis. Now that Kitty was
openly dating the mayor, she looked as giddy as a fifth-grader
with her first crush.

Meridee was congratulating Lewis and looking like a politician herself, talking to the media and laughing. It was her
radio station, too, after all, since she'd made such a huge in-
vestment in it. But she preferred to be the silent partner and
let Lewis have all the spotlight. That was her way.

Meanwhile, Dallas became more persistent to get that quote
from Vivi.

"Oh, my Lord, I cannot get that dung fly Dallas off me,"
Vivi said. "She is the most paparazzi-fied reporter in history.
And have you seen her skirt? My God, you can just about see
all the way up to the promised land."

Sonny reached over and hugged Vivi. "Congrats on the
ground breaking. Y'all got quite a future ahead. This is a great
day," Sonny said. "And, Vivi, I don't think I have ever seen
you glowing like you are today."

"That's 'cause I'm sweatin' my ass off, Sonny. Now, if I

could just have you put a restrainin' order on the Mouth of the South, the day would be perfect. Dallas is driving me crazy for a statement."

"Then give her one," I said.

"Yes, a good one," Bonita added as she rejoined the group with her sweet cold lemonade. "A shocker that'll shut her up."

Just then we saw Dallas heading our way, tiptoeing on the dirt with her stick-thin stilettos.

"Here we go again," Vivi said. "While I do love all this attention, something about that woman's attitude just rubs me wrong. I'd rather talk to a rattlesnake."

"Vivi," Dallas snapped, coming up beside us. "Are you ready to make a remark regarding today's dedication yet? It is hot as hell out here and I have to prepare for my newscast. I can't wait all day."

"Why, Dallas," Vivi cooed, in a falsely sweet voice, "I would be happy to give you a statement. I am just so proud of Lewis Heart and everything he has done for the city of Tuscaloosa that I could strip him naked and ride him like a bull, right this second." Vivi smiled innocently. "How's that, sugar? Will that work for you?"

All of us broke out in embarrassed shocked laughter.

"Oh, crap, I didn't have my mic on," Dallas said. She thrust the newly powered up mic into Vivi's face. "Can you say that again?"

"Of course, sweetie. Anything for you. I love my Lewis and I am extremely proud of him." She stopped and smiled.

"That's not quite what you said before," Dallas insisted. "Could we try that again?" She repositioned the mic under Vivi's nose.

Vivi shook her head. "Sorry. Gotta go see my man now. He's busy saving the day and I wanna be with him. Bye, y'all." She winked at me and took off toward Lewis.

L ater that afternoon, I was sitting in the cool of my office with Wanda Jo. Harry hardly ever came in anymore since the campaign had taken over his life. But I was okay with that. I liked working on things by myself, much more than I ever thought I would. I had several cases going, and I was glad to be so busy. Otherwise, I might find myself hanging over at the police station in a certain investigator's office, which would simply not do.

I was meeting with Wanda Jo concerning a file when Vivi came flying in, literally running down the hall and straight into my office. "Blake, oh, my God, you'll never guess what happened after you left the press conference. It is unreal!"

"Sit down, girl. You gonna deliver that baby right here if you don't," Wanda Jo said, getting up and giving her a chair, then pulled up one for herself.

"What the hell, Vivi?" I asked her. "What happened?"

"Blake, you are gonna die. In a million years, we never would have seen this comin'."

"Are you gonna tell me or are we practicing telepathy?"

"After you left, Harry came over to Lewis and asked to talk to him. Lewis looked surprised and nervous. I mean, you know how it is between them. I moved closer to Lewis for support when Harry *asked me for privacy.* Can you believe it? I am carrying Lewis's baby, and Harry had the nerve to ask me to give them a minute alone. I was immediately suspicious."

"You aren't the only one. What did you do?"

"I walked over to Meridee and Kitty, who were still talkin' to Mayor Charlie. Harry said something to Lewis and he plopped down on the bottom step in shock. Then Harry sat down next to him."

"Oh, my Lord," Wanda Jo said. "It must have been serious for Harry to risk getting his pants dirty. What the heck did he say?" She knew Harry pretty well herself. Well, actually, everyone knew that for Harry to sit on anything other than a proper seat in his perfectly pressed pants was way out of character.

"I'm getting there, I'm getting there! Anyway, I wanted to run over when I saw Lewis sit down, but then I saw them shake hands. A minute later—you won't even believe this— they hugged. Hugged!"

"No way," I said. My heart sank. I knew Harry would be up to something with Lewis in the spotlight today. He just couldn't stand it.

"Yes, way," answered Vivi. "I almost fainted. With the heat and all, I thought I was seeing a mirage, but Meridee confirmed it. She was watching with me, and you know how she never misses a thing."

"Vivi, spit it out. What happened? I'm about to die here," I said.

"Harry walked away, and Lewis sank back down on the steps. I ran over to him and sat beside him. Blake, you aren't gonna believe this, but Harry wanted to make amends. He actually apologized to Lewis, said he was truly sorry. Harry said he had misjudged Lewis for years and had been wrong about him. Can you freakin' believe that?"

I sat in silence.

"Blake, you can close your mouth now," Wanda Jo chimed in. "It's not like Harry apologizing is a sign of the apocalypse, though it's pretty damn close, for sure."

"This is just not the Harry I know," I said. "What else happened?"

"Harry asked Lewis to forgive him, and said he wanted to make up for lost time. Wanted them to act more like brothers. You know Lewis. He has been so hungry for family since the big fight all those years ago, and Harry not speaking to him ever since. Lewis said he was ready for them to start over, and he asked Harry to be best man at our wedding."

"Okay," said Wanda Jo. "It's officially the apocalypse."

I couldn't believe this. Lewis and Harry had gone for over six years without speaking, all because of money and what to do with their mother after their father died. While Harry was the practical, serious one, Lewis was always going for the big dream, like owning his own radio station, though none of his schemes had ever worked out until now. He had lost the majority of the family fortune and went to Meridee behind everyone's backs to ask for loans. But while the rest of us had spent our time judging Lewis based on his failures, Meridee saw something special in him, as she did in everyone. She helped him get this radio station going and he has been able to fully pay her back. But Harry has never ever apologized to Lewis. Till now.

"I can't believe Harry came around," I admitted. Was it

real? I wondered. Was he genuinely wanting to make amends? Or did he just want something, now that Lewis was Tuscaloosa's golden boy.

Vivi seemed happy, but I detected a hint of confusion from her, too. We sat there in shock and silence for a few moments.

Wanda Jo broke in first. "Look, y'all, we can sit here all day long wonderin' what the hell he's up to, or we can just be glad this happened. Whatever the motive, Lewis has got his big brother back. Just in time for the wedding, too! I have known those boys since they were knee-high to a grasshopper, and I know their momma would be proud."

"You're right, Wanda Jo," I ventured warily.

"'Course I am. But I can't just sit here whistlin' Dixie. I got to get home and watch my VCR. I hope all my stories taped. Y'all just be grateful for good news and have a good evenin'. I know I will. That new widowed preacher's stoppin' by for some spaghetti." Wanda Jo got up and pushed her chair back up against the wall.

Vivi laughed. "Oh, my word, Miss Wanda Jo, I thought you swore off all men of the Lord when you left your last preacher man."

"Well, at my age, I can't be too picky. Ever'body deserves a chance, you know. Only problem is he's a damn Baptist, and you know I still can't bake a pound cake. What good will I be at a funeral? All those Baptists bake like a son of a gun." She winked. "Better get my cookbooks out in case somebody kicks the bucket. Wouldn't wanna disappoint my new man. Now remember," she added, "you two let these boys alone. It will all work itself out. We don't need you being like Lucy and Ethel stirrin' the pot."

It was true; we did have the reputation of always being up to something. But when Wanda Jo left, Vivi and I sat looking at each other. We both knew Harry, and this turnaround was, at the very least, a tad fishy.

"I swear, Blake, I want Lewis to be happy. I don't want to say anything to him, you know, just be supportive—but I have one eye cocked over my shoulder. Harry can't be for real, can he?"

"I don't know," I said, "but for now, I guess it's okay. I mean, how bad could it be?" In truth, I knew it wasn't real. My prediction was that Harry probably thought it would be good for his campaign since: 1) it fit perfectly into Harry's family values platform, and 2) Dan likely suggested it and told Harry to smarten up. With Lewis being near royalty as the voice of the Tide, Tuscaloosa really *liked* him. Lewis was a really likable guy in general. So it was pretty brilliant for Harry to buddy up to him. And the timing was way too perfect, with all those reporters around to capture the moment. I was sure Harry knew exactly what he was doing. Lewis was so happy, he would be receptive to Harry's gesture. For Harry, being a politician through and through, this reconciliation was likely all in a day's work. For him, it was a double bonus. He'd get all the votes from the Lewis fans, and he would be standing up as best man in the wedding of the decade for Tuscaloosa.

But also, I knew deep down he was actually proud of Lewis. Probably surprised his brother had finally pulled off one of his grand schemes, but it was an important one, and now Lewis was somewhat of an equal. Someone Harry was not ashamed of anymore. Harry was proud to be the brother of our new town hero and be able to show him off, especially on air. All good stuff for a future senator. And if the end result was that he would stand up for Lewis on the big day, then I guess this charade wouldn't do any harm.

Vivi sighed. "I just don't want Lewis hurt. He's not the type to put up walls, you know? He's an all or nothin' type of

guy. That's what I love about him. I feel like I want to warn
him, but at this point, I can't. He was so happy, and, after all
the fanfare today, this was just the icing on the cake. It would
be so cruel to tell him his brother might be using him. Anyway, I'm goin' home. Lewis said he was comin' in a bit, and
I gotta help Arthur get the place ready. Miss Bonita's coming
over for dinner, and Lewis says he's bringin' me a surprise."

"What do you think it could be? He already gave you one
surprise..." I waggled my eyebrows at her burgeoning belly.

"Ha-ha. Very funny. Lewis wants to commemorate this
day in a special way, so we'll just have to see what that means.
You comin' tonight?"

"Yeah, I'll be there. I'm sleeping there these days, remember? I really wanna stay with Sonny. We even talked about
it last night, but I'm so afraid Tabloid Dallas will be lurking
around. I decided it'd be best to wait until the election is over."

"Hey, why don't you bring Sonny out? If anyone asks, he
could be out there with Bonita, visiting us after work."

"I already asked him...."

"The more the merrier!" Vivi rose from her chair. "Blake,
I know you're busy and I hate to push, but when do you think
we can get up to Birmingham to find Tressa? I am having
sleepless nights over this."

"I know you are, honey. I think we can get up there and
back the day after tomorrow. I'll work it out with Wanda Jo
so my meetings are scheduled around it."

"The Fru Fru guys are coming out that day, first thing, to
walk around the property and lay out the plans for the wedding. We can leave right after lunch."

I walked her to the front office and hugged her goodbye.
As I returned to my office to pack up, I was back, as usual,
to thinking about Sonny. Instead of being satiated from last
night, I felt hungry for more. Harry and I never made love

the way Sonny and I did, full of passion and a deep emotional connection. I needed to focus on so many other things right now, but all I wanted was Sonny, shirtless and in my office right that second.

12

I sat down at my desk and dialed Sonny's cell. He picked up on the first ring. "Officer Bartholomew. Does someone need to be searched?"

"Why, yes, Officer, however did you know?"

"Are you finally alone in your office?" he asked.

"Yes, are you spying on me?"

"Always," he said.

I could hear the smile in his voice.

"I'll be right over. My legs are walking right now, and I can't stop them. Uh-oh, here they go out the door. Here I come. I'm coming now."

"Well, come in the back door. I've already locked up the front."

Before I knew it, he was walking in the back door, his cell phone still to his ear. "I'm here now, gorgeous." He hung up and stood in the hallway.

"I see that and I like it, handsome." I beckoned him closer, wrapped my arms around him and walked him backward to my office. I locked the door behind us, then kissed him all over his face. All my pent-up passion from earlier in the day at the dedication let loose.

"Oh, my, did you miss me or what?" Sonny asked, enjoying the heat of my excitement.

"No, not at all," I said nonchalantly. "I'm like this all the time."

I was biting him lightly on the neck, reveling in the powerful surge of my emotions, when something inside me just snapped. Suddenly, I was out of my mind with cravings for him, filled with a lust and passion I'd never felt before with anyone. I grabbed his belt and tugged him against me.

Sonny responded like a force of nature. With one hand, he was trying to take his jacket off, while his other hand wandered down the back of my skirt. We reached my desk, and I raked my arm across the surface of it. Everything fell to the floor.

"I wanna eat you alive right now." Sonny pushed my skirt to my hips before lifting me up and settling me on the smooth surface. He slipped his fingers under my panties, hooking them in the crook of his finger, then slipped them down my bare legs and right off. He unbelted his pants with one hand, allowing the other to pull me even closer.

This was a different Sonny than I'd seen in the few times we had made love before. He was fierce, wild and white-hot in the moment.

He didn't take the time to unbutton my sleeveless blouse. He untucked it from my skirt and lifted it over my head, exposing my lacy white demi-bra. In seconds, he'd slipped the straps from my shoulders and pulled the bra down, my breasts now fully out and pressed against him.

Sonny yanked his still-buttoned shirt over his head, followed by his white T-shirt. He devoured me, licking my breasts, his hands all over my bare rear, caressing my inner thighs, then positioning himself between my legs. He was on fire, fast, furious and hungry for me, and I let him have his way.

He picked me up off my desk, my high heels still on and dangling, and I wrapped my legs around his waist as he thrust inside me. Then he set me back on the desk, his hands gripping my waist as he found a steady rhythm.

He never stopped consuming me, inhaling me. His touch was genius. He reached over and closed the blinds behind me without breaking his steady movements within me. It was like he had been living for this moment his whole life. It was the hottest lovemaking I had ever known. In fact, I had never known *anything* like this.

I had never seen Sonny so out of control. I felt like he was the most masculine person in the history of life. He was so big, overpowering me in the best way possible. He was breathing heavily as he worked toward his passionate release.

I was like an animal. He brought out something in me that I had no idea was even there. We reached that moment of bliss together and I found myself yelling out and digging my nails into the flesh of his back.

Sonny groaned, throwing his head back in ecstasy. When he finished, he looked into my eyes, little beads of sweat running down his forehead, his chest heaving up and down. "I love you, Blake—I do. God, you are so beautiful."

I held him to my naked breasts. It was the most emotionally charged moment I could ever remember. It was a huge release on so many levels. "I love you, too, Sonny. So much. Oh, my God, I have needed everything about you for so long."

He stood in front of me, and we held the embrace for a minute—until we heard a car pull up in front of the building.

Both of us looked bug-eyed at each other. Then Sonny scurried to put his pants back on, hopping around the room on one foot and grabbing his shirt. He reached back over, kissed me on the lips, and then ran from my office, disappearing out the back door, still half-dressed, like the superhero of passion. I could barely wrap my head around what had just happened. Or what was likely to happen any minute.

I slammed my door shut and pulled my skirt back down, pulled my bra back up and quickly threw my shirt over my head, tucking it in as I heard keys opening the front door of the building.

Shit! I thought, realizing it must be Harry.

"Blake, you here?" he called out. I grabbed my powder and lipstick from my purse and straightened out my makeup. I put my hair back into a ponytail, hoping I could pull off an end-of–the-workday look, not an I-just-had-the-hottest–sex-of–my-life look.

"Blake, where are you?" he called as he made his way to my office door. "I saw your car outside." His voice sounded strained.

"In here, Harry," I called back.

He jiggled the handle. "Why is your door locked?"

Oh, my God, I forgot the door. I hurried around the desk before he came in with his own key, picking things up and trying to throw them into my closet and drawers, now regretting having tossed the entire contents of my desk onto the floor.

Finally, I unlocked the door and opened it.

Harry walked in and looked around. He was standing right where Sonny had been standing, pantless, minutes ago.

"The door must've gotten locked when Wanda Jo left. I was on the phone so she shut it."

He just looked at me.

"I heard you and Lewis talked today. He asked you to be his best man?" I said, nervously trying to change the subject.

"He did and I accepted," Harry said, still not smiling.

"Well, it was good timing, too. I mean Lewis had a great day and all."

Harry bent over and picked up my tape holder and my stapler from the floor.

"Here," he said, handing me the telltale items. "There are a few pens under the chair, too. Your desk looks remarkably clean."

I grabbed the supplies and set them down on my desk, smiling, but inside I was shaking. "Thank you, Harry. I've been clearing out files and wanted a nice clean surface to work on. Are you staying here to work?"

"No. I have a fund-raiser meeting with Jane and Dan tonight. I'll say you're working on a case." Bitterness tinged his words. "It's what I always say."

"Harry, surely you don't want me there tonight, especially with Jane going." Jane was the judge who had almost ruled to bulldoze the Brooks Mansion to make room for a shopping mall—and Harry had committed the final sin in our marriage when he sided with her to earn her election vote rather than sticking by me in my attempt to save the historic building.

"I'm not seeing Jane on a personal level. It's all business, unlike you and Sonny."

My breath stuck in my throat.

"Tell that cop of yours to be more careful crossing the street next time. A car nearly hit him as he ran from our back door. I'm running for senator in case you forgot, and you messing around with that cop right here in my own office is pretty sloppy of you."

"*Your office?*" I said, forgetting my blunder for the moment. "Since when have you darkened these doors to work on anything with me in months? This place is more like a closet to you. It's certainly not where you spend your workdays."

"What does it matter that I'm not around the office? You were the one that was so quick to move out of our house," he said. "Maybe if you waited till the election was over, we might have worked it all out."

"Maybe if you kept Dallas's breast out of your mouth, I might feel more guilty."

Harry was more than upset now. "Other than that, what have I ever done to you?"

"Are you kidding me? You went behind my back and voted for Jane's zoning change, as a political favor, against the very case I was working on."

"It was my job."

"Your job? You knew how important the Brooks Mansion was to me and you took the favor—and Jane's money and support—and went against your own wife! Our marriage was struggling before, but that was the shot that killed it. You showed me your main priority, and it wasn't me."

"You know what? Maybe I was right all those years. *Maybe you should have just married your cop.* Fine, go for it. But do me one favor and please keep your clothes on till after November." He turned and slammed my door shut behind him. I could hear him stomping down the hall and, a moment later, the front door slammed, too.

Shaking, I watched him leave. I peered out the front window, watching as he slid into the driver's seat of his silver Mercedes, slipped on his wire-framed sunglasses, started the car and drove away. Was he right? Should I have waited until after the election? This fight left me feeling confused and guilty.

But what about the day I caught him with Dallas in my backyard? And there was no way I believed that he and Jane

were platonic. I'd caught more than one suspicious look between them over the past few weeks.

Okay, no more confusion, I told myself. It was all right for him
to run around, but I had to remain celibate? He was expecting me to just keep right on being the good girl and take all
his crap. It wasn't going to happen. He couldn't control me
anymore. Maybe the bad girl in me was finally stronger than
the good girl. I was starting to like her.

13

I called Sonny from my office as I was gathering my things. "It was Harry," I told him. "But he left." I didn't mention that Harry had seen him. It would embarrass him. "Oh, and don't forget about supper at the big house tonight. Bonita will be there, and Lewis is bringing Vivi a big surprise. You think you can still come?"

"Sure," he said. "But I'll drive my car and meet you there. That way I can get home and no one will say anything 'bout you driving me home late at night."

He was thinking and doing everything he could to help me in this little situation I was currently in.

"Great. See you there."

"I'll be right behind you, and I believe that could be a very nice place to be. Later, sugar." He hung up, laughing.

I locked everything up one last time, then went out back to my car and drove straight to Vivi's. Sonny was right where he said he'd be, in my rearview mirror. I couldn't help but smile.

We parked on the circle drive out near the fountain, Sonny pulling in behind me. I caught the glint in his eye and knew he was thinking of his earlier risqué comment, too.

The sunset splashed the sky with orange sherbet and turquoise watercolors. It cast a glow over us as we got out of our cars and walked over to hug each other.

"This is the magic hour," I said. "It's the moment just after the sun sets and there is still light in the sky. I read about it in a movie magazine."

"All my hours with you are magic," Sonny said, kissing my forehead. I snuggled into his neck and turned to watch the final glimmers of the day pass over the edge of the horizon.

Vivi appeared on the front porch of her plantation home. "Hey, y'all. So glad you could come, Sonny. Bonita is on her way. And Lewis stopped by someplace to pick up this surprise he says he has for me. Lord, what in the world is he doing? It almost has me nervous. Y'all come on in and have some iced tea."

Sonny and I walked up the stairs and the scrumptious aroma of fresh biscuits floated under my nose and led me to the kitchen. I arrived in the doorway and saw Vivi had painted her kitchen walls a buttercream-yellow.

The huge, oversized long wooden table took up most of the center of the room. Eight chairs with sky-blue plaid cushions and high ladder backs surrounded the table. Over the table hung a big, cream-colored chandelier that Vivi had flown in from an antiques dealer in France.

In fact, her whole house was done in Country French, every single room in festive colors, lots of pattern and textures, stripes and plaids. But the scene in the kitchen tonight would forever stay in my memory. Arthur at the stove, with his full chef apron on, humming to himself. Vivi washing vegetables at the sink. Her pastel blue chef's apron covered with prints of big yellow peonies and tied above her baby bump like a protective shield.

Arthur was just taking the biscuits from the oven, and the creamed corn, green beans and black-eyed peas were already sitting on the table, steam rising above the antique French bowls.

Some people have that ability to make a house a real home. To become the go-to place for the family for all the holidays. For my family, it had always been my grandmother Meridee's house. "Mother's," as it was known, was our command center, the sun of our little universe. Meridee was always cooking and singing, and everyone felt welcome to just come in and sit at the kitchen table and be in the moment with her.

Vivi, I could see now, had that same ability, that special spark that drew people in. I had always wanted to have it, too, but in this moment, I felt the shift. Having this baby and getting ready to marry Lewis had made her feel settled and comfortable. Her happiness literally made her glisten.

Vivi's house would be next in line to the throne. It was her nature to always be real, to never put on airs. Like it or not, she was always herself and had always been comfortable in her own skin. That was the magic. And she was just like Meridee in that way.

I wondered if I could ever be that way, have a place like that. I hoped so.

Sonny and I entered the busy, delicious room. "Oh, it smells so good in here. I can't wait to dig in."

"Me, either," Sonny said. "Been a long time since I had some good home cooking."

Note to self—learn to cook...anything.

Just as we sat down at the table, Bonita walked in and went straight over to Arthur and kissed his cheek. "Hey, sugar, how's my man?"

Arthur's big eyes lit up and he blushed. "I'm wonderful now." Arthur and Bonita had met shortly after she accepted the position on Sonny's investigative team. They'd clicked right off the bat, and it was clear that they were crazy about each other.

"Not just *now*, honey." She smiled at him. "This all just smells so fantastic. What can I do to help?"

"Everything is all set. What's in the bag you're carryin'?"

Bonita set a brown paper sack on the kitchen counter. "Just some good ol'-fashioned orange-pineapple ice cream."

"Oh, my word," Vivi said. "Where in the world did you find that? I haven't had a taste of that since Pure Process went out of business. Do tell."

"Well, if you must know, I made it myself," Bonita said, obviously proud of her accomplishment.

Arthur turned from the stove where he was frying the last of the chicken. "You are kiddin' me?"

"Nope, I kid you not. My daddy taught me how to make it years ago, before he passed. It's an old family secret."

I looked over at Arthur the very minute Bonita said she made the ice cream herself. I knew what he was thinking. Vivi glanced at me. She knew, too. With Arthur opening his Moonwinx BBQ place out back in a few weeks, that ice cream would sell like crazy, since nobody could get that flavor around here anymore. This was a match made in barbecue business heaven.

"Miss Bonita, you sweet thang," Arthur said playfully. "What do I need to do to get you to share that recipe with me?"

"Well, now, Mr. Arthur, that's something we'll have to discuss in private." Bonita blew him a kiss. He pretended to catch it and put it in his pocket.

They were so cute together, and so old-fashioned. Arthur

was in his early fifties and Bonita was in her early forties, but they hit it off like high-school sweethearts.

Arthur had graduated high school and even had a little college before Vivi's daddy died years ago, and Arthur had come running back to care for Vivi and her mother. Arthur had been studying business at Alabama, and was in his second year when it happened.

Arthur had lived on the plantation more like a relative most of his life. His mom died when he was about twelve. She had worked as a cook for the McFaddens for as long as I knew, and Arthur was her only child. I remember something about his dad dying in the Vietnam war, but all I knew was that both of his parents were gone and he had a real close relationship with Vivi's dad, Mr. McFadden. Arthur was living there even before Vivi was born.

Vivi had money to survive on and tried to convince him to finish college, but he would hear nothing of it. He knew she needed him. Her mother was never a very good one, always a little on the crazy side and rather sickly. She was also very dependent and needy. Arthur felt he had to be there for Vivi. She was barely a teenager and he felt responsible for her upbringing.

Bonita, meanwhile, was as smart as they came and highly opinionated. What she loved in Arthur was that he was an old-fashioned gentleman. That was a rare thing these days. She and Arthur were cute as could be...and it looked like they were fixin' to have quite a business together.

We all heard the front screen door slam, and Lewis's booming voice shook the rafters. "Hey, Red, I'm home. Come see what Daddy brought for my babies."

With all the crashing and banging going on in the front hall, it sounded like he must have brought Vivi a bull. We all hurried from the kitchen and ran into the hall, then stopped dead in our tracks.

Bouncing and jumping all over Lewis was a beautiful, rambunctious golden retriever. A dog. Lewis brought pregnant Vivi a dog.

"I wanted to complete our family, and every family needs a dog." Lewis was so grown-up and such a little boy all at the same time.

"Oh, honey, I love him," Vivi cooed. "He is just beautiful."

"I got him from a shelter after Cal, a frat buddy of mine, said he saw him there and thought I might like him. I always wanted a dog, and, Vivi, I know you said you did, too. So I ran by this morning and paid the fees and picked him up on the way home. What do ya think?"

"I think you're fabulous," Vivi said. "He will be wonderful for the baby and I know he will be such good company for me, especially during football season. Thank you, baby." She tippy-toed up and gave him a kiss.

"We still have to name him," Lewis said, frowning. "No way I'm calling him by the one they gave him at the shelter."

"How about we name him Harry," Vivi suggested, "to commemorate the importance of this day?"

"Perfect! That works for me. That way we will always remember what happened today."

I doubted the real Harry would see the honor in being remembered this way, though. Something told me the idea of sharing his name with this new furry friend wouldn't exactly fit with his *image*.

Lewis and Sonny headed back to the kitchen with Arthur. Vivi and I stayed back with Bonita.

"Are you really okay with this?" I asked Vivi.

"Oh, sure, we got all kinds of space out here. That dog'll love livin' here with all the rib bones from Arthur's business.

You know, I'm kinda likin' all this domesticity. I missed a lot of this growin' up, and Lewis did, too. We're gonna try to re-create a Norman Rockwell scene out here. I'm into it big-time," Vivi said, grinning ear to ear.

Just then, the dog started humping Bonita's leg.

"Good Lord, have mercy, now he can't be doing that!" Bonita exclaimed.

"Harry, stop that right this minute." Vivi pulled the dog off Bonita. He started humping me next.

"Oh, my heavens, y'all, I am so sorry." She pulled the dog off again and he ran on inside to the men. "I can't believe he did that to both of you." She was blushing red when, suddenly, she started laughing out loud.

"What's so funny?" I asked her.

"It just occurred to me I named the dog Harry."

"Yeah, so?" asked Bonita.

"Well, his nickname will have to be Harry The Humper. He *is* named after a politician, after all. And all the politicians I have ever known seem to have the same agenda."

"Typical politico, if you ask me," Bonita added.

We rejoined the men and sat at the big old table. The feast was fabulous and the conversation warm and memorable. Afterward, as we began to pass around some coffee, Vivi mentioned to Arthur she'd like to ask him something important.

"Well, sure, Miss Vivi. Anything." He smiled at her.

"Arthur, you mean the world to me. You have been my caretaker, my housemate and my friend for so long, I can't even remember. But, most importantly, you are my family."

Vivi had tears in her eyes and was getting choked up. "I want you to know you are welcome to stay and live here always. This is your home."

Arthur teared up, too.

"My wedding day is coming, and the most important person in my family should be giving me away. You are that person for me, Arthur. I ask you now. Will you give me away?"

"Miss Vivi, I hate the idea of ever givin' you away to anybody. I like you just right where you are. But yes, I will happily walk you down the aisle to your Mr. Lewis. It would be my utmost honor." His voice was shaky as he wiped his cheeks with his napkin.

Vivi went over to him and hugged the only man in her life besides Lewis. Bonita had to get up and hug Arthur, too.

"You are such a good man," Bonita said as she kissed Arthur's head.

"I know he is, and I am so lucky to have him," Vivi added.

"Me, too." Bonita smiled and went back to her seat. "Now, let's have us some ice cream."

14

I woke up with Harry licking my face—the dog, not the politician and soon-to-be ex-husband. I had decided to stay at Vivi's house, much to Sonny's dismay. I stretched and flipped the covers off, touched my bare feet to the wood floor and headed downstairs with Harry The Humper following closely behind. I had to admit, he was cute and lovable—much more so than his human counterpart.

No one was up yet, so the early morning was quiet. The already humid air clung to the windows over the sink in the kitchen, dripping condensation down the panes.

I put some coffee on and padded around in a white oxford button-down shirt of Sonny's that he had given me back in May when I got caught in an evening storm while running across the street to his office. I had somehow *accidentally* never returned it. The shirt was now my favorite nightgown.

When the coffee was ready, I handed Harry one of the biscuits Lewis had brought home last night for his new pet, then took him out to the porch.

I sat down in one of the white wicker rockers and Harry took his new spot in the dog bed Lewis had laid out for him. Bees buzzed around the hydrangea and gardenia bushes as dandelion seeds floated past the screened door to my left. The fountain on the gravel drive splashed a morning melody for the birds to sing to and bathe in. It was lovely and relaxing. This was a home now.

I don't think Harry, the human, and I had ever created that. Sure, our house was a showplace, but this magical warmth had never been a part of it. I wondered if I even knew how to make a home. I knew how to work hard and stand by my friends, but I hoped I could create this kind of magic when the time came.

I patted Harry The Humper's head. He was still busy chewing his treat, but stood up to head back inside when Arthur appeared at the screen door.

"Mornin', Arthur," I chirped. "Sleep okay?"

"Mornin', Miss Blake. Yes, I did, and you?" He was in a great mood, as usual.

"Never better. You and Bonita sure are gettin' on well these days," I said with my eyebrows raised.

"We do have us a good ol' time together. She brings out the best in me, I do believe. She even said she's gonna share that orange-pineapple ice cream recipe when I open the Moonwinx. Can you believe that?"

"That's wonderful." I loved hearing him so happy about his new restaurant. "That was quite a feast last night. One of the best I've had in quite a while, I'll say. Her ice cream just topped it all off. It will be a great addition to your menu."

"I've shown Bonita my plans, and she says I got a good

head for business. It's what I was studying when I left school so long ago."

"Well, she's right. I'm already hearing a lot of chatter about the opening of Moonwinx in town. And folks are talkin' about you and Bonita, too."

"She sure is something special. Can I get you some breakfast 'fore you have to go?" he asked.

"No, I've already put the coffee on and I'll eat later. Harry here looks a little hungry, though," I said, gesturing to the dog.

"Yeah, I saved him some leftovers from last night." Arthur reached down and patted his head.

"He's the luckiest hound I know, with all the food that comes outta here. Now, with the barbecue place you're opening, Lord, Arthur, he just won the lottery." I opened the screen door to the house and went back inside.

Vivi greeted me in the kitchen. She poured herself a cup of coffee. "Someone's up early." She took a sip from the steaming mug.

"Yes, I have a crazy day ahead of me." I rinsed my cup out in the sink. "We've got a meeting with the Fru Fru boys first thing this morning to discuss the plan for the ceremony and reception, and then I've got a lunch date with Kitty, and a media stint I need to attend for Harry this afternoon. But listen, honey, I promise we'll get to Tressa, just as soon as we can. She won't be Lewis's estranged wife much longer. I tracked down the name of a club Tressa worked in at one time not too long ago. I'll call today, and if she still works there, we'll pay her a little visit tomorrow. All right?"

"What would I ever do without you? You're like Superwoman! I don't know how you juggle it all." Vivi smiled.

"All in a day's work, hon." I could tell that thinking about this other woman had made these past two days more stressful than she needed right now. While I still had my cases to think about, it was my duty as matron of honor to help her sort out this sticky situation.

"I can't wait to see that woman face-to-face," Vivi said. "She's just got to understand."

"We can only hope." I headed toward the stairs. "You'd better get a move on. Both of us have to get dressed, and the Fru Fru boys are on their way."

Upstairs, I slipped on a navy pencil skirt and my white sleeveless blouse, my pearls, my red sling-backs and my red lipstick. I was trying to stay with a patriotic color scheme to play the part of senator's wife. But even the outfits were getting mundane.

I brushed my long brunette hair back, fluffed it up and sprayed my Aqua Net. By the time I reached the hour of Harry's speech this afternoon, my hair would be a frizzy mess with all this humidity. So I sprayed a bit more and brought my hair clips to put it up in case of a humidity attack later.

"Blake," Vivi called from downstairs, "the Fru Fru boys are here!"

I ran down into the front hall. Vivi had opened the door and I could see that Coco and Jean-Pierre had arrived in style in their hot Pepto-Bismol-pink van. It was a new Mercedes commercial van, with broad white stripes stretching horizontally across the bright pink sides.

A Fru Fru Affair was etched on both sides in grass-green fancy cursive writing. I went around to the back double doors, and Jean-Pierre was there, pulling out the platters that were stacked on built-in trays. The words on the back doors listed all of the events they catered: Weddings, Showers, Tailgates, Bat and Bar Mitzvahs, Even Funerals. That's exactly how it read, word for word.

Somehow, I didn't think it would look right for this hot-pink van to pull up at a cemetery, but I kept that to myself.

"Hey, y'all," Vivi said as they approached the porch.

Coco ran up the front steps like it was Christmas morning and all his presents were inside. "Oh, my goodness, this place is fantastic. I am so gonna love redoing it all."

"Wait a minute," Vivi protested. "Exactly what do y'all plan to redo?"

"Oh, honey, we can have so much fun with all this space. How 'bout we have the porch widened a bit so your entire bridal party can all get up there for pictures?" Coco asked, sizing things up and thinking out loud.

"No remodeling. I love this place just like it is." Vivi was trying to smile, but she never could hide her real feelings.

Coco sighed. "If you insist…but just in case, I have the number for this gorgeous construction worker." Coco smiled at the thought, though I wasn't sure *gorgeous* was counted as a real job qualification.

Jean-Pierre took out a fancy pen with a pink feather attached. "Let's talk about the animals."

"Animals? Y'all are startin' to scare me." Vivi fanned herself. "I'm gonna need a seat."

"Well, you know we have swans comin', and that's just for starters."

"Don't swans need, like, a pond?" Vivi asked.

"Yes, sweetie."

"Have you noticed I don't have one?"

"Don't worry. We're having one dug, right over there," Coco answered, gesturing to the land near the pecan grove.

"What? Y'all are plannin' on diggin' up my yard?"

Jean-Pierre continued writing with the feather pen. "It will be quick and painless and we can even leave the swans if you like. They'll be for sale after the wedding anyway."

Vivi looked even whiter than usual.

I quickly took the reins and interrupted all the excitement.

"Okay, maybe we need to slow it way down. How about we take a moment to hear what *Vivi* wants."

"I want to sit down inside outta this heat, that's the first thing I want," Vivi said.

We headed inside for some iced tea. I poured us all a glass as Vivi sat at the table with the guys.

Coco smiled. "You'll love this, Vivi. We plan on having a huge crate of a hundred doves to release when your groom kisses you. How about that?"

Vivi looked nauseous. "I thought doves were only used in magic shows and funerals. This is sounding like I could have an awful lot of bird shit to duck at my wedding."

"Don't worry. We'll release them far enough away from the wedding guests that they won't hit anyone if they poop."

Merciful heavens. A bunch of squawking swans? A hundred possibly incontinent doves? What would the Fru Fru boys come up with next? Lewis had already volunteered Harry The Humper as ring bearer last night. Pretty soon, we'd have a full-fledged zoo.

Just as the Fru Fru boys were driving off, Wanda Jo called and said my clients had to see me. Since I had to rush out, I decided to call Vivi as I drove.

"Hey, just checking on you. Those boys are sure full of creativity. What are your plans today?"

"In all this confusion, I forgot I have a baby doc appointment today. I'm so excited, I'm heading over there right now."

"Oh, good. Can't wait to hear the progress." I was so happy to change the subject. The Fru Frus had us both going crazy thinking about all those animals.

"I may have a surprise for y'all," she said, all singsongy. "Ta-ta."

She sounded excited and happy. I was hoping the little surprise would be learning if she were having a baby boy or a baby girl as Vivi had been predicting all along.

I pulled into the back parking lot and got out. Visions of Sonny running across the street and in through this back door swam through my head. Just the thought of him sent heat up and down my body. The vision of him as he walked in the back door, smoldering and hungry for me... I had to shake it. I had an appointment inside.

"Hey, Wanda Jo," I said as I walked in, setting my bag down on the credenza and my keys in the pink glass bowl. I grabbed the mail and headed into my office.

"Hey there, Miss Blake. I got messages out the wazoo for you this mornin'," Wanda Jo said, joining me.

"The clients called and said they'll be here a few minutes early, so I'm glad you're here."

She stopped at the doorway and smiled. She was wearing red pants and a white short-sleeved blouse with long red beads. I guess *America* was the theme of the week. She handed me the file as she headed to the kitchen.

"Did you work late last night?" she called from the other room.

"No, I left about half an hour after you, but Harry dropped by just as I was closing up."

I was hoping she didn't see anything, but I guess I should have known Wanda Jo and her eagle eyes.

"Oh, crap," she said. "I sure as hell hope the cop was gone by the time Harry got here. That would've been a dee-saster just waitin' to happen." She returned from the kitchen, smiling and kept talking as she handed me my Diet Coke. I hadn't even asked for one, but that was Wanda Jo. She just knew.

"Yes, Wanda Jo, my worlds didn't collide if that's what you're asking. It was all very discreet. Though I guess not discreet enough if you knew what I was up to."

"Well, nothin' gets by me, missy. And you just got that look on your face."

"What look?" I asked.

"You know, that look of 'uh-oh, what am I doing?' I can see it a mile away."

"Well, I hope you're the only one."

I took a sip of my drink, remembering full well Sonny grabbing his pants up and running out the back door with his shoes in his hand and Harry finding my desk items on the floor—the ones I pushed off as Sonny lifted my ass up on it to devour me. No, my worlds did not collide, as long as you don't count near midair collisions.

I smiled at her and said, "Let me know when the Aarons arrive. I need to glance at the file."

Wanda Jo grinned and closed my door. I sat at my desk in the cool of the air-conditioning, and my mind wandered off to thoughts of Sonny and a time in college before I met Harry.

My sophomore year at the University of Alabama was the most fun I had had in school up to that point. I entered every beauty pageant on campus.

I had been a bit nerdy in high school; the debate team was my life if that tells you anything. But when college started I was able to reinvent myself. I was still focused on school, but I was also dating several guys that year, all very different, and that wasn't like me at all. I was having a moment. A man moment. I must have blossomed that year because suddenly everyone wanted to go out with me. It was fall semester and crisp blue-sky football Saturdays were what we lived for.

I was so confident, still tan from the summer, wearing my tightest jeans and tightest low-cut shirts, and loving riding on the back of a convertible in every parade, wearing my sexiest gowns with a crown on my head.

Pumpkins were on all the porches, and homecoming banners draped the doorways of all the fraternities and sororities on campus. It was the best time of the year, and I was at my peak as a college girl.

One of the guys I was seeing was a model. Yes, I said *model*. I met him in an acting class, and he and I were assigned scenes from *Cat on a Hot Tin Roof*. That is one passionate piece of literature. We decided we needed to practice—a lot. Though it seemed like Steve and I only practiced the passionate scenes. The ones that required him to lie on top of me, without his shirt on, and deeply kiss me for hours. Oh, wait, that play doesn't have any scenes like that...

Well, we wrote them in ourselves, reasoning that unless we were "comfortable" with each other, the real kissing scenes wouldn't look right. Ah, yes, all in the name of character development. That was serious method acting.

His body was luscious, ripped and hard. He had jet-black hair, dimples and dark brown eyes. He was delicious. We practiced for hours every day. Then, like a harlot, I would go out at night with another guy. I mean, I didn't feel like a skank, Steve was only "rehearsal," after all.

Later in that glorious semester, I ran into Sonny on campus. He was working for the university police and going to school at Alabama, too. It was a weeknight, about ten o'clock, and we were in the stacks at the main library. My heart skipped when I saw him. I hadn't spoken to him in at least a year. We were both at college doing our thing. For me, that meant sorority life and beauty pageants; for him, it was criminal justice classes and police training. Our circles never overlapped.

But I will never forget that feeling of seeing him and what he looked like when he glanced up at me. He was in a lightweight crimson sweater, tan corduroys and loafers with no socks. His long, golden-brown bangs hung over his forehead just a tad too long. He slid his fingers through his hair, pushing it out of his eyes when he looked up and saw me.

He grinned that trademark grin and walked over to me. I was standing in a little cubby at the end of the stacks. He was very close to me, propping his arm on the door frame and leaning into me. I could smell his cologne and peppermint gum, and I vividly remember tingling all over.

He hugged me hello, and we talked, trying awkwardly to catch up, saying how we don't know how we missed seeing each other all this time.

"You seein' anybody in particular?" he asked.

"Not in particular," I answered, smiling.

And I wasn't, really. I had been seeing several guys at the moment, but not one of them in particular, I reasoned.

"I would love to see you, maybe Saturday, after the game? I'm working the sidelines that day, but maybe after?"

He was looking at me in that way he did that would always make me melt. He had a power over me and he knew it.

"Sure," was all I could muster.

Sonny leaned down and brushed his lips across mine, then pulled back and smiled. A tease for sure. He knew I loved that.

"You've still got the most beautiful eyes I have ever seen," I said. He leaned down again and pressed his lips to mine, holding there for a minute, gently nibbling before he pulled away.

"I've missed you, Blake. I'll meet you at the main gate right after the game."

I smiled. "See you then." I was in a trance.

We had been on and off again since we were fourteen, and this encounter would lead to our final attempt at being together before I met Harry.

I went home that night in a daze. How did he do this to me every single time? He could make me forget everything. The two days went by in a blur and, by Saturday, I was giddy. I hadn't even held "rehearsal" with Steve in the forty-eight hours since running into Sonny.

I waited for Sonny at the main gate after the game. The crowd was crazy with the big Bama win over Ol' Miss. My sorority sisters scattered to local bars on the famous strip, meeting frat boys and football players. I stood under the entryway to Bryant-Denny Stadium, nervously fidgeting and glancing around.

Then, there he was, walking toward me with his familiar swagger and that precious grin, in his uniform. He looked so good. My heart skipped. I had never seen him dressed in his professional clothes. It somehow made me feel older, more mature. Serious in a way that was so above and beyond the rest of my friends.

I couldn't wait to get my hands on him.

"Hey, Blake," he said as he approached. "You look great." He leaned down and hugged me tightly.

"I have to go back to my apartment and get changed," he said.

I liked the sound of that.

"I promise I won't be long. Wanna go see where I live these days?"

"I would love that," I said, smiling and maybe sounding a little too enthusiastic.

His apartment was scattered a bit but not messy. Mismatched furniture, but tasteful. Muted masculine colors, his trombone in a corner, and outdoor paraphernalia here and there. His backpack, some binoculars, a telescope. Any visitor would know right away he liked being outside on an adventure.

"Make yourself comfortable, I'll be right back," he said, heading to his bedroom.

"Okay," I said, smiling as I sat down on his dark brown leather couch. Sonny disappeared and I could hear him rummaging through his closet. I wanted to get up and check things out some more.

"I'm gonna use the restroom, okay?"

"Okay," he said, "but I'm not sure how clean it is." He was

so nervous, but at that point, nothing would have made me not want that night. He could have clothes and dirty underwear strewn from here to Mississippi and I wouldn't have cared. I was blinded by the thought of being alone with him. We were grown-ups now.

"It's up the hall on the right," he said.

I walked up the hall and glimpsed Sonny in his bedroom. The door was half-closed but open just enough for me to see him standing in his boxer briefs and no shirt. My stomach dropped like on a roller coaster ride. I took a deep breath and headed on into the bathroom.

It was small but had matching towels and shower curtain. His aftershave and cologne were on the sink. His razor next to his shaving cream, I breathed it all in deeply. Sonny was so masculine, even at nineteen.

I was in his man cave.

"Okay, ready if you are," he said, emerging from the bedroom. The image of him in his underwear from moments ago reappeared in my head. Was I ready? Did I want to go out or stay in? I was sure we needed to go before we got out of control. Sonny and I had always had an unexplainable, raging, combustible chemistry. *Yes, we had better go out,* I thought.

Sonny lived right off the strip, close to all the bars and restaurants. We walked to a little pizza place and shared a pepperoni. Small talk and catching up and a few awkward moments followed until Sonny reached across the table and cupped his hand over mine.

"This feels really good, Blake. I, uh, well…" He stumbled. "I hope you feel the same way."

I smiled at him and placed my other hand over his. "Of course I do, Sonny. I always do."

"I wanted to ask you if you'd like to go somewhere with me next weekend," he said with a hopeful tone in his voice.

"I'm going with my ragtime band over to Georgia for a little concert. Wanna go with me?"

Oh, I was elated inside, just bubbling over. I knew Sonny played his trombone in an old-fashioned group and now I would finally get to see him.

"Yes, absolutely," I said. "Can't wait."

When we left the pizza place, he offered to walk me back to my sorority.

"Let's go back to your place for a little while, instead," I suggested.

Sonny raised his eyebrow and grinned. "I would've asked, but I didn't want to push you," he said.

"No, it's fine, I'd like to keep talking," I said, sure that my eyes were saying I wanted a lot more than just talking.

We walked back to his apartment, holding hands, as comfortable together as though we'd never been apart. When we got inside, I perched on his couch while he grabbed us a couple of soft drinks. Then he sat down in front of me, placing them on the coffee table among newspapers and school notebooks.

"Blake, I want to be honest with you," he said seriously. "All this time we've been apart... Well, I've missed you. I think we're right together, and I don't want to waste any more time. I want to get back together. What do ya think?"

I could tell how nervous he was from the way he kept running his fingers through his hair. It was his nervous tick, and I'd always thought it was so cute. My heart was racing.

"Me, too. I mean, yes, I think that's a good idea." We were both awkward, in that nineteen-year-old way. So full of emotions and desires, but so unsure about how to act on them.

Sonny leaned over and kissed me, softly, then with force and passion. We made out, touching and exploring for most of the night, before he walked me all the way back to my sorority house in the wee hours. He was a gentleman, and a sensual, generous lover. I knew one thing, I definitely wanted more, though I wasn't sure I was ready. But Sonny never pushed me. And in the end we never did actually sleep together.

For several months, things were amazing and I was happy. I was falling hard; something had happened to me over that semester that made me know this relationship with Sonny could be it. But then we went on that fateful trip to Nashville. It was spring and I had been going on little jaunts to see his group perform. That particular weekend we were just over the Alabama line, and it was about 11:00 p.m. when we stopped for a late bite at the Waffle House. Eventually, talk turned to my plans for the fall. I was hoping to spend the next semester in New York, but Sonny didn't want me to go.

"I love you, Blake. I always have. I think we've got a good thing goin' here, don't you?"

"Yes, I love you, too, baby. You know that."

"Then why are you leavin' to go so far away to New York?"

"I have to, Sonny. It's such an amazing opportunity and I'm so excited! They only chose twenty students from all over the country to study there and I am one of them. It will be so good for my career," I explained.

"I know, but I'll just miss you so bad. I was hoping we could take this to the next level, if you stay."

"Oh, Sonny, what do you mean?"

"I mean...I'm thinking about forever." He stopped, realizing the gravity of what he had just said. It threw me. We were barely twenty and he wanted to talk about marriage.

"I do think about forever all the time," I said.

"But Blake, be realistic. If you go to New York, anything could happen."

"Sonny, don't you trust me? I don't see why we couldn't continue things just like they are," I said, trying to make sense of what he was saying.

"But Blake, I can't do a long-distance relationship with you. And I know you'll meet people there, too."

"Sonny, please, I know we can do it."

"I can't. I'm sorry."

I started to tear up. "What does this mean?" I asked.

"Well, I guess we'll have to just see how it goes. See where we are when you get back." He was quiet, then, and we both sat staring at our half-eaten waffles. After a few minutes like that, it seemed there was simply nothing more to say. We loved each other and wanted things to last forever, but we were just too young to make the sort of commitments and sacrifices it would take to stay together. I could tell he was sad as he started the car, and we drove the nearly three hours back in silence.

Things faded away slowly after that talk. I knew he was hurt. I just didn't know how much at the time. I went on to New York and that's when I met Harry. Sonny went on and finished his police training and met Laura, his now ex-wife. But I never forgot that familiar feeling I got every time I was near him, comfort like I've never felt with anyone else. It was hard to believe it has taken us all these years to finally find our way back to each other. But now that we had, it sure felt like coming home.

Wanda Jo announced the Aarons and showed them in. They had all the paperwork they could find and even said they had information on Walter's girlfriend.

"Hey, y'all, so glad to see you. Come right on in and have a seat," I said, motioning to the chairs in front of my desk.

"Y'all need anything else, just holler." Wanda Jo stepped out and went back to her desk.

"We found all of Walter's papers. I can't believe he wouldn't tell us this, but…well, it seems he did get married and it was just a few weeks before he died." Wayne handed me the paperwork. It was all of Walter's insurance papers and his will.

"I should tell you," I began as carefully as I could, "that I found out just recently that the homicide investigators have evidence to the fact that foul play may have been involved in Walter's death."

"I knew it," Wynona said. "There was no damn way he would jump."

"What does this mean, Mrs. Heart?" Wayne asked.

"Well, it will hold up the settlement until we find out just what happened. But the police think someone wanted him off that boat."

I went through the insurance papers to see who was listed as the beneficiary. I was looking for the name of Walter's wife, when I noticed something quite strange. His wife's name was Tamlyn M. Hartman. It took about a minute before I realized why the name sounded so familiar. Lewis's estranged wife also had the last name Hartman. *Another Hartman?* I wondered. Well, Tuscaloosa did have a few of them. I remembered I'd even gone to school with a Katie Hartman.

"Do y'all happen to have a picture of Walter's new wife?" I asked.

"No, nothing. As we said, we had no idea who she was or that their relationship was so serious. And there were no pictures in the paperwork and files we went through, either," Wayne answered. "Is there a way to know if she ever filed to get her settlement?" he asked.

"I'll be checking in with the insurance company later. I know y'all are trying to settle his will as soon as possible, so I'll go over all of his papers. My guess is that he never had time to change his will if all of this happened so suddenly."

But even if that were true, the Aarons still had a lot to be concerned about. While the will might state that they were the ones to get his estate, this revelation about the new insurance beneficiary meant we'd have a lot more to straighten out.

"Y'all just hang on. We will get to the bottom of this." I was trying to be reassuring but this case was getting messier by the day.

Wanda Jo interrupted and handed me a message on a piece of paper.

Call Sonny. They have turned up some evidence on the barge.

I told the Aarons I would call them the minute we could track Ms. Hartman down, and then walked them to the front office where Wanda Jo showed them out. I hurried back to my office and called Sonny.

"What's the news?" I asked, breathless.

"We found a cell phone. I think it may be Walter's. Bonita found it out there today. She went out there for one more look and found it on the barge itself. I'm not sure how we missed it before, but I guess that's why I hired Bonita. Anyway, the battery was dry. We're charging it now to see if there's anything else it can tell us about what happened to Walter Aaron."

"Great news, baby. I'll be there in ten minutes."

I grabbed my purse and told Wanda Jo I had to get to the station. I ran out without hearing her say goodbye.

16

I made it to the station in record time and ran into Bonita
and Sonny talking in the front lobby.

"Hey, y'all. I heard there was some excitement out at the
barge today."

"Yep, Bonita is determined. And she was right. There was
more to find out there. The Aarons have gotta be on the edge
of their seats."

"Speaking of which, they turned up some good information y'all can probably use. They found the wedding certificate
and the new wife's name matches the beneficiary on Walter's
updated insurance policy. It's a woman by the name of Tamlyn M. Hartman."

"Hartman?" Bonita jumped in. "Isn't that the last name of
the woman Lewis is supposedly married to?"

"Bonita, you have a brain like a lockbox. It sure is. I haven't
had a chance to look into it to see if, by some wild chance,

the two are related. But I brought the Aarons' copies of the documents with me, in case you want to look at them now."

"We're meeting with them tomorrow," Sonny said, "but if there's something we can work with today, that would be great."

We made our way into a conference room and spread the papers on the table. Sonny went over to where the cell phone they'd found was charging to check its status.

"I'm so glad you were persistent, Bonita. The cell phone could be a real break in the case," I said.

She shrugged off my praise. "I just had this nagging feeling that there had to be more out there. Keys, or something."

Sonny joined us at the table. "Okay, we got us a phone, y'all. Let's take a quick peek." He turned on the cell. They both wore white gloves to protect the evidence and the phone was in a plastic bag, but we could still see through it and make out the names in his contacts list.

"Pull up the pictures, in case we got lucky," Bonita said.

"Your wish is my command," Sonny said, bringing up the most recent photos Walter took.

We gazed at a picture of Walter with a blonde bombshell. The woman had long, straight blond hair and a deep tan. She wore a white dress and was standing, in profile, next to Walter. The next shot was a close-up of wedding rings. This had to be Tamlyn Hartman.

Sonny turned to me. "Does she look familiar to you?"

I hesitated. Maybe I just had the whole Lewis situation on my mind, but this woman definitely reminded me of the photos we'd found of his estranged wife—though not nearly as redneck as I remembered from the camo bikini picture. But it seemed a pretty big leap. Just because they were both blonde and had the same last name didn't mean anything. And I didn't want to jump to any wild conclusions in front of Sonny and

Bonita. "I can't see much of her face," I told them, "but she does look familiar."

"I'm gonna call Lewis's friend Cal, out at the university. He's a computer guy with some pretty impressive tracking skills. We may need him." Sonny passed the phone to Bonita for further inspection. Cal, I remembered, was one of Lewis's gorgeous frat brothers from college. He was smart beyond reason and an athlete to boot. The complete package. He played football at Alabama with Lewis, but now ran the entire computer science department there. He was one of those rare finds—a handsome, sexy jock but with the smarts to back it all up.

"Yes," Bonita said, flicking through the phone's call directory. "Cal needs to find us Mrs. Tamlyn M. Hartman Aaron. From what I can see here, the calls to her number only go back a few weeks."

We said our goodbyes, and then Sonny and Bonita headed out to the campus to talk to Cal, while I went my separate way. I'd been shocked they let me into the investigation as much as they did, but I was thrilled I'd been able to help.

I knew one thing: if Walter *was* pushed to his fate, this new wife couldn't have done it herself. A busty blonde that attractive would certainly have been noticed on that barge full of men. It seemed this case was far from closed.

Kitty met me for our lunch date at the Fifteenth Street Diner right at noon. I loved the fried green tomatoes, and Kitty loved their fried chicken. Though to be fair, Kitty loved everybody's fried chicken. The small café was so homey and comfortable. Decorated to look like a 1950s diner, it had laminate tables and vinyl chairs with chrome accents. And they had some of the best home cooking in Tuscaloosa.

Kitty was already there when I arrived, sitting in a booth and talking to the waitress. I walked over to her and hugged her hello.

"Hey, Mother, I am so glad we could meet. I don't have long, but this place is just what I needed today."

"You need comfort food?" Her eyes narrowed. "What's going on, Blake Elizabeth?"

God, she always could read me like a book.

"Can't a girl just call her own mother for lunch without a deposition?" I asked, sitting down on the red leather cushion.

"Why, of course, my dear, but I know my daughter. Now spill, sugar. You got that look."

"What *is* it with everybody today? Wanda Jo thought I had some look, too, this morning. Maybe it's the heat."

"I don't think either of us were talkin' 'bout the weather." She bit the arm of her bedazzled reading glasses like she always did when she was thinking, raised her eyebrows at me, then glanced down at the menu.

"I know. I do need to talk, and you were the safest bet." And truth be told, I did need my mother's advice. She had a way of making things simple and less dramatic.

"Well, that's what mothers are for." She smiled, and I knew it made her happy that I still needed her. After the waitress took our orders, we talked small talk until she showed up with the deep-fried Southern treats. Once she'd left us alone again, I took a deep breath and told Kitty all the confusion I was feeling.

"Well, Mother, the thing is, I know it's no secret to you, but I'm in love with Sonny."

"Did you think I needed a plate full of fried food for you to tell me this? I have known that as a fact for over twenty years," she said, popping a pickle in her mouth. "And guess what, I've got a news flash for you. Sonny is in love with you, too. Now that that's all settled, let's hear the real story."

I took a bite of a tomato and cleared my throat. "I just have a lot on my mind, you know? I mean, I know my marriage with Harry is over, and he knows it, too, but we're in this really awkward period where he's running for office, and I'm playing the part of the happy, supportive, politician's wife."

"I know, baby, and I know you hate pretending, but it's all just temporary," she said.

"But, Mother, it feels like an eternity. It's gotta last all the way till November. I just can't stand it! I wanna be with Sonny so bad."

"Who says you can't? You just gotta be careful, is all. It is a sticky situation for sure, with the campaign, the TV reporters, and in the middle of it, your marriage ending. Trust me, honey, I understand. But, as with everything in life, *temporary* is the word of the day. It will get you through anything."

I knew that was Kitty's mantra. All four of her marriages were just that—temporary. It was scary and reassuring at the same time. Yet she'd survived. In fact, from the look of her, she'd done better than survived. She'd thrived.

I guess I was just a bit spoiled. I wanted what I wanted. And what I wanted was Sonny. And I didn't want to wait till November to have him. But I had no choice.

"Let's just play this out," Kitty said, thinking out loud. "The worst-case scenario is that news gets out that you and Harry are splitting up, right?"

"Mother!" I said. "Keep it down. We are in public and people will hear you." I looked around nervously. "No, actually that is not the worst that could happen," I said. Kitty stopped eating and looked up at me. She raised her eyebrows. "The worst that could happen is—" I leaned forward to make sure no one could hear me "—is if anyone hears that I'm sleeping with Sonny. If it gets out that Harry Heart's wife is having an affair with the chief homicide investigator, all three of us are ruined."

The magnitude of the situation suddenly nauseated me. I put down my fork and looked up at my mother. I could see the concern in her eyes. She leaned forward and placed her hand on mine.

"Listen to me, baby. Nothing of the kind is gonna happen to you. You simply make sure you and Sonny are never caught. Try to limit your time with him and always stay behind closed and locked doors. Be careful in public. Once again, *temporary* is the word. It won't be easy, but, baby, the best things never are. It will all be over before you know it."

She patted my hand and smiled a Sassy Belle smile at me. A sign of unity and strength that I'd recognized since childhood. It told me it would all be okay.

"But, Mother, what about Dallas?" I asked her point-blank. "I got the feeling last time we talked that she knew something about my…situation. Maybe I'm just being paranoid, but I just don't trust her."

"Well, I wouldn't put anything past her, so be careful. I'm sure she already knows what's going on with all three of you. You know Dallas. If there's gossip to be heard, she's already got the details. What she doesn't have is the proof. But I don't think you need to be so concerned about her. I'm sure she's got enough going on that she isn't consumed with thoughts of you and Harry every minute."

"No, but she would love nothing more than a good juicy story, so she can get her face back on a billboard. She could build a three-ring circus with all of this," I said, shaking my head at the thought.

"Still…without solid proof, she's got nothing to report. And it seems to me there's plenty of juicy stories that would be easier for her to dig up," Kitty said.

"What do you mean?" I interrupted.

"Well, Harry is seen pretty often these days with that self-absorbed Judge Shamblin. And he did vote with her on the rezoning of the Brooks Mansion. I don't know for sure, of course, but if it walks like a duck… Well, you just never do know."

"Maybe," I said. "But it still wouldn't be as big as the news about me and Sonny."

"Oh, really? I beg to differ," Kitty said, putting her chicken leg down and wiping her mouth. She leaned into me again.

"Harry, the senatorial candidate, having an affair with the most powerful judge in town? Come on, no one would even be interested in your story." She smiled.

Kitty had a way of putting it all into perspective. I relaxed and took a swig of tea. She was right. And I suddenly felt better.

"Look, sugar, all we can do is all we can do. Be careful. It's temporary. End of story." Kitty sat back and motioned to the waitress for more tea.

"Now, you've got a rally to get to, so put on a Tony-winning performance and make sure you don't get caught doing anything stupid. I was gonna say, 'don't do anything I wouldn't do,' but, hell, it's too late for that." She laughed at herself, and I laughed with her.

It was a release of all the tension that had built up over the past few days. And I wouldn't forget it. I was starting to value my mother on a whole new level. Not just as my mother, but also my friend. I needed her. And that felt good. She supported me unconditionally. I wanted to be like that when I became a mother.

I paid the bill, though in typical Kitty fashion, she argued with me about it. I walked Kitty to her car and hugged her.

"Now remember, put your red lipstick on and stand by that soon-to-be ex-husband of yours and perform like your life depends on it. The sooner we get that man to Washington, the better." Kitty got into her white Lexus and waved goodbye with her bangles jingling.

Okay, I said to myself. *Curtain up. It's showtime.*

18

As I drove through the center of town, I saw the billboards announcing the big citywide celebration at Lewis's new radio station and the grand opening of the Brooks Mansion in just a few short weeks. We'd have Vivi's shower then, too. And by that time, surely Lewis would be a free man.

On the billboard, Lewis was pictured by the wonderful old antebellum home and the new call letters WCTR in the center of the sign. It was one of many billboards going up all over town.

When I arrived at Snow Hinton Park, the tents were up and grandstands had been erected for the crowds to sit and listen to all the rhetoric.

The two white canopies were full of campaign banners and bumper stickers, buttons and little flags, all for sale. Cold soft drinks and bottles of water were in large metal buckets filled with ice and were free to anyone who made a donation or bought a piece of memorabilia.

A large stage was constructed facing a little grove of trees, so the voters could sit in the shade to listen. A wooden podium was placed right in the middle of the stage and a huge banner hung motionless in the stagnant hot air. Follow Your Heart to Washington. Harry's slogan was all over town, on cars, on billboards and in the media. He and Lewis both were the new favorite sons of Tuscaloosa.

I tried to keep in mind what Kitty had said: *The sooner we get that man to Washington, the better.* So true. I decided to get out there today and do my best to make that happen.

Temporary. My new mantra.

I made my way over to Dan, since Harry was busy talking with voters. His sleeves were rolled up, his shirt open at the top button with no tie. He was casual, and Harry was never dressed casual. I knew he had to be uncomfortable without his tie and trademark cuff links.

I guess this would be a Broadway show for both of us.

He looked up and caught my eye as he shook hands with a supporter. He smiled at me, obviously glad to see me there to help stage the performance. "Hey there, Mr. Campaign Manager," I said to Dan, deciding to be really friendly and agreeable. It would shock both of them, but it would make my acting job easier. "How's it going?" I leaned in and gave Dan a sideways hug.

"We're good," Dan said. "You look great. Perfect for a hot summer day in the Deep South and perfect for a future senator's wife."

I guess Dan just had to size me up. It was his nature, assessing the image and figuring how well it would play to Harry's public. Dan was the spin doctor, and I seemed to have passed his exam.

"Go over with Harry, if you want. I'm sure he'd like you to meet his supporters. But after that, Blake, we need to talk."

That didn't sound good. "Great. Can't wait," I said with my award-winning grin.

I walked over to Harry, and he welcomed me into the little circle of people.

"Here's my lovely wife, now. Blake O'Hara Heart, she's my rock," he said, smiling. Okay, contest over. He'd win the Tony for sure. Everyone reached out their hands to shake mine. I smiled and shook back. Harry put his arm around my waist. We looked like the happy political couple.

"Nice to meet, y'all," I said. "Thanks so much for joining us today in this unbearable heat."

Once I'd had a chance to greet most of Harry's biggest supporters, we headed back together toward the stage.

"Thanks for coming today, Blake," Harry said as we made our way to the podium where Dan was waiting. "I know you had a busy morning, but I needed you here today."

I smiled at him and nodded, letting him know it was okay.

"We do what we need to do," I said, envisioning him in Washington. "I am here for you."

"Well, I know you could be elsewhere, so I appreciate it. It helps," he said, then headed over to Dan.

I watched him walk away from me, his stride still as confident as it had been when I'd first fallen for him. But now, I realized, standing there in the dripping heat, I felt so differently about him. Maybe we could be friends eventually, once some of the hurt between us eased, but it was clear that what I had with Sonny already felt deeper than what I'd ever had with Harry. I watched him shake Dan's hand, a two-handed shake that was Harry's calling card. He could look you in the eye as if no one existed but you. He had that political way about him, and he and Dan made a great team.

The reporters began to arrive, and crews set up cameras alongside the stage. Newspaper people and TV journalists from all over the state were propping up tripods and doing test shots. Of course Dallas was also there claiming her spot.

The election was still three months away but Harry made sure he was at every dog and pony show he could find, since that's where you'd find opposing candidate Bullhorn McGraw. His real name was Robert James—Bobby J. for short—but ever since he began campaigning he'd been called Bullhorn because he stumped from the back of a pickup truck using a bullhorn and making a ton of racket.

As Harry found himself amid another group of supporters, Dan took the opportunity to approach me.

"Blake, how about that chat?"

"Sure, Dan. What's up?"

"Well," he began, as he walked me away from the podium to the back of the stage, "we both know you and Harry are all but done." He was whispering. "The thing is, no one else knows. We've kept up the show pretty damn well if you ask me. But we gotta be careful. We're only a few months out and everybody's gonna be snooping around, looking for dirt."

Harry must've told him about the near collision with Sonny in my office. So much for that being a "private" meeting.

"I know, Dan," I said, sounding a tad defensive I was sure. "I think I've been keeping up the show pretty damn well myself."

"I think you need to talk with Harry and make this plan official. Nothing changes. Nothing is filed, whatsoever, until after the election. Divorce and campaigns just don't mix well, unless it's the divorce of your opponent."

I was starting to feel like he didn't trust me not to blow this whole act. "Look, Dan, I'm not the one who took a little nibble on the breast of a certain reporter last spring. Out in broad daylight, mind you. I know what I have to do and I think I've been doing it rather well, thank you. And I think you should also keep in mind that I am doing you and Harry a pretty big favor here. There's no law that says I have to keep up this charade, but I'm doing it because I think Harry deserves to win this election. Despite everything that's happened, he *is* technically my husband and I do care about him. I don't take this situation lightly, you know."

"Fine, you and I may have an understanding, but maybe you need to have a little chat with Harry. With the election so close, he gets really wound up about these sorts of things." He nodded toward the stage.

"Yeah, he looks really wound up...." I said, looking at Harry, who was standing with a certain Judge Jane Shamblin, his arm around her waist and his lips on her cheek. Jane wasn't all that attractive, but maybe that didn't matter to Harry. Her blond hair was always in an impeccable chignon, and she wore skirt suits everywhere. Add cuff links and she could be a female version of Harry. He wanted to win this senate race as much as he wanted his next breath, and Judge Jane Shamblin was his secret weapon. She came from a long line of judges, all very wealthy and successful. Harry was smart to align with her. She could make sure he got elected. Her family had that kind of power.

Dan frowned. "Okay, you do have a point. I'll talk to him. Take care and thanks for being so...understanding." He nodded, then turned and walked toward Harry at a clip, mumbling something about not being a fireman and hating having to constantly put out fires.

Just then I heard the loud nauseating bellow of the bullhorn. Wouldn't you know it; there was Bobby J. and his entourage. Without fail, wherever Harry was, Bullhorn McGraw showed up in the back of a green Ford pickup truck. He sat in a lawn chair with his son, who doubled as his campaign manager. Bobby J.'s wife, Doralyn, was also by his side.

"Hey, y'all, my good citizens of Tuscaloosa! Sho' is hot out here. Wanna fan?" He bellowed the greeting through his bull-horn as he passed out paper fans with his big face pictured on the front. This was not good.

Oh, the fans were a fabulous idea, but seeing as how today's temperature hovered at something like ninety-nine degrees with ninety-nine percent humidity, I was starting to envision Bullhorn's face waving all over as Harry tried to speak. There were hundreds of them. Bullhorn's motto, Send Your Bull-horn to Washington, Have Your Voice Heard, would be fan-ning back and forth in rhythm to Harry's great stump speech. For someone who acted so dumb, Bobby J. was pretty smart.

He was a rotund man, and he wore a white short-sleeved shirt and khaki gabardine pants. The pants were a tad too long, his shirt a bit too tight, and he was wearing his ever-present suspenders. He was about forty-five years old, but looked older.

He used to own a car dealership and starred in all the TV commercials himself. At the end of each one, he would say, "Bobby J.'s got your new car in stock right now." Then he'd snap his suspenders and wink to the camera. Those suspend-ers were part of his image, just like Harry's cuff links were part of his.

Noticing the commotion Bullhorn had created, Dan rushed over to his interns and gave them instructions. Harry had ob-viously been *instructed* to leave Judge Shamblin's side and get his butt behind the stage for his grand entry.

I decided to go chat with Harry while Dan and the interns handled Bullhorn.

"Harry, let's talk for a second, okay?" I began. "I want you to know I will not do anything to hurt your campaign. I am not planning on moving ahead with our divorce until after the election."

"I know, Blake, I trust you."

"Well, Dan thinks we need to make it official, like with a secret handshake or something. Just so we're both on the same page."

Harry laughed and offered his hand, and it lightened the mood.

"I know you, Harry, and even with all that has happened between us, I still think you are the best candidate for the job. I don't have to put on a show when it comes to my faith in your ability to be a wonderful senator."

He stopped and looked into my eyes. We had reached an understanding. I could see I would always have a relationship with him. Maybe not a marriage, but at least an understanding.

"You mean you're not worried Gomer Pyle out there is gonna beat me?"

I laughed. Harry walked over to a fold-up chair where he had his satchel and took out his speech. "So, we're good?" I wasn't really asking, just affirming.

"Yes, we're fine. I'm sorry about the other night. I just, well, I was just tired and didn't see it coming so soon." He started flipping pages, his attention drifting off as he started silently mouthing some of the harder sections of the speech.

Clearly he had turned the page and was only thinking of his audience. He had a way of doing that, turning emotions on and off like a faucet.

I peeked around the stage and saw a huge crowd gathering. It was ten minutes to speech time and the place was like a circus. Dan and the interns were hurriedly swapping cold water bottles for the fans, with Bullhorn just passing more out again.

Then, without warning or goodbyes, Bullhorn's truck drove off, and as it rolled away, I saw Sonny standing under the trees where the truck had been. My heart skipped and I almost stepped from behind the stage, but caught myself.

What was Sonny doing at the rally? This was patrolman

detail, not investigator territory. Still, whatever Sonny said to Bullhorn got him to leave, and awkward as it might be if Harry noticed him here, he'd be thankful for his intervention.

Dan came backstage to make sure we were ready.

"Okay, you two, look, we've got this thing with Bullhorn covered. We managed to get rid of most of the fans, and the cops seem to have convinced him to disappear for now." He smiled his winning smile at us. "Okay, y'all ready to do this? Let's go." Dan didn't wait for an answer. He turned and led the way.

I was nervous. Not because of the crowd or the acting job I was about to do, but because Sonny was out there and I knew he was taking a chance on seeing me.

Dan went onstage first to do the introductions. I stood silently next to Harry. He looked at me and offered his arm and smiled gently. I wrapped my arm under his.

"Showtime," he said.

I smiled back, suddenly realizing we got along much better as *fake* husband and wife. Maybe this would work out, after all.

19

"I give you your next senator from the great state of Alabama, Harry Heart and his wife, Blake O'Hara Heart."

Dan moved aside and the crowd erupted into applause as Harry led the way onstage, his left arm extended in a permanent wave, and me, still locked in the crook of his right arm. He stepped to the podium. I dropped off and stepped back a little. My part was just to play the role of supportive wife, and believe me, that was even more than I wanted.

I looked directly across the tops of all the heads, and there, standing in the back, leaning on a tree, was my knight in shining armor. I locked eyes with Sonny and he smiled. I wondered what he had said to Bullhorn to make him leave.

Harry was talking and the crowd was cheering intermittently, but I didn't hear a word. He sounded like Charlie Brown's teacher from the cartoon. *Wa wa wa...wa wa wa.*

I kept my gaze locked on Sonny and never heard a word of Harry's speech. The conversation with Kitty was playing in my head, *Be careful in public.* Then the talk with Dan, *No one else needs to know.* My head was swimming in the heat.

Suddenly, Harry gestured toward me, inviting me to the podium. Surely, he wasn't going to ask me to speak?

"Now I'd love to introduce my wife and greatest supporter, Blake O'Hara Heart." Harry stepped away from the mic and gave me a little shove toward it.

"Don't be shy, honey," Harry said.

Shy? Me? Come on. I was once the debate champion. Had he forgotten that about me?

I smiled and stepped in front of him.

He leaned over and whispered in my ear, under the guise of giving me a kiss. "Do you have any idea what I just said, or were you in Never Never Land with your cop over there?"

"Honey, I heard every word," I lied. "I've got this." I stepped up to the mic. "Thank y'all so much for coming out here on this blistering hot day." The crowd was smiling and applauding, and I thought, *I kinda like this.* Something about being at the podium in front of an audience felt pretty good to me, so I continued.

"I just want to say, you have the best man for the job right here on stage with me." I gestured back to Harry. "Your heart knows it, too. Dig down deep and ask yourself, who do I want speaking for me and representing my family in Washington, D.C.? Listen well. You'll hear the answer, then do what it says, and Follow Your Heart to Washington!"

The crowd cheered and I stepped back. Harry draped his arm around my back, then leaned in and kissed my cheek, for real this time. We both had earned our Tony Awards with these performances. I looked over to the tree where Sonny was. He was still standing there, looking good enough to eat. Everything seemed to be going as smoothly as we could have hoped for when, out of the far corner of my eye, I spotted Dan

The Man with Dallas, and they were kissing! Never in all my worrying about this day had I thought to be concerned about Dan and Dallas. I was completely stunned.

"Harry, look!" I whispered urgently. "That's Dan…kissing Dallas! What in hell is that all about?"

"Oh, that… Well, she's been really after him lately." Harry kept smiling and waving as we walked back across the metal grandstand, never once breaking the calm, confident soon-to-be senator character.

"What?" I was dumbfounded. "You knew about this and it's okay with you?"

"Sure, why not? They're both adults." Harry was being surprisingly nonchalant. I, however, nearly lost my fried green tomatoes from lunch right then and there. But we were still onstage waving. Puking would not be attractive.

"Harry, she is after something. I have always liked Dan just fine, but…well, he looks like James Carville on a bad day. And Dallas looks like…you know, kinda like Jessica Simpson in a beauty pageant. Her standards are pretty high when it comes to appearances. There's no way she'd go for Dan. Something's up with this."

"It's fine, Blake. She's not as shallow as you think. And Dan seems to really like her. And, if you think about it, it helps the campaign. This definitely puts her on our side."

Well, that was typical. He always found a way to make everything about him and his campaign. I wondered if Dan had the same plan in mind, or if there was something real going on between him and Dallas. We gave a final wave to the crowd and began the descent toward the side and back of the stage, straight into Dan and Dallas, midembrace. I was about to tell them to get a room, when Dallas came up for air.

"Well, hey, Blake, how are you doing?" She was smug as ever.

"Not as well as you seem to be. I see you're making the

rounds on the Heart campaign," I said, referring to the time a couple of months ago when I caught her in a similar embrace with my husband. "Should I alert that cute little intern over there that he's next?"

"Oh, Blake, that's all water under the bridge now that I found Dan." She turned back to him and draped her arms all over him like a serpent.

"Dallas, you are a piece of work. I have afternoon appointments, so, Harry, take care. Dan, well, my list of advice for *you* is far too long for this moment. I'll have to send you a memo. Bye, y'all."

I turned and left before I said anything worse that could end up in print. It was all just too nauseating. These men were so stupid not to see she was playing a game, and her games were not known for being fun or harmless. As she rounded up her crew and sent them on their way, I was reminded more and more of the Wicked Witch of the West dispersing her flying monkeys.

Well, this was one Dorothy who had no intention of surrendering without a fight. Besides, I wanted to find Sonny. I grabbed my bag from the intern who was watching our area under the stage and fumbled for my cell. I had to call Vivi this minute. This time *I* had the headline, and Dallas was the lead story.

20

I dialed Vivi the second I grabbed my phone. Voice mail.
"Hey, little mommy, you will never in a million years guess what is headlining this performance I just gave at the rally. Call me ASAP. Can't wait to hear what the baby doc had to say. Love you." I dropped the phone back down in my purse and walked back to my car. I looked up as I approached the lot near the park, and there he was. My port in the storm.

Sonny was leaning on my car with his hands in his pockets and his legs crossed at the ankles. He was adorable. I wanted to run to him and kiss him but I knew better. We couldn't even hug.

"Hey, baby. You were brilliant," he said as I approached the car.

"Hey, baby, yourself. I saw you standing under the trees and practically missed Harry's entire speech," I said. "But I have huge news that will blow your mind."

"Oh, really? I like to think about you blowing my mind."
He grinned and cocked his eyebrow.

"Oh, don't tempt me like that," I said, imagining the same
thing. "Now, listen. You won't believe this in a million years."
I reached around him to the door and opened it, his shirt
touching my face as I leaned in and threw my purse across to
the passenger side and turned back around. The scent of his
cologne sent another tingle through me.

I smiled up at him and he looked down at me, ready for
the conquest. Being careful was just agony. But I knew there
was no seeing him tonight. I had too much work to do, and
at some point, I knew I had to heed Kitty's advice.

"You'll never guess who Dan Donohugh is seeing."

"Dan The Man, Harry's campaign manager?" Sonny asked.

"The one and only," I said.

"Who?"

I paused for dramatic effect, and then said in a conspirato-
rial whisper, "Dallas."

"As in, Dallas Dubois? You cannot be serious."

"I know. I nearly passed out when I saw them making out
under the stage. Harry said he knew about it, though! Thinks
it's good for business, even. Such a *Harry* response," I said.

"Well, he does have a point," Sonny said.

"How do you figure?"

"Well, if Dan is doing Dallas, they have control of her. And
therefore they have a TV station in their pocket. It's sleazy,
but it works. And it actually works for Dallas, too. This way,
she gets all the leads on the campaign, breaks all the stories
first, and her career could skyrocket as a result."

"If anyone ever thinks they have control over Dallas, they're
kidding themselves… Dan does Dallas, huh? Sounds like a
porn film to me," I added with a giggle. "I don't know why

I'm surprised. Those people are all cut from the same cloth. But I mean, Dallas and Dan? I thought she had better taste."

"What? You think Dan is unattractive? Aww, c'mon, Blake." Sonny laughed.

"Well, him, too," I continued. "I mean Dallas is a bit…" Sonny seemed to have stopped listening and was looking at me seriously. One step closer and there would be no daylight between us.

"What? I mean, I guess if you like that centerfold look…" Sonny was smiling and was moving so close that it was dangerous. I backed up and cleared my throat for emphasis. "I need to get to Vivi's. She may have some big news today. She's been at the baby doc all afternoon."

"How 'bout you swing by my office for a quick…uh, meeting. Park in the back. If we go in different cars, no one will know." Sonny was looking like the wolf in *Little Red Riding Hood.* He was offering to put me in danger, but with the promise that I would enjoy it. Unfortunately, it was an offer I had to refuse.

Just then, my cell rang. It was Wanda Jo.

"Hey, what's up?"

"Can you swing back by here? The Aarons are here and they need to see you. I told them you were at the rally and they said they'd wait. Been here half an hour."

"Okay, I'll be there in ten minutes." I hung up.

"Doesn't sound like you'll be in my office in ten minutes," Sonny said, disappointed.

"Maybe later this week. We have to at least try to be careful. So hang on to your horses, cowboy." He winked and walked away with that familiar swagger. He couldn't even kiss my cheek goodbye.

When I arrived at my office, the Aarons were in the waiting room.

"Thanks so much for seeing us without an appointment, Mrs. Heart," Wynona said, taking a seat in my office.

"What's up? Did y'all find something else?" I asked as I put my things on the credenza and sat down at my desk.

"Yes, actually. We found out something today and we wanted you to hear it right away," Wayne said. "We were talking to a friend of Walter's this morning after we spoke to you, and he said he knew a little about that Tamlyn girl he just married."

"Great. Anything will help. What did he say?"

"He said he met Tamlyn just a few weeks ago and for sure it was a whirlwind romance. We thought it might be important to know where Walter met her. This friend said it was in a bar up in Birmingham. He said she was a singer."

The coincidences kept mounting. "Did you get the name of the bar? Did he remember that?" I asked.

"He said he wasn't sure of the name but that it was some kind of strip club. Apparently, she didn't strip, though, she just sang a little."

"When was he up there last? Did he mention anyone else from the bar that might be of some help to us?" I was jotting down notes as they spoke.

"He said Walter was up there a good bit and he got buddy-buddy with the manager. Walter never said anything about the place to us, but I guess he was a regular there. At least for a few months." Wynona took a tissue out of her purse. "I am so embarrassed."

"These were Walter's actions, Ms. Aaron. You have nothing to be ashamed of."

"Ms. Heart, I feel so bad that we don't have any more to tell you about our own brother. But he did things like this and we just had no idea."

"It's okay, Ms. Aaron. This is good information. Y'all have anything else?"

"Apparently this girl is beautiful and seemed to have her own money, too. It made Walter feel relaxed around her, knowing she wasn't a gold digger. That was everything his friend told us." Wayne Aaron looked at me full of anticipation, hoping I could string something together from all of this.

"I'm so sorry we just jumped in on your busy day again. We just want this solved so we can go back to our lives," Wynona said.

"Well, thank y'all for being persistent. It's no problem, especially if it helps to move things forward." I got up and showed them out. "I'm certain the police will want to talk to this friend of Walter's. We'll let you know."

They both seemed to feel genuinely upset that they weren't closer to Walter when he was alive. I could tell they wanted to do right by him in death, but I was also sure, since Walter had gotten the entire inheritance from their uncle, that they were hoping to get at least a little something back on this settlement. I had put in a call to the insurance office to see if a check for the death benefits had been issued to Tamlyn. I was still waiting for word back.

The good news was that the Aarons had given me the perfect excuse to go see Sonny with all of this information. Sonny needed to know about this new witness, so it was my responsibility to fill him in.

Okay, maybe I was bending the rules a tiny bit. I promised myself I would only run in for a second. But I was pretty sure myself wasn't listening.

_21_

I was at the police station before I knew it. It was after five o'clock, so I thought I would sit in the car till I was sure I could sneak in without being seen. I sent Sonny a text. Coast clear?

Yes, clear and waiting, he answered back. I got out, taking my purse, so if anyone wanted to peek in my windows they wouldn't see my bag. I wasn't thinking that someone could actually see _me_ walking in. This is proof that hormones actually do make a person crazy. I knew this meeting was anything but careful, but the state of my mind that day was questionable to say the least. I slipped inside the back door and walked down the hallway, sliding into Sonny's office door sideways, shutting it behind me.

"C'mere, gorgeous." He was sitting on the front of his desk, leaning back on it with his long legs crossed. "I knew you couldn't resist," he said in his lowest voice.

I immediately leaned into him, pressing my body against

his. He kissed my forehead, and when I looked up into his eyes, he pressed his lips to mine.

"I need to tell you the news," I said, as his lips slid down my neck.

"What could be a headline right now?" He kept kissing me.

"The Aarons, remember? They were at my office a few minutes ago."

He slid his mouth down my jaw and rolled his tongue around my neck. I was delirious. He pulled me from around my waist as he walked backward, falling into his desk chair, me straddling him. His suit coat, hanging from the back of the chair, hit the floor as we moved.

"Sonny, I can't concentrate like this," I managed as I kissed him back.

"Tell me, I'm listening," he said, but he kept tasting me.

"Tamlyn Hartman, Walter Aaron's widow, is a bar singer in Birmingham. Or at least she was a few months ago."

"Okay, I'll write that down in a minute. Remind me."

"Okay, I'll remind you," I said, rolling my head from side to side, slowly becoming intoxicated in the moment. "My legs are gonna go numb if we keep this up."

"I have an idea," he said as he inhaled my skin.

"What's that?"

"I have a cot here in the closet for the nights I have to stay. Wanna try it out?"

"Sure," I said, "anytime, anywhere. Are you sure it's safe?" I asked as if I actually cared. My blouse already unbuttoned to my waist, his hands hot on my skin. I knew we were taking a chance no matter what.

"You locked the door when you came in and all the chiefs have left for the day. This part of the building is empty. What-dya say?"

I knew I should've been more concerned about being

caught, or heard at least, but something in me just didn't care right then. Maybe because he was removing his shirt as he spoke.

"I say yes," I murmured.

Sonny walked over to the closet, his belt open and hanging loose, his shirt untucked and unbuttoned. He pulled a rolling cot from the closet and laid it out flat in the middle of his office. It was already made up with sheets and a lightweight blanket.

"Well, it's no Ritz-Carlton, but it's more comfortable than the chair."

"It works for me," I said, laughing as I slipped my red heels off and unzipped my skirt. After pulling off my shirt and bra, Sonny let his pants fall to the floor next to my skirt. I lay down and he crawled on top, running his hands all over me. We were just getting into heavy kissing and exploring when, from the silence of the station lobby, we heard a door slam.

"Sonny, you here?"

Bonita! Damn.

We froze, face-to-face, me under Sonny, with our mouths dropped open and our eyes bugging out in shock.

"Oh, my God, we have the worst luck! She'll be back here any second."

Sonny scrambled up off of me and grabbed his pants, hopping around for his shoes, tucking his shirt in and trying to buckle his belt, all in one move.

I was still there on the cot, lying mostly naked, wiggling like a fish out of water trying to get up when all of a sudden, the whole cot collapsed into itself with me in it.

I was folded up like chicken in a taco, my legs flailing, one arm stuck out over my head.

"Shit! Shit! Oh, God," Sonny said as he was scurrying to pull the office back together. He grabbed my clothes and shoes in one hand and tried to pull me out with the other, but Bonita was knocking now, more and more insistent.

"Sonny? You in there?" She jiggled the door handle. "I see your car out there, so I know you're here somewhere."

"Oh, my God, get me outta here," I said, wiggling all my free limbs like an animal in a trap.

"I'm trying, baby." Sonny was pulling me, and the bed was rolling all over the room as he pulled. "It's jammed. I'm sorry, but bear with me. Don't be mad!"

With that, Sonny opened the closet door and kicked the entire cot, with me in it, back into the closet and slammed the door.

Well, Blake, I thought, *this is what you get.* I was stuck in the pitch dark, half-naked and shoved into a roll-away bed in Sonny's office closet. I held my breath as I heard Sonny open the office door.

"Hey, Bonita, how in the hell did that damn door get locked?"

"Am I interrupting something?" she asked.

I could see her shadow on the floor as she entered the small office.

"No, I was just catching up on my paperwork, had my headphones on. Guess I didn't hear you. That stupid door has been sticking. Sorry. What's going on?" I knew Sonny was trying to get her out as quick as he could, seeing as how I might not be breathing well from my taco in the closet.

"Well, the results on that river drowning are back. You know, the one from that birthday party last week? That poor boy did die of drowning like we thought. But the tests show positive for alcohol poisoning. He was drunk. That will help the lawsuit, I'm sure," she said.

"Okay, thanks, I'll look over the file in the morning. I appreciate you staying late to bring me these." Sonny was walking over to the door to show her out when I saw the shadows on the floor stop.

"Sonny, there's an earring on your floor," she said. I immediately tried to move my hand to check if it was mine. Shit, my earring was missing—well, not missing, *found* is the better word. Found by Bonita.

"Oh, I'll take that," Sonny said. "Maybe it belongs to the woman I was interviewing on that murder case this morning."

"I could swear I saw Blake wearing those earrings the other night at Vivi's dinner. Hmm, wonder how they could've gotten here?"

Damn! Didn't she ever take that investigator hat off? Ever?

"Must be a popular style. Thanks again for the file, Bonita. You go on home for the night. I gotta get finished up and get home myself." Sonny gave a fake laugh.

"Okay, if you say so, Sonny. I'll see you tomorrow. Get a good night's sleep now. You look like you need it."

"You, too, Bonita. G'night." I heard the door to Sonny's office shut and click locked, and he ran over and opened the closet.

I sat, still topless in the taco cot. I knew for certain Kitty would tell me this was *not* the definition of *careful*.

"Oh, baby, I am so sorry." He pulled me by my one hand that was caught outside the cot, and when he did the entire bed rolled out at such a speed it nearly knocked him over. He went back in the closet and grabbed my blouse and bra, my skirt and shoes, and then pried open the bed like a superman, freeing me from its grip.

He helped me up and I dressed in a hurry, laughing as I zipped up my skirt.

"I am so sorry, Blake. I tried to get her outta here as fast as I could."

"This was way too close. What were we thinking?"

"I know what I was thinking. I couldn't wait another second to have you," Sonny said, kissing me softly and pulling me into him for a tight embrace.

"What are we gonna do?" I whispered in his ear. "At this rate we're never gonna make it to November without being discovered."

"I'm sorry," he said again as I reached for my purse. "I just can't stop thinking about being with you." A little smile crept across his lips. "You did look funny in that cot."

I straightened my skirt and smoothed my hair. I knew I needed to go. Vivi probably had news about what color the nursery would be. And I knew if I didn't start being sensible, it might be me that needed a nursery.

22

Finally, I was back at Vivi's. I had changed into my cotton navy shorts and white tank top and was sitting at the kitchen table. Arthur was out back, working with some contractors on the finishing touches of the Moonwinx.

I was exhausted. It had been quite a day, starting with that meeting with Coco and Jean-Pierre, which now seemed to have taken place ages ago. I had to laugh. Even Vivi would not believe the things that happened to me today.

She breezed in a minute later and ran upstairs, saying she'd be right down. I got up and filled two big glasses with ice and poured us some tea from the fridge. Vivi had a saucer of sliced lemons covered in plastic wrap on the second shelf, so I grabbed it, along with the Ziploc bag of fresh mint, which she grew in pots on the big wraparound front porch. I set everything alongside a plate of chocolate chip cookies on her huge wooden table.

I was ready for some serious girl time.

Vivi waddled into the room, having changed into a comfortable pair of cute pink shorts with little white polka dots. "Honey, I am so hot I felt like a firecracker lit on both ends."

"Sit down and tell me everything," I said, leaning toward her with excitement. "I can't wait."

Vivi pushed a small picture of her sonogram across the table to me.

I tried to decipher the little blob in the picture, and Vivi helped by pointing out the tiny features of her baby. My eyes welled up. For some reason, this photo made everything more real, and it brought a lump to my throat. I looked up and smiled. "Oh, Vivi, I am so happy for you."

"I'm so happy, too." Her eyes glistened.

"Do we know what it is yet? Is five months too early?"

"Blake, can't you tell? Look at the picture. Do you see a little penis?"

I looked closely. I turned the little picture around and around. "No."

"Exactly!" Vivi said. "That's because there isn't one."

We both burst out laughing.

"Oh, my gosh, Vivi, you're having a girl! We are gonna have so much fun." I ran around the table and hugged her.

"I know," she said, squeezing me back. "That's why I'm wearing pink. I stopped by Belk and bought as many pink things as I could find. I wanted to call you so bad, but I knew you were finishing up at the rally. I ran by the radio station to surprise Lewis, though."

"How did it go?"

"He had wanted to come with me, but I told him I didn't think we'd know today. I wanted to tell him myself so it would be special. I took two long, wide satin ribbons with me to the doctor. After I found out, I was so excited I drove straight to the station. I tied the pink satin ribbon around my waist, like a big ol' present, then draped my purse in front of me and walked in, looking for Lewis.

"Well, I finally found him in the new studio among a bunch of construction workers. He led me out to the veranda, away from all the noise, and asked if we knew anything about the sex. I opened my arms, revealing the pink bow on my belly and smiled my biggest smile, and do you know what he said?"

"What?"

"He goes, 'I'll have to buy me a shotgun to keep all those boys away from my little princess.'" Vivi laughed and I could just picture Lewis being the doting and protective father.

"Blake, he had tears rolling down his face. I have never seen him so emotional. He literally lifted my pregnant ass off the floor, and that's not easy these days."

I reached across the table and squeezed her hands. "Oh, Vivi, your fairy tale is all coming together."

"I know! I have to pinch myself to make sure I'm not dreaming." She pulled off her necklace, which held her daddy's wedding ring, and held it out. "I got it sized for Lewis. I can't wait to slip it on his finger on our wedding day." It was an heirloom ring in the Celtic design of love never ending. It was part of her Irish heritage and had been in Vivi's family forever. She'd been wearing it on that chain around her neck ever since her father had passed away.

Just then, Harry The Humper came wandering into the kitchen. Vivi put the necklace down and reached over to a clear glass jar on the table. He jumped up on her, licking her face as she handed him a dog biscuit. "I have to keep his mouth busy at all times. He chews on anything that doesn't move."

Once she had Harry busy with his treat, she turned to me with a serious expression. "Okay, what happened at the rally? You sounded out of breath with excitement."

"Vivi, wait till you hear this. Dallas was kissin' on Dan The Man!"

"You've gotta be kiddin' me! That is unreal! What's the man thinking of?"

"Her double-Ds?"

Vivi cracked up. "Oh, my God, that has to be the incentive!"

It was times like this I would always remember. Our girl time. I wondered if these moments would continue after Vivi had Lewis and the baby to care for every day. Her priorities were rearranging, her new life blossoming right before my eyes. There had been so much change this summer, and I had no control over any of it, but I sat back and let it wash over me. We giggled and gossiped like old times, and I savored every minute.

Still laughing, Vivi got up and went to the sink to wash her hands after petting Harry and sending him outside with another treat. The sun was slipping lower in the sky and dusk was settling in, a welcome respite from the unbearable heat. I felt a cool breeze as she opened the screened door off the back porch. Rain was in the air.

"I love it just before the rain. It smells so good," Vivi said.

The hot day had melted into a cool evening, but the humidity was still hovering over us like a wet blanket on a clothesline. Since it was such a peaceful summer night, the window over the kitchen sink was left open and the damp air drifted in along with the music of summer; an orchestra of frogs and crickets hummed as we sat laughing and remembering. I was fully engulfed in this special moment. When I became friends with Vivi on the first day of third grade, I knew she was special. I always knew we would grow old together.

We used to daydream and talk for hours about our weddings. Vivi always wanted a huge magical affair. I did, too, but

I'm more of a romantic. When we were thirteen, we drew up our plans for the perfect fairy-tale wedding day. I think Vivi actually wanted to arrive in a pumpkin-shaped stagecoach, just like Cinderella, then walk through a tunnel of palace soldiers holding their swords over their heads.

I loved the stagecoach idea, but I wanted my prince to ride in on horseback. Maybe both of us would get our fairy tales one way or another. For now, I was working hard at making all of Vivi's fairy-tale dreams come true.

The rain was moving in and Arthur came through the back door just as the skies began to darken.

"Hey there, ladies," said Arthur as he made his way into the kitchen. I could hear the contractors' trucks pulling out of the driveway. "It's a comin' up a cloud out there I see. I'll get us some pork chops frying for dinner. Won't take a few minutes." He picked something up off the floor. "This yours?" He held up a dangling broken chain.

"Yes, but where is Lewis's ring?" Vivi asked. "It should be on there."

We looked under the table and all around.

"Oh, no! I can't get married without that ring. It's an heirloom."

"Miss Vivi, I'm sure the ring will turn up. We'll tear the place apart if we have to. After all, it's not like it could up and walk away."

Vivi slumped at the table, her brows furrowed. "I can't believe this happened. I was having such a good day."

"Don't worry, honey," I said. "We'll keep looking."

The rain had started with a light sprinkle, and Lewis came running up the steps with a bouquet in hand. Vivi turned to him just as he entered the kitchen and she gasped at the sight of the flowers he carried.

He must have had it custom-made because it had all of

her favorites: peach roses, orange gerber daisies, sunflowers, pink and white hydrangea, and of course, pale pink peonies, the most prized of all. It was gorgeous, bright and colorful, just like Vivi.

"Thank you, baby. They're beautiful." She took them from him and pulled out the card, reading it out loud.

"For Vivi and Tallulah, I love you both so much. I am the luckiest man in the world. Love, Daddy."

Vivi now had tears running down her cheeks.

"Miss Vivi, you're having a girl?" Arthur asked. "That's wonderful."

"Yes, I just found out today. I was gonna tell you, but I got distracted."

"Tallulah," he said. "That's a good name."

"I picked it because of Tallulah Bankhead, the silent-film star. She was from Alabama, too."

"It's perfect."

Just as we all sat down, Harry came in and did a big doggy shake and splattered us all with muddy water. His sopping feet pranced all through the room, leaving wet brown paw prints everywhere.

Vivi grabbed a rag and wiped down the dog's paws. "Go on now, Harry. Get outta here." Vivi shooed him to his bed in the corner. "I can't believe I left him out digging in the rain. Oh, what a mess. I guess we still have some training to work on."

I grabbed a dishcloth and started wiping up the floor with my foot. Arthur and Lewis were laughing and washing off all the spots they could see.

Finally, we all sat down together to eat, all of us talking about the new nursery. The thunder was loud and the rain was pouring by the time we finished the cobbler. We had the kitchen window open, and the lullaby of the sudden summer thunderstorm was like a sedative on this overly stimulating day. The storm continued through the night, lightning ripping flashes of light across the wood floor, the blustery heavy downfall eventually dissolving into a gentle, steady rain.

I snuggled down into my bed at Vivi's. I would call the Fru Fru boys first thing in the morning to get them going on everything pink. Coco and Jean-Pierre would love this news.

In between visions of pink tulle, thoughts about tracking down Tressa kept me on edge. That was our big task for tomorrow, and there was no telling how it would play out. I rode an emotional roller coaster all night long and barely slept. What if Tressa refused to sign? What if she made things even more difficult for Vivi and Lewis? And worse, why did I have this nagging feeling that there was some connection between Tressa and Mrs. Tamlyn Hartman Aaron?

23

The next morning, I shoved the last of my makeup in my bag while sandwiching the phone between my ear and my shoulder. "Hey, Wanda Jo. I'll be up in Birmingham all day with Vivi, trying to track down this Tressa girl, so I'm not going to be in the office. I need a quick letter drafted to the Historical Society. I left the file on your desk."

"Got it. Now, y'all be careful, okay? We don't know this Tressa."

"I promise, we'll be okay. How's that new preacher of yours doin' these days?" I asked. "Still seeing him?"

"You better believe it," Wanda Jo gushed. "Can you believe he don't seem to mind my cussin' every now and then."

"Wow, that's a switch."

"And guess what? He'll even throw back a few. Jesus *did* drink wine, so alcohol can't be *all* bad, you know? It's in the Bible, after all. I might just be able to hang on to this one."

We laughed. "Okay," I said, "I'll check in this afternoon and let you know when I expect to get back."

"I'll hold down the fort."

I hung up, thinking how much I loved having her around. We made a good team and she was my real partner here. Harry never came in on a regular basis anymore, and I never even called him about any cases. So it was just us girls.

Vivi and I put the last of the things in the car. I wanted to make sure we had all the proof we needed when we finally confronted Tressa. We jumped in the front seat and slammed the doors. Vivi had filled Arthur in on all the details. He stuck his head in her car window.

"Okay, Arthur. We'll be back late tonight."

"I'll be here. You girls drive safe. Now look here, Miss Vivi, don't you worry about anything. We'll find that ring today while you're out, so rest your head and focus on what y'all got to do." He reached in, and she grabbed his hand and squeezed it.

"I'm so glad I've got you, Arthur." She smiled at him.

"Of course you do. And you always will." We both smiled at him as I started the car.

"Okay, Vivi, let's put this to bed and get you married."

"I'm with ya, honey. Let's roll!"

We drove down the long gravel drive to the gate of the McFadden Plantation, turned right, leaving dust flying behind us as we headed for I-59 North. Next stop, Birmingham. With Tuscaloosa fading in our rearview mirror, I told Vivi we needed to make sure word of this never got out.

"Dallas can't even get a whisper of this news. What a huge story it would be for her. Play-by-play Announcer and Radio Station Owner Lewis Heart in Bigamy Battle."

"I know. I've already thought about that. You know the Fru Fru boys are going to the media today about the wedding announcement. I'm already getting calls from the paper and the TV stations about covering the event." Vivi was fidgeting in her seat.

"Oh, no. They don't know about this, do they?"

"No, I'm sure they don't, but they'll be spreading a little info today on where the media is allowed to set up on the property. You know, stuff like that."

"Well, as long as we keep this between us…and Arthur and Lewis, of course. Dallas is notorious for pushing till she gets her story," I said.

"I'm starting to feel like I'm in a circus."

"Starting? I've been playing ringmaster for several weeks here. Where have you been?" I looked at her and smiled, but she was still shifting her weight around in her seat, pulling the air conditioner vents toward her.

"I'm sorry, but I'm gonna have to pee. It's a side effect of carrying Tallulah around."

After several pee breaks, we finally arrived at the Puss and Boots Gentlemen's Club. It was early afternoon, so the mood was a tad awkward as a very pregnant lady and I stepped inside the men's club. My research had shown Tressa still worked as a dancer, the very same thing she was doing when she met Lewis back in college.

The place was dark, but looking around I was forced to admit that it wasn't the sleazy hole-in-the-wall I'd been imagining it to be. There was a huge dark cherry wood bar lining one side of the building. The new-looking carpet was a cranberry color, and the stage had four bronze poles for the dancers. A maroon curtain hung behind the stage and was swept up in a swag with golden fringe. A microphone stood at center stage, ready for a singer.

This certainly didn't look like a place where a girl like Tressa would be working. The photo I had printed off the internet was of a girl with stringy blond hair and a camouflage bikini. She looked like she might be working at some truck stop, not a higher-end gentlemen's club like this.

Vivi took a seat at the bar and ordered a ginger ale. I walked around, checking things out. I suddenly wished I had Sonny with me, a knot forming in my stomach. He was the investigator, and I felt a little out of my element.

I showed Tressa's picture around but no one seemed to recognize her. I was told to come back around six o'clock when a woman they called T would be there. She was their singer, and maybe she might know this girl.

Just then, a man walked over to me.

"Can I help you?"

He was a little greasy-looking and wore a dark suit with a crimson shirt. He had a mafia look about him with his long black hair slicked back and his tiny barely there mustache, a bit too long near his mouth. He wasn't very tall, but he made up for that in his bulk. He looked like a former bodybuilder, but only about five foot seven.

"Yes," I said, mustering my confidence and looking him straight in his brown eyes. "I'm looking for this woman." I showed him Tressa's picture.

"I've never seen her. She doesn't work here," he answered, a little too quickly.

"Do you have a singer everyone calls T?"

"Yeah, what's it to you?"

"Someone said she might know the woman in this photo. She's coming in later I heard."

"You heard a lot, lady. T don't know her, either."

I was crowding him. "You're sure about that?" I asked.

"Yeah, I mean, you're welcome to stay, but she don't know nuthin'."

"Fine, we'll hang around for a while. What's your name, you know, just in case I need anything?"

I was trying to lighten things up and just get back to Vivi.

"Dwayne. Dwayne Martin. I'm the manager. You can talk to T during her break if you're gonna stick around."

"Thanks."

He walked away, and I scooted over to Vivi, who was looking really out of place.

"Blake, this just feels weird. I am so pregnant, and this is a men's club. I look like I'm scoping the place for a sugar daddy *and* a baby daddy."

"Well, you're in luck. It looks like that's just what the clientele is around here. Loaded old men. That guy I was speaking to was the manager, and he says he doesn't recognize Tressa, either."

"Oh, Blake, what if we can't find her before my deadline? Lewis and I have to get our blood test and wedding license before the wedding."

"Well, we still have a month. We'll find her."

I said that to calm Vivi, but I was starting to have my doubts.

"I have to go," she said, looking nervously at Dwayne. He let go of her and began to walk away, assuming she was right behind him. "I hope you find those folks you're lookin' for." Her voice was soft.

"Yeah, thanks." I slipped her my card without Dwayne noticing. "Call me if you think of anything," I whispered. I walked back over to the bar. I knew it was time to get Vivi home.

I helped a disappointed Vivi back to the car and we settled in for the hour drive back to Tuscaloosa. We picked up some Taco Casa for the road and drove home in the dark…in more ways than one.

Late that night, everyone in the house was asleep. I was wide-awake, still tossing and turning, hoping Sonny had made contact with Cal when I heard my phone jingle. I turned over to see who would be texting me at this ungodly hour. To my surprise, it was T.

I couldn't admit it in front of Dwayne but…I am Tressa. I had a little work done before I started working at this club, and I go by T now so no one will recognize me. I remember that night at the frat house and the fake wedding, but I won't sign the annulment papers till I meet my husband. Take it or leave it. And please keep this to yourself if you want my help.

I sat up in bed, sick to my stomach. There was no sleeping for me. I texted her back.

Meet me in Tuscaloosa ASAP. I will let Lewis know. I was trying to stay calm, but everything inside me wanted to scream in the dark silent house. Tressa and T were the same person! Did that mean this woman was also Tamlyn? She hadn't admitted it, but if it was true, then that meant Lewis might be

married to a woman who was also a suspect in a possible murder case. So much for this being a simple paperwork issue. My
phone jingled again.

Tomorrow night. Where?

   Text me when you get here, I typed. I wanted to make sure
I had it all lined up so Lewis could get these papers signed.

See you then.

   I had to get up and pace the room. I was a frantic mess. I
wanted to tell Vivi right then, but as far along as she was, I
knew it was a bad idea to wake her with this stressful news. She
and Lewis would both overreact. They would talk to Tressa
tomorrow anyway, so there was nothing I could do but wait
for daybreak and count the minutes till this lap dance diva
would finally sign over Lewis's freedom.

25

The minute I heard Vivi up, I ran downstairs and told them everything. Vivi, to my surprise, was actually excited. She and Lewis felt like it was almost over. They'd get the papers signed tonight and away Tressa would go. Somehow I wasn't feeling quite so confident.

"I had a feeling she knew more than she said! She looked shifty even from where I was sitting," Vivi said as she ran around the kitchen, getting breakfast.

"I know, but she wants to meet Lewis and I can't figure out why," I said.

"Probably just curious," Lewis mumbled, sitting down at the table, still partly asleep.

"Lewis is kinda famous and she probably just wants a look. If she's a Bama fan—and seriously, aren't we all?—she's bound to remember who he is. I'm sure she just wants an autograph or something as a memento."

I was thinking the same thing, but it was a lot less reassuring. Lewis was famous, and maybe Tressa wanted a little more than his signature. If this girl happened to be Tamlyn, too, she could not be legally married to Walter, since she was still technically married to Lewis! Maybe she wanted a little cash bonus from the famous star announcer, since she knew she'd get no money now from her deceased "husband," Walter. Or maybe she didn't understand any of that and was just being greedy. I knew one thing. We all had better be careful. Looked like this spider would bite anyone for money.

I had been so busy with work and Harry's campaign and planning Vivi's wedding and shower that my life had become even more than a circus—it was an entire carnival. I needed help, and I knew just the woman for the job: Bonita.

I knew she and Arthur were becoming much closer and that she was going to be a big part of his barbecue business. Oh, she was still very much an investigator on Sonny's team, but she was helping Arthur all the time and, therefore, was out at Vivi's a lot. I always knew Sonny was a big fan of hers and now, as I had gotten to know her better, I understood why. She was seriously one of the smartest people I had ever met. And nothing stood in her way. She was just what I needed to make sure all of these celebrations for Vivi came off without a hitch. I had a meeting planned for lunch with Jean-Pierre and Coco, and I had asked Bonita to join us. We were meeting at Wintzell's Oyster House on the Warrior River, where much of the menu is made up of delicacies from the Gulf.

Tuscaloosa isn't too far from the Gulf, maybe about five hours. I spent every summer of my life down there. We had a beach house, and Meridee, Kitty and my daddy loved being there better than anywhere else. We almost stopped those trips to the Gulf after Daddy died in that boating accident when I was six. But then Kitty's girlfriends starting coming with us and I always brought Vivi. Those summer vacations became major girlfriend getaways. It made those days without Daddy a little more bearable. I learned at a tender age how important your girlfriends are and that my Sassy Belle sisters were forever. I had a feeling that with Bonita, I was fixin' to induct a new member.

Bonita arrived in style as usual. She was known around town for her impeccable fashion sense. Frankly, I didn't know anybody that dressed like Bonita. She loved her designer labels, so I knew she was going to get along with Coco and Jean-Pierre just peachy.

Bonita was wearing a gorgeous black-trimmed Chanel suit in lightweight, banana-cream-colored fabric. She had on dangly pearl earrings and a yellow pearl necklace. Her makeup accentuated her doll-like eyelashes and perfectly shaped pink lips. She wore strappy high heels and, even at her weight, she walked like a pageant queen. Curvaceous and confident, this woman was a Sassy Belle without a doubt.

"Hey, Blake, how are you doin'?" She gave me a hug as she sat down. The planners weren't there yet so Bonita and I had a chance to talk while we waited.

"So much better now that you're helping me out. Thank you so much for doing this, Bonita. I'm seriously running out of steam here and I think you will have some great ideas. The shower's in a week, and then the wedding is just a month after that. I want Vivi to be the center of the universe and feel like a princess at both events." I smiled and she nodded.

"You know I love that Vivi," she said. "My Arthur loves that girl like she was his own flesh and blood, and now that I know her, I can tell you she is nothing but pure good. I will be happy to help you make her feel like a queen." Bonita stopped to order sweet tea and ask for extra lemon.

"Oh, Bonita, I knew I could count on you! Now let me tell you all about A Fru Fru Affair. These guys are great."

"Guys?" she asked. "And a business called A Fru Fru Affair? This just gets better and better."

"I've known them since high school. They're a bit younger than me and they were always very creative. Their names are Coco and Jean-Pierre."

"Blake, are you gonna sit there and tell me that a momma actually named her boy child Coco?"

"Well, his real name is Craig but he changed it for the sake of business," I said, smiling.

"And Jean-Pierre? Did his momma name him that or did he name himself, too?" She took a sip of tea, grinning.

"His name is John-Paul. See, they both just love France."

"So, don't tell me, Coco named himself after Coco Chanel? C'mon, Blake, are you for real?"

"Actually, Coco's real last name is Channels."

"His name is Coco Channels?" Bonita burst out laughing; she had the loudest, most robust laugh I had ever heard. "Lord have mercy, me, you have got to be pullin' my leg," she said. "I can't imagine a more perfect duo to work with. Good thing I wore my Chanel suit!"

"Y'all are a perfect fit," I said, laughing. "You're gonna love them."

I saw Coco at the hostess desk. I waved my hand so he would see me. And right behind him was Jean-Pierre.

"They're here! I can't wait for you to meet them." Coco was waving his arms as he and Jean-Pierre made their way to the table.

"Hey, honey! Don't you look a-*ma*-zing." Coco sang it out as he came over and gave me a hug.

I did the introductions. "This is Bonita Baldwin. This is Coco Channels."

"Oh, my word, honey, look at that fabulous outfit," Coco exclaimed, reaching out to hug Bonita. "You are a vision, my dear. I have heard so much about you. And you're wearin' my namesake, aren't you? Chanel. I just love you already!"

"I've heard so much about you, too." She winked at me and smiled. "I like you already, you obviously have excellent taste," she said.

"Well, I guess Coco has a new bestie." Jean-Pierre was feeling left out.

"Aww, no, Jean-Pierre, no way. Are you jealous? Get over here and meet Miss Bonita," I said.

"So nice to meet you, Jean-Pierre. I am just thrilled to be working with y'all."

"Y'all have a seat and let's get going," I said. The waitress came back and took our orders.

"Miss Bonita, let's hear your ideas on this bridal-baby-bash. We gotta do double duty on this, you know," Jean-Pierre said.

"I do have some ideas," she said. "What do y'all think about makeovers?" Bonita asked them, grinning.

"Oh, my gawd, she is talkin' my language," Coco said, laughing. "I love it."

"Ain't no Southern girl who won't love a good makeover and a fashion show," Bonita continued.

"A fashion show, too! Where in the world did you find her, Blake? She is a natural at this."

"I thought we'd set up a little salon in Meridee's living room and the whole theme will be princess-based," Bonita continued. "Then we can stage a fashion show for momma and baby, look-alike outfits since we know it's a baby girl."

"Oh," Coco interrupted, "do tell Miss Vivi thank you from the bottom of my heart for havin' us a baby girl. That makes this so much easier for us."

"I'll let her know she has done her duty." I smiled at Bonita.

"Well, she had already picked her wedding colors as pink and blush and cream, so now with a girl on the way, we don't have to worry about coordination. The bridal-baby-bash can all be the same color—pink!" Coco did love his work, it was slightly obvious.

"Now, how do we fit the psychic in?" Jean-Pierre interjected, bringing the excitement to a screeching halt.

"Say what?" Bonita set her tea down.

"Well, Vivi has us all goin' in a caravan down to the river to visit her mystic friend, Myra Jean. I personally think it sounds like a hoot," Coco said.

"Blake, I don't know about a clairvoyant. Those people scare me," Bonita said.

"Oh, c'mon, Miss Bonita, it'll be fun. She's just a show, right, Blake?" Jean-Pierre put his pen down.

"Well, if you're askin' me if she can make things float through the air and speak to the spirit world, I don't think so. She's just an old friend of my grandmother's. But she does have a knack for sensing things the rest of us don't," I said, not wanting to reveal how right she'd actually been on her last prediction. "Besides, Vivi wanted this visit as her wedding gift from me, and I'm not gonna disappoint her."

"Does she have a crystal ball?" Coco sat up in his chair and raised his eyebrows.

"Oh, I don't know," I said. "I never saw her use it if she does." I smiled, trying to downplay the whole thing.

"Okay, but how does a psychic reading fit in to the whole princess-for-a-day theme we got goin' here, other than I'll be in royal freak-out mode?" Bonita asked.

"Okay, here's the plan," Jean-Pierre said, taking charge. "We'll have the makeovers and then a fashion show, and then we'll have desserts. Once all that's done, we'll head down to the river to the magician. Didn't everyone in the olden days believe in witches and magic and all that? We'll consider it part of a princess's privilege to know what her future holds. It'll be different, and I know Miss Vivi loves different. I think it'll work."

"Me, too," Coco said. "I love it. All the guests will have their fortunes read, and maybe we can get the wizard to predict someone's engagement." Coco was grinning.

"She's not a wizard, she's a psychic," I said.

"Well, whatever, magician, wizard, psychic… We're gonna have us a fortune-telling."

"Okay, but I don't want my fortune read," Bonita said firmly. "I'm plenty fortunate enough. But I'll go. I always wanted to see if I could tell how they do their tricks." She was smiling as she took a sip of tea.

"She's not doing any tricks, I promise. She doesn't pull rabbits out of hats, either," I said.

The waitress brought our lunch, and we ate while finalizing the details.

"The invitations have been sent, and we are on our way," Jean-Pierre said.

"Awesome," I said. "So now Bonita and I will work on the makeover artists and…"

Coco interrupted, "And we will get the fashion show together. I *so* can do that. *Thrilled,* that is the word today, y'all. Thrilled!"

"He is all over this. He got up, practicing his bend and snap—he just loves to pretend he's Reese Witherspoon in *Legally Blonde,*" Jean-Pierre said. "I am gonna have to calm that man down." He rolled his eyes like this was a daily duty.

I paid the bill and left a generous tip, and we all said our goodbyes.

"Honey, those two are a hoot. I just love working with

them," Bonita said as she opened her car door. "Thank you for asking me to be involved, Blake. It really means a lot."

"You're so welcome, honey. I need you for this, so I thank you, too," I said sincerely.

"No, Blake, it's more than that." She looked serious for the first time that afternoon. "This really makes me feel like family, you know?"

"Oh, Bonita, but you are." I smiled and hugged her. "I'll call you later. We have a cake tasting set up for later this week at Vivi's house. We want your opinion."

"You think I would ever miss a cake tasting?" She laughed. "Seriously, you don't have to ask me twice."

She started her car, waving out the window as she drove out of the parking lot and headed across the river toward the police station. I knew we were in for quite a joyride with Bonita and the planners working together now, and it took a load of stress off my shoulders. It was going to be a bridal-baby-bash that would go down in Fru Fru history.

I was just getting in my car when Jean-Pierre circled back and pulled in next to me. "Blake, we need to talk. I didn't want to say anything before, you know with Bonita here and all, but I was at the TV station yesterday making sure the media understands all about parking at the wedding. They all wanna be there because our voice of the Tide, Mr. Lewis, is the man of the hour. Anyway, I overheard something I thought you might like to know."

"What?" I said, full of concern.

"Well, I know how you and Miss Vivi are always dodging that TV reporter Dallas Dubois. I remember she was always just awful back in high school. So I thought you might like to know that when I was dropping off the media info yesterday, I heard her talking to that news director about something rather…interesting."

"Oh, really? What's going on?" I asked.

"Well, the news director told her she needed to get to the

bottom of this Harry Heart affair or else she could lose her job."

"What? Affair?"

"Oh, Blake, I hope I didn't say too much. I don't want to upset you, but you're his wife and I felt you ought to know."

"No. No. Tell me everything."

"Well," he said, leaning out of the car window slightly, "it seems that the TV station is having cutbacks and two reporters will be laid off. A third reporter will be getting the anchor seat, but two of them are getting the ax by the end of the year."

"Well, that is very interesting." I was trying not to overreact, but inside, I was sick.

"Yeah, and I heard the news director say she can come at it from both ends, too. Whatever that means. I'm sure it doesn't mean what it means in *my* world." He laughed. "But really, the idea of anyone fooling around behind *your* back is just ridiculous. There's no way a man would cheat if he landed a catch like you. So, I just wanted to make sure you had the heads-up about what those sleazeballs were up to."

"Thank you so much. I did need to know this. I think my husband needs to know this, too. If Dallas's job is at stake, she'll do anything she can to get a story—even if there isn't one," I added.

"You're welcome, Miss Blake. Just know Coco and I are on your side. We just love you and Miss Vivi. Oh, we're starting work on that pond tomorrow."

Uh-oh. "Is that okay with Vivi?"

"Yes, she said she kinda liked the idea, after all. So the bulldozers will be there bright and early."

Great, I thought. I love bulldozers at 7:00 a.m. It's my favorite. I wish they would bring a jackhammer, too.

I said goodbye and then called Sonny to let him know I might be late. We had an appointment with Cal, who was gonna use his tech-wizard skills to see what he could dig up on Tressa, Tonia and Tamlyn. But not before I stopped by at Harry's to tell him we were being run over at both ends by a bulldozer named Dallas.

Suddenly this whole affair with Dan and Dallas made sense. Her job was on the line and she was in a panic. Not only was she trying her best to get the details on Sonny and me, she was also following Harry and Jane, and Dan was her best way into that circle.

I pulled into the driveway and ran inside on autopilot. Once inside the front door, I stopped dead in my tracks. It felt so strange being back inside my own home. It took my breath away. I was struck like I had run into a haunted theater, the ghosts of my life with Harry hovering overhead. I stood motionless for a second before I was physically able to dash up the stairs. I called out to him. Everywhere I looked, I could see images of us.

I hadn't even looked to see if his car was parked outside. My stomach was suddenly in knots as I climbed up the stairs to our bedroom. My mind was in another world: inside the fairy tale of Blake and Harry. A flood of emotions came rushing in and I found myself unprepared for the sensations I was feeling. I was filled with confusion.

And then I opened the bedroom door. Jane and Harry were just finishing up. The bed a mess, sheets and duvet in a heap, the two of them buttoning their crisply pressed shirts.

"Blake! What are you doing here?" Harry exclaimed.

"Well, it's my house, too, isn't it? Nice to see you, Jane. Enjoying my husband? My bed?"

I was infuriated, but instead of ripping them to shreds— luckily for them—I turned to sarcasm.

"Blake, I'm so sorry," Harry said.

"Yeah, right, Harry. Stow it. I guess you think it's okay

for you to screw around and jeopardize your senate run, just as long as I don't. Well, guess what? I'm here to tell you Dallas is after you and your little *friendship* here with the judge."

"What do you mean?" Jane asked as she looked for her heels.

"I prefer to speak directly to my husband, Your…Honor," I replied.

I walked on inside the room, seeing my dressing table, my mirror and my things still in their place. It shook me. As my heart fluttered, I tried to stay focused on why I was there. But all my emotions suddenly stuck in my throat.

"Harry, Dallas is rubbing up on Dan so she can get the story on you and Jane. I told you something strange was going on with them. I have a good source who's heard her news director threaten her job if she didn't break the story of our marriage. Or lack thereof."

"Jane and I have never…"

"Stop!" I interrupted. "Are you honestly going to try and say nothing is happening after Jane has clearly just finished her ride on the bologna pony? I mean, really, Harry, how stupid do you think I am? I just wanted you to know and to try to be careful. The snake is out there."

I turned and walked out, feeling sick to my stomach, when something caught my eye from the large window over my vanity. I moved closer and I saw the top of a very recognizable bottle-blond head. Dallas was out on that rose trellis I, myself, had fallen off last May.

"Oh, my God! Dallas is peeking in that window right now! That's her cameraman. Oh, Lord. They've gotten all of this on video."

"Shit! You gotta be kidding me!"

Harry tore out of the bedroom while Jane stood frozen, her mouth dropped open. I was sure she had never been in a situation like this, the reputation of her family name suddenly hanging in the balance.

I ran out after Harry, ready to confront Dallas and her cameraman in the front yard. The hot sun was dripping down and both of us were yelling in front of the whole neighborhood. I knew even if the video was never seen, anyone could grab their cell phone and have this battle on YouTube in minutes. This one moment in the driveway could destroy Harry's entire campaign.

Harry was barely dressed, shirt untucked, his belt hanging to one side as he swung open the front door. Dallas and her cameraman ran to the TV van parked down the street. We were too late. They were gone.

Harry grabbed his cell phone and called Dan. I jumped in my car and headed to the TV station, following close behind the van. I ripped into the parking lot right behind them.

"Dallas!" I screamed at her as she got out. "Listen to me. There is no way you can use a frame of that footage. I will sue you for invasion of privacy."

"Harry is a public figure, Blake. I'm sure you know the law."

"In fact, I do, and Harry wasn't *in* public. He was in the privacy of his own home and you were shooting inside his windows. I can and will put a stop to this and subpoena that tape."

"What do you care, Blake? He was screwing someone else. Last I heard y'all are still married. Why would you defend him?"

I ignored the question. "Not one bit of this is for public consumption. I do know the law and I will go after you. Don't push me."

I was so wound up and I was about to snap. I was shaking all over. I wanted to scream, I wanted to cry. It was overwhelming me. But I had to keep it together until I knew I had her agreement.

"Do what you need to do, Blake. And so will I." She turned on her five-inch heels and headed inside.

I got back in my car and called Harry. He knew the privacy act as well as I did. My grandfather himself set the precedent and wrote the privacy laws for the state of Alabama. I knew she couldn't use any of whatever she got.

"Hey. Did you get her?" he asked me.

"I threatened her. I still think we need to call the news director." I was driving and realized I was headed straight to Meridee's.

"That will get her fired. I think she must be in a panic over her job."

"She is. That's what I was trying to tell you. The TV station thinks they know about us splitting up and they are pushing her to get the story. I think if you call her yourself, maybe even have Dan get ahold of her, you might be able to talk some sense into her. Tell her we *will* call her boss and we *will* pursue legal action against her and the station. I'm sure she knows she's gone too far and her job would be over before any of the proceedings got started."

"I will take care of this," Harry assured me.

"I hope so," I said, my voice cracking. I was starting to break down.

"Blake, I'm so sorry. I guess we're both screwing up."

Typical Harry. Never, ever able to accept the blame for himself. "Speak for yourself," I screeched, then hung up and parked my car in Meridee's driveway.

27

I sat in the car and checked my watch. I needed to get to Sonny. We had an appointment in half an hour with Cal, yet I'd wound up at Meridee's, where I always seem to find myself during a crisis. I called Sonny and told him I'd meet him at the university.

I got out of the car and ambled for the house in an emotional daze. My only thought was to sit at that table and tell Meridee what was going on. I just wanted to hear her voice and be near her. She could always make the world go away, and I needed that more than anything right this minute. That, and the comfort of her treat corner in the kitchen.

I scooted up the redbrick steps and onto the back porch. I heard laughing as I stepped up into the house, but the kitchen where everyone usually gathered was empty. I moved near the hallway leading to the bedrooms. There it was again. But this time it was a man's rolling chuckle.

Was Meridee with a man? *Please, dear Lord, no more bed-*

room surprises today. I decided to take off my high heels and tiptoe down the hall. I felt like a burglar. Meridee's door was cracked open. I peeked in, but her room was dark except for the sunlight slipping through the widow curtains and splashing across the walls of the small room.

But the giggling continued.

I moved slowly, treading quietly along the tapestry carpet. I arrived at the door to Kitty's childhood bedroom. Door cracked slightly, the sounds were definitely coming from here. There had been another car outside, but it wasn't Kitty's. I steadied my breathing and peeked inside.

I almost passed out right there in the hall. There was my mother in her childhood bed with the mayor! I gasped at the awful sight, at which point Kitty immediately looked up and caught my eyeball peering in on her afternoon delight. I felt nauseous. Mayor Charlie and his big white rear end rolling all over my chubette mother, and both of them laughing out loud. Well, at least *they* were having a good time.

I ran back up the hall into the kitchen, thinking I either needed to throw up or have a stiff drink. No one wants to see their mother naked with anyone! *What the hell is with everyone today?* I thought. *Everybody is having a nooner except me!*

"Blake!" I heard Kitty screaming from down the hall. "Come back."

"No, Mother, I wouldn't come back down that hall for all the diamonds at Tiffany's! I have seen enough today to keep me up for a month of Sundays."

I ran straight to the snack corner of Meridee's kitchen and shoved a stale Krispy Kreme into my mouth, chasing it with a swig of Jack Daniel's straight from the bottle that was sitting on the counter. Where in the heck was Meridee? And why in the world would Kitty come here for her afternoon *conference*—as she liked to call these visits—with the mayor?

Kitty entered the kitchen a bit disheveled and saw me downing another swig of Jack.

"Blake, I am sorry you had to see that, but my God, girl, why would you sneak in like that?"

"Mother, excuse me, but I was looking for Meridee 'cause, you know, she lives here," I said.

"I know, darlin', but Meridee had some errands to run and we thought we'd take our opportunity while we could. We figured no one would recognize the mayor's car here, and he surely couldn't come to my house in the middle of the day. What would my neighbors say? I'm supposed to be out sellin' houses. I missed our weekly caravan for this deliciousness."

She was smiling and obviously just coming out of a state of euphoria.

"So we came here thinking we'd get some time alone."

"Why in the world would you ever think that, Mother? Everybody drops by Meridee's. It's like Grand Central most of the time. Why not just go to his house?" I asked, thinking this was an obvious question.

"Oh, Blake, don't be silly. The mayor's supposed to be at work, too. He can't be seen home in the middle of the day." She laughed as if I were the stupid one.

"So are you telling me that Meridee's place is your, um, humping grounds?"

"You got it, and I don't see why it has to be a problem for anyone. Meridee is not even here and so no one has to know."

"Well, Mother, I *do* know, and please, for the love of God, do not elaborate." I shoved the last bite of the doughnut into my mouth.

"What are you doing here anyway?" Kitty asked. "I thought you had a meeting about that case you're working on."

"I do. I was on my way there when I thought I would drop by and talk to Meridee."

"Well, talk to Momma, baby. I'm here." I could tell she was genuinely concerned for me. I guess, in a pinch, she would have to do.

"I ran by my house and found Harry and Jane just finishing up."

"Finishing up what, baby?"

"You know. Seems like you and Harry were both on the, uh—same page this afternoon."

"Oh, darlin'. I am so sorry. That must've been awful to walk in on."

"You're tellin' me. And that's not even the worst part."

"You mean it gets worse? It's a fact then, you are totally over him."

"Yeah. I caught Dallas on the trellis with her camera in the window."

"Oh, sweet Jesus! That is over the top! Even for her."

"I told her about our rights to privacy and all of that. I'm not sure how much she got on tape, but I do know she can't use any of it or we can sue the entire station. Harry said he would call and threaten her."

"Oh, wow, the preppy SOB has finally decided to be your partner in *something*. Well, wonders never cease." She smiled.

Maybe Kitty was just what I needed. I took a deep breath and kissed her on the cheek.

"Maybe they weren't really doing anything. Maybe they just lie there in bed and puff each other up." We both burst out laughing. It occurred to me right then that that's how we belles deal with trouble. We are sarcastic as hell and use laughter—and some good Krispy Kremes—to solve all our problems. Okay, and maybe a good splash of Jack. And Kitty was right. I was more concerned about the big picture than about the fact that my husband had just had sex with another woman. That proved I was over Harry.

As she spoke, Mayor Charlie meandered down the hall, smoothing his hair, and stopped right behind Kitty in the hallway door frame. He had been there all of a second when Meridee arrived back home and stepped up into the kitchen from the back porch.

"Hey, y'all, what's ever'body doing here? My God, Kitty, you look a fright! Your clothes aren't even on straight. And… Mayor Charlie, what are you doing here? Oh, my, my, my…" She set her purse on the table and walked over to the fridge. "Anybody want a Coke?" she asked. "Or possibly a cigarette?" She smiled, knowing Kitty had been selling more than houses to the good leader of our fair city.

"Yes," I said, "actually, I could use a Coke about right now." Kitty turned and kissed Charlie on the cheek as he finished tucking in his shirt.

"None for me, Miss Meridee, I have to get back to the office," Mayor Charlie said. "Somebody might miss me." He laughed a deep, hardy giggle. He was cute, I had to admit. Tall and big all over, longish gray hair and a big belly. He was a likable guy and I was actually happy for Kitty, though still a tad nauseated. Maybe this one would stick. I hoped so, for her sake. I knew Kitty was looking for love. At her age, I admired her for still believing in it after four tries at marriage.

Just then her cell phone rang from her oversized Michael Kors bag. She fumbled through it, setting things on the table as she searched for the ringing device. I was sure she was gonna pull a toaster out before she found the phone.

"Hey, darlin'," she finally answered. Kitty answered that way for everyone, so it could be Charlie, a client or even one of her ex-husbands.

"Oh, precious, I know y'all are so nervous, but it's gonna be okay, I promise."

I still had no idea.

"Okay, baby, now no more tears, everything will turn out just fine, I promise. I'll see y'all in a few. Okay, bye, darlin'." And she hung up.

"Lord have mercy, these first-time buyers—they need so much hand-holdin'. I hate to have to run, but somebody needs me even more than you two do. That poor girl is pure ol' dee falling apart. The closing is this afternoon. I gotta go calm her down."

"Mother, where is your car?" I asked. "I didn't see it in the driveway."

"Oh, honey, I parked it across the street in Ms. Collins's driveway. I knew she was out of town because Meridee asked me to grab her mail for her the other day. No one needs to know any more than we want them to, you know? That's a lesson for you, Blake."

She smiled and headed down the stairs to the driveway. Why did I always feel like she was the one outsmarting me? I decided I had a lot to learn from her.

I checked my watch and realized I was late to see Cal and Sonny. I got up and kissed Meridee on the cheek, then left right behind Kitty. Maybe following in her footsteps wasn't all that bad.

28

Sonny and Bonita were still sitting in his squad car in the parking lot of the computer sciences building when I pulled in. I kept thinking about meeting T at the nightclub and her late-night admission that she was, in fact, Tressa Hartman. It was a relief to have half of the mystery solved, but one question still lingered: Was Tonia/Tressa also Tamlyn Hartman? From the cell phone picture I saw, it might very well be possible. But then, T also admitted to having work done, so maybe it was just that plastic-looking similarity I was noticing. Or perhaps Tonia/Tressa and Tamlyn were related somehow...though that would be a pretty wild coincidence at this point. Regardless, something was brewing, and I was hoping Cal could help us figure it out.

Cal was eager to get right to it when we arrived in his office. "Hey, y'all," he greeted us with a precious Southern accent, from the upper crust. His family had been Alabama alumni forever. Cal had only recently come back home. He had been getting his master's and doctorate and then taught for a while at Georgia. Lewis was so glad to have his best buddy back in town. And just in time, too. Cal would be one of the groomsmen at the wedding.

"So, there are issues with this Tamlyn Hartman y'all asked me to check on."

Sonny sat up in his chair. "Like what kind of issues?"

"Like…she's dead, for one."

I was dumbfounded. Bonita frowned. "But she is the sole benefactor of Walter Aaron's estate."

"That's quite a trick then, since Miss Tamlyn died at age six in a car accident with her mother. She and her sister were born to Tonia Hartman in Tennessee. They were twins. I found their birth records and Tamlyn's death record, too."

"Tonia! Oh, Lord, now I see. And what's the sister's name?" I asked, though I think we all knew already.

"Tressa Mae Hartman," Cal said. "Both sisters' identities and social security numbers have been used off and on over the past few years. Tamlyn's name is the one with the money socked away and the nice high-rent apartment."

Sonny shook his head. "So Tressa has slipped into her sister's identity from time to time, most likely for some wicked purposes."

There was our wicked witch.

"And not only that," I added. "The woman I met at the club yesterday? She goes by T for Tonia, which she said was her mother's name. So not only does Tressa borrow her dead sister's identity, but she also hides behind her mother's!"

"Sounds like a black widow," Sonny said.

"Yep," Bonita said with a smirk, "and he ain't talking about the spider with eight legs, either. So what do we think? Tressa/Tamlyn comes in, marries someone rich, then knocks 'em off?"

"Or has someone *else* knock him off," Sonny added.

"So, y'all think she married Walter Aaron, then had him killed for his inheritance?" I asked them.

"It's a possibility," Sonny said, "but we still have a lot of unanswered questions. Like who's the person working with her? And has she done this before?"

"This must be why Tressa wouldn't sign the annulment papers right away. She says she wants to see Lewis again before she agrees to do anything. Maybe she thinks Lewis could be her next victim? She wouldn't even need to trick him into marrying her, since he already did. All she'd have to do now is figure out a way to..." I couldn't even finish the thought.

Sonny scowled. "She must know *exactly* who Lewis is—and what he's worth."

My stomach churned. "Sonny, Tressa is coming here tonight to meet Lewis. What are we gonna do? If he dies right now, she would inherit everything. In the eyes of the law, they have been legally married for thirteen years."

"Oh, my Lord," Bonita said. "This woman sounds dangerous. We need to pull together enough proof to arrest her as soon as possible."

"We can talk about that after we leave," Sonny said. "Cal, document everything you can, and I'll get official copies of any legal forms. If you find anything else that connects to this woman, let us know."

"Will do," Cal said. As he walked us out, he said to me, "Tell that redheaded friend of yours to take care of my buddy. Lewis was my best friend during our football days out here. I love him like a brother. I'll see you at the wedding, if not before." That was now one day I couldn't wait to see coming.

He turned to Sonny. "If you need more backup, just let me know. This woman has pissed me off."

"Best thing you could do, Cal, is nail her at this end,"

Sonny said. "The sooner, the better, so we can pull her off the streets."

I followed Sonny and Bonita back to the police station, and we made plans for the meeting with Tressa that night. By this point, I felt like part of the team. I had come up with quite a few leads on my own.

"I think we need to take this slow and careful," Sonny said. "We don't know how far this woman will go. Everything is just speculation right now and we need solid proof."

"Right. I think a wire might be a good idea. If we can get her to admit something, we'll be a lot closer to building a solid case." Bonita was always thinking.

I sat, listening to them go through the details. It was time for me to prioritize things. Chaos was all around me. I had so much to do for Vivi's shower, which was now just a week away, and I had another appointment with the Aarons in a few days. I had promised them we could get to the bottom of this and, well, all I really wanted to do right now was run away from all of this with Sonny. While I was thinking, my phone jingled from a text message.

"Hey, y'all," I interrupted them. "It's Tressa. She says she wants this meeting tonight to be at that park near the mall. Snow Hinton Park at 7:00 p.m."

"Perfect. We'll wire Lewis and see if we can get a hint about what this girl is up to," Sonny said. "Honestly, if we're right about this and Tressa and Tamlyn are the same woman, we need to make sure Lewis is ready for anything."

"Yes, I think it's time to get Vivi and Lewis up-to-date," I said.

The mood was frantic now. The sooner we got tonight over with, the sooner we could go back to the wedding-related chaos that I had come to welcome. Meeting with the Fru Frus was a piece of cake compared to this stress.

I called Vivi and told her she needed to come down to the police station. "Bring Lewis and tell him we need to talk about Tressa. I'll be here waiting."

I sat with Sonny in his office, his eyes showed me his concern.

"You okay?" he asked.

"I'm fine," I lied. "Just want this to end. I mean really, who does this Tressa think she is? I don't think she realizes who she's messin' with." I smiled at him, but I knew he could see right through me.

He reached for me and pulled me into him, hugging me tightly.

"And, no, in case you were wondering, I don't really give a damn who sees this," he said.

I hugged him back, resting for a minute in his arms. I didn't kiss him, though I wanted to. The smell of him, and the feel of his face touching mine was such a comfort. I almost let down and had a good cry. It was all just too much.

Lewis and Vivi must have arrived, because I could hear Vivi's voice coming from the lobby. I knew she would flip out once she found out Lewis was possibly in danger. But we had no time to dwell on it. Tressa would be ready to meet us in just a few short hours and we all needed to be ready.

29

By 6:15 p.m. we had Lewis wired. It was almost showtime. Both Sonny and Bonita were ready to go, the tape recorders running between them in the squad car.

"I'm gonna park across the street at Arby's. We'll do a test first and make sure we can get everything," Bonita said. "If I need to move, I'll let you know."

"Okay," I said, taking a deep breath. "Here we go." I walked away to my car and slid into the front seat.

"Y'all, ready?" I said to Lewis and Vivi who were already in the car. Vivi and I planned to stay in the car and let Lewis do all the talking, but when Vivi is involved, things don't always go as planned.

"Well, if ready means feeling like I might vomit, sure, I'm ready as I'll ever be." Vivi was always so direct.

"I'm the one with this wire. I feel like all y'all are gonna hear is my heart beating outta my chest," Lewis said from the backseat. "I have no idea how to get her to say what we want her to say. Anybody wanna enlighten me?"

"Just act natural, be yourself, and we'll see what she says. Make sure you ask her to sign the papers. What we need to hear is anything that might link her to the Walter Aaron case. If we play this right, she might just walk right into it all by herself," I said.

"Yeah, baby. Just play it by ear. I'm gonna be right here," Vivi said, trying to be reassuring.

"What if she sees this wire?" Lewis was making sure he was all tucked in.

"She won't, but if she asks anything, just tell her you were rehearsing for the kickoff and doing sound checks. She'll believe you," I said. We hadn't given him much warning with this little stunt we were about to pull. But we had no time to do this any other way.

We arrived at the park early so we could get everything situated. Bonita and Sonny were parked across the street at the fast-food restaurant in an unmarked car.

"Okay, Lewis. Give us a sound check," Bonita said through the mic in Lewis's ear.

"I hope I don't piss my pants," Lewis said for her. "How's that?"

"Perfect," she said. "You're gonna be just fine."

From my seat in the car, I could see Bonita and Sonny across the park. It was good to know we were all in this together.

We all waited in the air-conditioning of the car until we saw Tressa pull in. Lewis got out and stood a few steps from the car to wait for her to approach. She actually looked a little nervous herself. She made her way over to my car, stopping by a trash can to toss out an oily fast-food bag.

"Hey," she said, making a beeline to Lewis. She was dressed in a black miniskirt and a red halter-style top. Her perfectly pedicured toes peeked out of a pair of high-heeled sandals. Long, straight blond hair hung down her back and her heavy makeup was caked on like a mask. I guess she was used to wearing whatever face suited her at the moment.

"Hey," Lewis said. Their greeting was awkward to say the least. "I'm Lewis Heart." He stuck his hand out to her.

"Oh, honey, I know who you are. You haven't changed much since college, and I've seen your picture all over town. Don't be silly, I can't shake your hand, we're married."

And with that she laid her lips right on him. His eyes bugged out as she held his face between her hands and pressed herself against him as she kissed him. Vivi sat there for a moment in complete shock. I needed to tie her down, but it was too late. She was out of the car in three seconds flat, with me following close behind.

"You are most certainly not married. It's all a big mistake. You don't even know him." Vivi was livid, her face almost as red as her hair.

"Oh, I think you just might be mistaken," Tressa crooned. "We most certainly are married, and y'all have that paper to prove it."

"I am sorry," Lewis interrupted, "but I hardly even remember you, ma'am. I mean, I have a vague memory of what went down that night, but I would hardly qualify that encounter as a proper marriage. What I need is for you to sign this paper right here." Lewis handed her the annulment document. He rubbed his ear that the mic was in and made a face at Vivi. I looked across the street and saw Bonita move the squad car to the front of the restaurant. Lewis must be getting feedback that made it difficult to hear.

"Oh, I know all about that little piece of paper. But what I wanna know is what's it worth to ya." Tressa was standing there smugly, her weight on one hip, twirling her hair. "I mean, I know you and your reputation, Lewis. You've always been quite the ladies' man. Maybe you wanna try this out for a test drive?" She thrust her breasts forward and gave him a coquettish little grin.

"What it's worth?" Lewis asked. "You want me to give you something to sign this annulment paper?" Lewis didn't even realize that he was playing this just right. I doubted she'd reveal anything about Walter Aaron, but if we could catch her on extortion charges, it could be enough to bring her in and dig a bit deeper into the dark dealings she was involved in.

Lewis rubbed at his ear again, but he kept on smiling. Vivi was standing next to him and I knew she wanted to pull Tressa's hair out of her head. I was just hoping Bonita and Sonny were getting all of this through the wire.

"I don't know. How much you got?" Tressa moved a little closer, thinking she was turning Lewis on. "Maybe you wanna consummate this little marriage of ours first?" She moved closer, talking low and slow, pretending Vivi and I weren't even there. "You know, I can make sure you're always happy."

I wanted to say something, but I didn't dare mess up this moment. I grabbed Vivi by the hand and squeezed the life out of it, trying to keep her from exploding. Then Tressa turned to face us. "I need some privacy with my husband, please. Y'all need to get outta here for a second."

Vivi lost it right there. "I have just about had enough of you, you untalented little slut. Now sign that damn paper or I'm gonna make you wish you had never laid eyes on my Lewis!"

I knew I had to get ahold of Vivi so we wouldn't lose this chance. She was fixin' to blow this whole thing. "Tressa, seriously, get to the point. No one's going anywhere," I said in my most serious tone. I could see she was getting nervous. But I was feeling pretty slick.

"Fine. Okay, here it is. I will sign that there paper for ten thousand dollars."

"Ten thousand dollars!" Lewis shook his head in disbelief. "I can't possibly do that. I don't have that kind of money just sittin' around."

"Well, if you wanna be free to marry that red bull over there, that's my price." Tressa was fidgeting. I could tell she wanted more than money, but she gave up on the idea with Vivi in her face.

Lewis ran his hands down his face in defeat. "Okay. Fine. But I can't pay you right now. Listen, can you meet me to-morrow?"

"Perfect," she said, a grin spreading across her plastic-perfect face. "What time?"

Lewis looked at me like he had no idea what to say. The poor guy was just making this up as he went along. "Um, how's one o'clock?"

"Fine. Where?"

"Do you know where the old Brooks Mansion is?" he asked her.

"Yeah, your radio station, right? I saw your billboards. I'll see you then." Tressa winked at him, then turned and winked at Vivi.

I let go of Vivi's hand, which was turning purple from the vise grip I had her in. As soon as Tressa was gone, I went to the trash can and dug out the fast-food bag she dropped in earlier. If Sonny and Bonita could find fingerprints that would place her at the scene of Walter Aaron's death, we might be one step closer to closing this case. We all jumped back into my car and drove across the street to Arby's, where Sonny and Bo-nita were sitting in the car fiddling with the wire equipment.

"Did y'all get that?" Vivi asked. "Oh, my God, Lewis was perfect. He even set the drop-off so y'all can grab her!"

"Well, let's not get ahead of ourselves, Vivi. We didn't get anything that would link her to the Walter Aaron death," Bonita said. "Every few minutes, all we could hear was someone ordering a giant roast beef."

"I know," Lewis said. "I was hearing that, too. One second I've got Tressa offering herself up to me, and the next I'm hearing, 'I'll have a large roast beef and some of those potato cakes.' It was hard enough to concentrate. Plus it made me hungry."

"Well, y'all will be happy to know I got this." I presented the fast-food bag from my purse.

"You got KFC? Now?" Bonita asked.

"Don't be ridiculous. I saw Tressa throw this away and I thought you might be able to find something on it that could tie her to the Aaron case." I handed the bag to Sonny.

"That's my girl. Smart as a whip, just like you always were." He took the bag from me and handed it to Bonita. "We need to get this tested right away."

"Here, take my watch, too," Lewis said. "Her hand touched it when she reached over to kiss me," Lewis said.

Vivi made a face, but Bonita put on a pair of white gloves from her purse and took the watch and bagged it, as well.

"Let's play the tape back," Sonny suggested.

We listened and, luckily, it was pretty much all there, the most important parts, anyway. Every so often we heard someone ask for extra Horsey Sauce, but there was enough information to get the job done. Tressa had attempted to extort Lewis—for ten thousand dollars, no less. And now we had it all on tape. It wasn't what we came here for, but it was certainly the best progress we'd made so far.

"Y'all know I don't actually have ten thousand dollars to give this woman, right?" Lewis said. "I was willing to say just about anything to get her to sign that paper."

"That's okay," Sonny said. "We're gonna be there when the

transaction takes place so we can bring her in. All we need is to catch her taking what she *thinks* is the money from you. We'll get fake bills to use, so you don't have to worry."

"It's gonna all be okay," I said to Vivi, putting my arm around her. "We will get that wedding license in plenty of time. And if we can get lucky and tie her to Walter somehow, we can put this whole thing to bed."

"Y'all don't really think my Lewis is in real danger do you?" Vivi's rage had passed but now she looked worried out of her mind.

"No, baby. Nothing's gonna happen to me," Lewis reassured her. "Sonny and Bonita got this, right, y'all?"

"We sure do. When you meet her tomorrow, we're gonna have a patrol car out at the mansion, just for safety. But there will be enough of us there to make sure nothing terrible goes down," Sonny said.

"Great idea. See, Vivi? Everything's okay. Promise." I was starting to wonder whether I could keep all the promises I'd been making lately.

30

The next day, Vivi and I were at the Brooks Mansion at noon with takeout for everyone. Arthur had sent over some barbecue sandwiches along with all the fixin's. I called the Fru Fru boys and confirmed the cake tasting for the next day. Meanwhile the pond was being dug on the McFadden property, and the shower guests were sending in their RSVPs for the big event. For one split second, it felt like I had all the balls in the air.

Then one came crashing down.

All of us were gathered in Lewis's office waiting for Tressa, but one o'clock came and went and she still hadn't showed. By two we still hadn't heard anything. All of us, especially Vivi, were a bundle of nerves. I decided to send Tressa a text.

Are you on your way? was all I said.

A text came back almost instantly.

No, she ain't. This is her manager, Dwayne. T is busy today. She'll get back to you.

My stomach dropped as I relayed the message to the group. Vivi started to cry, and Sonny and Bonita stood up from the sofa in Lewis's office.

"Who is this Dwayne?" Bonita asked.

"He runs the Puss and Boots Club in Birmingham," I explained. "He's the reason she didn't seem able to tell me much when we went out there to see her. Something must have happened for him to find out she was coming here. She told me not to let anyone know. To be honest, I think she's scared of him," I said.

"Did you get a look at him?" Bonita asked.

"Yeah, we both did," Vivi said.

"Well, I'd like to figure out a little more about him and his influence over Tressa. But if she isn't showing up today we might as well go on home. Why don't y'all meet me at the station tomorrow after the cake tasting," Bonita said, grabbing her bag. "I've got a few things I'm working on, including trying to pin down everyone who was working at the dock the day Walter Aaron died. Maybe we'll have some more information. Meanwhile, I'm going to ask for surveillance on this club of Dwayne's, see if anything fishy is going on with his business."

"I know the force up there pretty well," Sonny added. "They'll work with us. I'm gonna have them bag something of Dwayne's for fingerprints or DNA in case our stuff doesn't connect the dots."

"I'll go get the ball rolling," Bonita said as she headed for the door. "I won't be far, so give me a call if you need anything."

Once she'd left, Vivi and I sat together on the couch while Lewis took Sonny around on a quick tour of the station.

"Blake," Vivi said. Her voice had dropped. I could sense a seriousness in her tone.

"Yes, sweetie?" I answered.

"Do you think I'll be a good mother?"

I grabbed her hands in mine and looked into her eyes.

"Yes, Vivi, of course. You are going to be the best mother. You're a natural caretaker, and so loving and nurturing. I just cannot wait to see you taking care of our Tallulah."

"I know what they say, though," Vivi continued.

"What? What do they say?" I asked.

"They say that you mother the way you were mothered. And, well, my mother wasn't around too much, you know? I mean, she was so sick so much of the time, remember?"

"Yes, Vivi, your mother was sick, so who mothered you in her place?"

"Cora did most of the time," Vivi said, recalling her nanny who really did raise her right alongside Arthur. Cora was about twenty years older than Arthur and had died a few years ago.

"Exactly, and you wouldn't trade those memories for anything. She taught you to cook and sew and make things. And she always encouraged you to write. She's the whole reason you got your degree in journalism. She was your mother as far as who you have to emulate. Right?"

Vivi had tears streaming down her rosy cheeks now. I got up and grabbed a paper towel from the counter and handed it to Vivi.

"It's okay, sweetie. She was wonderful and you will be, too."

"Thanks, Blake," she said. "These hormones make me so emotional about things at the most random times. I just wish Cora could be here to see all this. She would love this baby like it was her own."

"Just like she did you," I said.

Vivi smiled at me and nodded. As we talked, I pictured myself as a mother and was suddenly filled with the idea of family and just how important it was to me. I guess it had been lying just beneath the surface all along. Maybe it was being with Sonny, but I was really starting to feel more and more ready. And I just loved thinking about it.

Just then the boys returned from their tour, so we all gathered our things and headed home for the night. I gave Vivi and Lewis a ride back to the plantation, but after everything that had happened today, I craved the reassurance of spending some alone time with Sonny. It would be just what I needed to get my head back on straight, so I decided to head directly to his place.

He must've heard me pull up, because he came outside before I even knocked. Seeing him warmed my heart.

"Hey, baby," he said, folding me into his arms. "I missed you so bad."

"I'm home now, sweetie." My throat closed with emotion, realizing what I had just said. It felt like it'd been so long since something really good had happened, but my whole being sensed that having Sonny hold me close was a really, really good thing. I reached up to his cheek, then pulled his head gently down toward me for a kiss. We walked into the house together, our arms around each other's backs.

Once inside, we were extremely careful—keeping the lights dim and staying away from the windows. We wanted to go out on the porch, but decided not to take the chance. Being trapped in the house was tough for an outdoor guy like Sonny. He would rather make love under a canopy of a million stars than in a bed any day. But tonight, it was okay to just be with each other.

"Are you gonna stay tonight?" he asked, hope in his eyes.

I knew I shouldn't, but I couldn't force myself to leave. We'd been having a comfortable night of just quiet relaxation. Even our usual mad rush of passion seemed muted a bit, and we took simple comfort in each other's presence, laughing and talking for hours. With each moment we spent together, it felt more and more natural to be with him here. I loved the easiness that had taken over our relationship, and when we finally made love, we fit together like two pieces of a puzzle.

Afterward, I smiled and cuddled against his big strong chest, and his heartbeat lulled me into sleep. I just wished I didn't have the nagging feeling that this was the calm before the storm.

Late the next morning, bulldozers were working away and water trucks were filling the little pond at Vivi's. It was beautiful, really, all that water, calm and serene, reflecting beneath a weeping willow near the front gate of the property. New sod still sat on a big truck, waiting to landscape around the pool of water with soft green grass.

"Hey, ladies," Coco said as he jumped out of the big pink van in the driveway and trotted around to the back to help Jean-Pierre retrieve the cakes.

"You boys come on in. We got the kitchen all set up," Vivi called from the front porch.

I helped carry the testing cakes inside and set them up all over the big oak table in Vivi's kitchen. Meridee and Kitty popped in and joined us. Bonita was coming in from helping Arthur at the barbecue place.

Everyone looked so festive. Bonita was in a lemon-yellow sleeveless top with her collar popped up, lime-green pearls tight around her neck. Mother and Meridee wore different shades of pink. I had been at a Preservation Society meeting early that morning so I was still a bit dressed up in my sleeveless wraparound lavender silk top that tied with a sash that dripped down the leg of my cream-colored pants.

Vivi, though, was just stunning. She was in a strapless white sundress with purple polka dots and a satin purple sash tied in a bow under her breasts. We looked like little wedding cakes ourselves, and everybody was in a great mood. When you're fixin' to eat that much cake, who wouldn't be happy?

"Oh, I am so excited," Bonita said. "Blake, thanks so much for including me. I just love me some good desserts. I'm helping Arthur with a few new recipes for cobbler right now." She shifted her plump rear end in her seat at the end of the table near the door to the butler's pantry. Kitty and Meridee took the two chairs by the stove, and I sat with Vivi on the other side near the sink.

"Now, ladies, we are happy to have y'all sample our delicious array of cakes for all of the upcoming events," Jean-Pierre announced as he and Coco presented the first of the sweet confections. And one after another, we stuffed ourselves with their amazing recipes. Strawberry, chocolate, red velvet, lemon, peach. The flavors were endless and all of them delicious.

Just as we were at the peak of our sugar high, a loud crack exploded from outside. The sound seemed to come from near the willow tree where all the construction was happening, followed by cries of "Oh, shit!" from the various workmen. We all jumped up and looked out the window to see a geyser was shooting up like Old Faithful from the center of the hole they'd been digging for the pond.

"Oh, my God, what in hell have they done to my pond?" Vivi headed out the back door, all of us running after her in our pretty cake-tasting clothes.

"We've hit a water main," the worker screamed.

"No shit!" Vivi screamed back, her hands in the air.

"What can we do?" Jean-Pierre stepped up, feeling responsible I was sure, since he had insisted on the pond for the ten swans that were coming.

"I've got a great idea, Vivi!" Coco announced. "How 'bout

we make a fountain in the middle of the pond?" He was trying to mitigate the damages, but I appreciated his attempts to smooth things over as best he could.

"Very funny." Vivi turned her attention back to the construction worker. "Now turn that water off before you flood my whole damn house."

The man ran up to the side of the house and shut the water off. We all stood looking at the humongous mud puddle that was supposed to be swan lake.

"You know, maybe there's a silver lining here. I do sorta like that fountain idea," Kitty said. "Don't all royal castles have some sort of extravagant water feature? Seems to me Coco's right. This fits right in with your theme, doesn't it?"

"Hey," shouted a construction worker, running up from the pond. "A bunch of odds and ends washed up from the dirt when that main broke. Most of it was just random junk, but we found this and thought you might want to see it." The man handed Vivi her daddy's ring, muddy from where they found it.

"Oh, my goodness. Daddy's ring! Thank y'all so much." Vivi clutched the dirty heirloom to her chest, holding it tight in her fist. "That damn dog. He's taken everything that's not nailed down and buried it out there in the yard. No tellin' what else they'll find by the end of this."

"Oh, sweetie, I am so happy you have that back. Lewis is gonna just love it." I hugged her.

"See?" Kitty said with her eyebrows up. "Silver linings. They're everywhere."

We made our way back up to the house and all of us stuffed ourselves with more cake. About an hour later we were all full and on a sugar high.

"Oh, my Lord, I am gonna go into a diabetic coma if I have one more bite," Bonita said, patting her ample belly.

"I have never eaten so much cake in my entire life, and I could keep goin' here if they let me," Meridee said, sliding her index finger alongside her saucer for the last bit of icing.

"Me, too. This has been fabulous! I think I want them all," Vivi said, laughing.

"All?" repeated Jean-Pierre. "We showed you fifteen kinds."

"Why not have all fifteen, then? No one should go through life without a chance to taste all these. We can have the strawberry pink for the main wedding cake for me, and, for Lewis, the red velvet with creamy frosting, so the groom's cake will be in Crimson Tide colors. I want it to be done in the shape of Bryant-Denny Stadium. Lewis will be so excited. Then we can have several smaller cakes for the shower, and a few extra at the wedding and the Brooks Mansion grand opening." She might regret that order once the effects of the sugar wore off, but the Fru Fru boys were all over it in a hot second.

"Honey, we can so do that," Coco responded, dollar signs flashing before his eyes. "Just make a list of where and when." He nodded over to Jean-Pierre and started taking up the plates while we all sat in a sugared stupor. Jean-Pierre's pink feather note-taking pen was flying again.

"I need some caffeine. All this sugar's gonna make me sleepy," Vivi said.

"Yes, that's a great idea. A sugar high followed by a caffeine chaser, while pregnant. I don't think so," I said. I got up and grabbed the pitcher of ice water from the counter and poured her a glass.

Once Meridee, Kitty and the Fru Frus had left, Vivi went to freshen up while Bonita and I did the last of the dishes. As we were finishing, her cell phone rang. "It's Sonny," she said as she pulled it out of her bag to answer it. She went into the hall and spoke quietly into the phone, but she looked excited when she returned.

"Some tests are back from that fast-food bag you found, Blake. And there might be some more information waiting at the station, too. I've got to get over there now."

Just then Vivi came out of the powder room. "I heard y'all and I'm ready," she said.

"We'll be right behind you," I said to Bonita.

Bonita got up and kissed Vivi on the cheek. "Thanks for having me be part of this. What an afternoon! I'll see y'all later. The new information should be there by the time y'all arrive."

31

We parked in back of the police station and went in quickly. Bonita was already in Sonny's office and they had pulled in two extra chairs for us.

Lewis was busy at the Brooks Mansion overseeing the renovation and the hiring of employees. Sonny had an undercover officer watching him for protection, but I was worried about how much stress he was under.

Lewis was one of those people who always looked like he had it together, but he was such a good actor that he could be falling apart and no one would know. Well, no one except for Vivi. She was a genius at making people talk. She could read you and know if something was bothering you and then she'd get it out of you before you even realized what you were saying. They were good for each other.

Vivi and I sat down and Sonny poured us some water from his bar on the credenza. Bonita pulled some drawings from a manila envelope.

"So, one of the things I've been looking into is who exactly was working on the barge the day Walter Aaron died. As it turns out, the company had hired a day worker for the day Walter disappeared. Only trouble is, the arrangement they had with him must've been something under the table, because they didn't have a record of who he was or where he lives or anything like that. It all sounded a bit fishy to me, so I brought along our police sketch artist to draw up some facial composites based on our interviews with the other staff. Here's the renderings from the descriptions the tugboat captain gave our artist."

I sat silently, staring at the face in the sketch in front of me.

"Seems the barge company hired day workers on a regular basis," Bonita continued. "And on the day Walter was pushed off, this is the man they had hired. He was stocky, broadchested like a bodybuilder."

There was something familiar about him.

"That looks a little like that manager from the strip club," Vivi blurted out.

"I was thinking the same thing," I agreed. "I mean, if we remove the hat and add that mustache he was trying to grow." I moved my hand over the drawing, careful not to touch the pencil marks. "This is that guy Dwayne who texted me yesterday to say Tressa wasn't gonna show up to sign the papers. He called himself her manager."

"Yep, looks just like him." Vivi leaned back in her chair. We were all silent for a second as we put the pieces of the puzzle together in our heads.

"We're also doing another swipe of the boat to see if there's anything we can run against the samples we get from Tressa and Dwayne. So far we can't find anything out there but Walter's prints and they're on everything. He fought for his life," Bonita said.

"If we can directly tie these two to the boat, this case will wrap itself up in a pretty tidy bow," Sonny said.

"Except," Bonita interjected, "it's looking more and more like Tressa might be in real danger from this Dwayne character. It's clear they're somehow working together, but I'm thinking he's the one pulling the strings. And if he did the actual killing, he can't afford to let Tressa talk, which is probably why she was a no-show yesterday."

"If we can't place either Tressa or Dwayne at the boat, I'm afraid we have a dead end," Sonny said, getting up and pouring himself some of the water.

"But we can prove Tressa married Walter," I protested.

"*Tamlyn* married Walter, and she doesn't exist. We don't have a strong enough case to prove that Tressa actually stole her sister's identity. At least, nothing strong enough to stick in court," Bonita said, putting the drawings back in the envelope. "We haven't been able to track down the person who married the two of them or anyone who actually knew them when they were together, so all we have is a couple of pictures on his cell phone and a license that may or may not be valid. Even more interesting—no one, not Tressa/Tamlyn or anyone, has applied to receive Walter's benefits yet. We're still waiting to hear."

"What about the annulment?" Vivi asked, visibly upset.

"I think Tressa is looking for a way out of her arrangement with Dwayne," Sonny said. "Maybe she was hoping to score some money off Lewis and skip town."

"So that's why she was sneaking off down here by herself?" I surmised. "She told me no one could know she was coming here to meet Lewis, that no one could know T was really Tressa. Maybe Dwayne has no idea about any of that. She's hoping she can swing this deal with Lewis quietly and then slip away with the cash before Dwayne can catch her. It fits."

"I'd love to talk to her myself, see if she's willing to spill any dirt about this guy to save her own hide," Sonny said. "But I've gotta make sure her manager is nowhere around when I do."

"Well, clearly it's not safe to text her," I pointed out. "He has her phone now, remember? How are you gonna do it?"

"Looks like I'm off to Birmingham tonight. Dwayne and Tressa have no idea what I look like, so I can hang out around Puss and Boots without drawing any suspicion. Hopefully I'll be able to sneak a little alone time with Tressa without Dwayne breathing down her neck, so long as he thinks I'm just a regular customer." Sonny got up and grabbed his suit coat off the back of the chair.

We all stood up and said our goodbyes, but I hung back in Sonny's office as Vivi and Bonita headed up the hall to talk to the sketch artist. "Please be careful," I said to him as I gazed deep into those familiar dark brown eyes. "These people are dangerous. They killed Walter."

"Don't worry, baby. It's all in a day's work for me. I'm a homicide investigator, remember? Careful is my specialty." He smiled and winked at me, gathering his things. I began to think he lived for moments like this. His excitement was palpable.

He leaned down and kissed my lips. "I love you, Blake. Don't worry. I'll be back tonight."

I was counting on it.

32

I barely slept that night while I waited for Sonny to call and let me know when he was on his way home. By 3:00 a.m. I couldn't take it anymore. I called his cell. Voice mail.

"Call me, text me. Something. I'm a wreck."

I got up and walked through the silent darkness to the kitchen. Harry The Humper, asleep in his bed, barely stirred when he saw me. He'd probably lick the burglars on their way out of the house with the goods before he'd let out a bark. Unless they had one of his bones. He wasn't exactly watchdog material.

A thunderstorm had crept up, and the lightning ripped the darkness open like a horror movie, illuminating the kitchen in shadows and stark light. I pulled my robe across my chest a little tighter and sat down at the big kitchen table, fingering my cell phone. *Where could he be?* I needed my own police scanner if I was gonna be with Sonny. Something, anything, that would help me keep an eye on him and know that he was all right.

I grabbed my laptop from my bag on the chair next to me and decided to check if there was any breaking news from Birmingham. What if Tressa or Dwayne had recognized Sonny? Tressa did have ties to Tuscaloosa, so it wasn't a big stretch to think he could be in real danger. The anxiety choked me.

I began to think, *This is what my life with Sonny is going to be like. Every single time he goes out on a call, I'm going to be eaten up with worry.* I could see it all playing out, me sitting up till all hours of the morning by the phone with a knot in my stomach. Just like right now.

My mind began to fill with doubts. *Maybe I'm not cut out for this. Maybe I'm too selfish. Maybe I'm too much the nervous type. The more I love him, the more I worry. What kind of life will that be for either of us?*

The thunder crashed and made me jump in the still hush of the wee hours.

My cell lit up.

"Oh, my God, I've been worried sick," I said as I answered.

"I'm okay. It took a little longer than I thought. Dwayne never left her side," Sonny said. "But I followed them home. Dwayne is staying right there with her, though from the look of it I don't think it's by her choice."

"I have been so worried," I said, exhaling.

"Blake, baby, I told you, this is what I do. C'mon, if I know you're at home falling apart it makes it harder for me to get my job done. I need to know you trust me not to be stupid enough to take unnecessary risks."

"Okay, I know. It's all still new to me, that's all. And I didn't expect it to hit me so hard."

"I know, baby. I just hate to think of you upset."

"So, what happened tonight?" I asked, desperate to change the subject.

"I met Dwayne. He's an interesting character. I can't wait to see what his prints reveal, probably a secret rap sheet a mile long. He was very curious about me, though, especially after noticing I tried to talk to Tressa alone."

"That must have pissed him off."

"He was like a pit bull guarding her. I think you're right. She's under his control."

"What do we do now?"

"Wait for her to get back in touch with you about signing those papers and getting the money from Lewis. That's all we can do."

"I'll get the Aarons up to speed in the morning and tell them we're still investigating. That will keep them feeling like they are in the loop."

"Sounds like a good plan. Now go get some sleep, beautiful. It's all gonna be okay. We got this. And we're doing it together. Although, I can think of better things to do together."

"'Night, handsome." I hung up, smiling. God, I did love this man. But for the first time I realized that, even once we were able to go public, this relationship wouldn't be trouble free. Eventually, Sonny and I would have to have a talk.

The next week was hectic for me. I was so busy with clients and the wedding that I wasn't able to see Sonny at all. We were still waiting for any developments on the Walter Aaron case and even Dallas seemed to be making herself scarce. I had several appointments at the office this morning, and the Fru Fru guys were coming over to finalize the last few details of the bridal-baby-bash, which was happening tomorrow.

"I'm here, Wanda Jo," I said, coming in the back door.

"Good. Those boys from A Fru Fru Affair called to say they're on their way."

"Great," I said. "I'll be in my office."

I walked up the hall and closed my door. I sat down in my desk chair and stared at my red Chanel bag on the credenza, thinking about my cell phone inside. I wanted to call Sonny so badly. This whole issue was still bothering me, gnawing away at me almost constantly this whole week. I knew I was seeing him in just a few hours, but I was reaching the point where I couldn't think of anything else. I didn't want to mess up this relationship. But I also never wanted to see Sonny in danger. And I knew I couldn't keep all that worrying locked up. Besides, he could always read me. I pulled out my files and began to work, my purse staring a hole through me as I typed on my laptop.

Then I heard my cell ringing. I pulled it out, and the caller ID read Sonny. I took a deep breath and decided now was not the time to have a deep talk with him. It would just make him worry about me. No, the timing was off. I decided to play it cool and light.

"Horny Hotline, do you have a passion?" I answered in my most seductive voice.

"Why, yes, I do as a matter of fact," he said, playing along.

"How can I be of service?" I asked.

"Well, I'm craving a sexy little thing, about five foot four, with the most beautiful blue-green eyes and long dark hair. Her breasts should be magnificent, and her skin like silk. I need her right now, this second," he said. "What can you do?"

"Well, we'll have to see what we can do. I believe she's a bit tied up at the moment."

"That's exactly what I was hoping for," he said, "so I can eat her up and down while she squirms in pleasure."

I almost dropped my phone. My heart was racing. "No, I

mean she has other engagements until later this evening." I shifted my weight in my chair.

"Well, maybe I can make an appointment for later then. I can meet her anywhere."

"I will have her call you later. How's that, sir?"

"I can hardly wait, ma'am. Tell her I'm starving for her."

"Will do. I hear she's pretty famished herself. Ta-ta, lover."

And I hung up. I was in a daze as I got up and put my phone back in my purse. I went into the bathroom and shut the door. I wet a paper towel and dabbed my forehead, my neck and chest, then took a good look in the mirror. I was changing right before my own eyes. At one time, I had been all career and money and achievement. I was Harry's wife and partner. But that life had become so lonely. Now I wanted exactly what Sonny was offering: flirting and playfulness, passion and romance. I looked again at my face in the bathroom mirror and I could see it in my eyes. Happiness.

I actually liked what I saw. A fuller, more satisfied woman was looking back at me. And the source of this change was a man I had known most of my life. Why was I changing so much? Maybe it was Vivi and her baby. Maybe it was my new deeper understanding of Kitty. Vivi was making a family, and my need for Kitty was changing and growing. It seemed family was what I wanted, too. Deep down it's what I knew I had always wanted, but life with Harry had become an exciting roller coaster ride for our careers.

I swallowed hard as I began to realize that maybe some of the fault for my marriage ending was mine. I never talked to Harry about anything I really wanted, other than to be his partner. I let him lead. I had become lazy. Following him was just easier than thinking for myself. I could go on autopilot and not have to worry. I did love him so much at one time.

He was my ideal dream man on the outside. Preppy, outgoing and confident.

I exhaled, thinking of Sonny, who was my dream man inside and out. It would be a fresh start for me. But could I do it? Was I about to fail at this relationship, too? Was I cut out to be a cop's wife? That's why I knew we had to talk as soon as we could.

I headed back to my office just as Wanda Jo was ringing to announce the Fru Fru boys' arrival.

Coco entered the conference room first and leaned over for a quick air kiss. "Hey, Blake. My, my, don't you look like a Ralph Lauren magazine ad today."

"Yes, you need to be on a runway, my dear," Jean-Pierre said as they both took their seats for our final meeting before the big bridal-baby-bash.

"Let's get right to the list," I said, so glad that this shower was almost behind me.

"We are prepared to have Miss Meridee's house decorated first thing tomorrow morning. An ice sculpture is being delivered at 2:00 p.m., with the party starting at 2:30. We've arranged for a fashion show of mother-daughter outfits, and then we'll have a full makeover done on every guest." Coco finished up with a big smile. "Then we all head down to the river to see the genie."

"My God," Jean-Pierre said, "she is not a genie, she's a soothsayer."

At this point, I decided to give up on telling them Miss Myra was a psychic. They could call her a witch at this point, so long as we pulled this bash off for Vivi.

"What time is the wizard expecting us?" Coco asked.

"Meridee tells me around four o'clock, so that should give us lots of time for the makeovers," Jean-Pierre replied.

"All of that sounds great," I said. "What are the decorations going to look like at Meridee's?"

"Well," Jean-Pierre said, "it has been a teeny bit tricky with it being both a baby shower and a wedding shower. We don't get too many of those." He smiled and peered over his glasses. "The pink theme worked for both, so we've ordered pink glitter wedding bells and, trying to be tasteful, we will be hanging little baby girl clothes on a little clothesline as a back drop behind the cake."

"We thought this was a much more aesthetically pleasing idea than that baby piñata," Coco added. "I mean really, who wants to beat a baby till all the candy falls out? Ridiculous."

I laughed out loud. Who knew where they came up with this stuff. I was just glad they'd steered away from the piñata idea.

Jean-Pierre crossed his legs and continued. "The cake has been ordered and will be picked up early in the morning. It's pink, of course. And it will require a little time to construct it. We want it to be a surprise, though, so that's all I can say for now." His eyebrows went up and he grinned. I hoped I was smart to trust him.

"Anything else?" Jean-Pierre began to put his things away.

"No, I think we are right on track," I said, relieved.

Coco checked off the list. "Now, as far as the wedding plans go, we've got the restaurant booked. Hotel rooms reserved. Flowers ordered. Videographer and photographers slated. There are a few nitpicky things left, but we still have over a month to work 'em all out, so we're doing fine."

"Then we're all set. I will meet y'all at Meridee's at ten o'clock tomorrow!"

I hugged them goodbye and Wanda Jo took their numbers in case she ever had to call them for me. She got up and showed them out.

"Those two are a sight. I actually thought I was seeing a fashion show when they walked in. They were dressed better'an me." She laughed. "Here are a few messages. Your next appointment cancelled. They'll come next week instead."

"Thanks, Wanda Jo. What would I ever do without you?"

"Luckily, you'll never have to know," she said. "Now listen, I need to tell you something. A friend of mine overheard Dallas asking someone on the phone why you're never seen with Harry, except when stumping. She's convinced you're not living at home. My friend was asking me about it, but I just played dumb."

"Thanks for the warning."

God, that Dallas was a menace. I tried calling Harry to tell him, but ended up leaving a voice mail. I tried Sonny with the same result. He and Bonita were busy working on Walter's case, but another murder had also come in several days ago, so he was doing a lot of running around.

After a few hours of work, I got a text message from Sonny.

Hey, babe, what's up?

My fingers flew over the little keyboard. How about we meet at your place for some dinner? I thought I'd swing by and grab some Chinese on the way. How does that sound?

Sounds like fun, sugar. I'll wrap it all up here and meet you at home later.

I could almost see him smiling. I loved what he'd written next.

Meet you at home.

A home with him was what I truly wanted, but we still needed to talk. Maybe now I was uncovering the real reason I had never married Sonny in the first place.

33

I arrived at Sonny's as dusk settled in, his wooden front porch lit with the last peeks of sun. His house was set way out from sight, down a one-lane gravel road. Trees and overgrown shrubbery bending in on either side, making it even more private.

Sonny lived on about seven acres. His parents had owned it before him. His property was covered in trees, wooded, like a small forest. No one would even know there was a house down this dirt road if they were just out for a drive. It couldn't be seen from any street. It was secluded and private. But Dallas knew where it was 'cause she'd crawl through kudzu a mile thick for a freakin' story. She was determined like that. But unless she was out there specifically trying to spy on us tonight, my car shouldn't be seen where I was parking it.

I could see Sonny in the living room through the glass door. He caught my headlights and stepped out onto the porch. A knot formed in my stomach when I thought about revealing all the doubts I'd been having.

"Hey, beautiful, get in here and give this old boy some lovin'," Sonny said, reaching out to hug me. "Gosh, you're a sight for sore eyes. So we eatin' in bed or we gonna be civilized?"

"Let's eat in the kitchen," I said as I pulled away and walked inside with the bag of Chinese food in one hand.

"Sounds good and smells even better." Sonny kissed my cheek and followed me into his kitchen and helped me set up the takeout. We ate and kept the conversation light. I knew he was confused that I didn't jump to react to all his sexual teasing.

We finished up and I walked around the center island and slipped my hand in his.

"Sonny, let's go to the swing," I said, trying not to let him see through me.

But of course he did.

"What's that I see in those beautiful eyes, baby?" he asked, kissing my hand as he held it.

"I need to ask you a few things and, well, let's just go outside and talk for a while," I said, pulling him toward the porch. The night air was wet and sultry. We sat on the swing in the dim amber light.

"What's botherin' you, Blake?"

"Am I that obvious?" I asked, looking up at him.

"I always could see right through that 'I'm tryin' to be brave' smile. Besides, your eyes give you away every time."

"I'm scared, Sonny. The other night, it really hit me that I could lose you. Anytime. Any second. Bad guys don't care whether or not someone is at home waiting on you to return."

He pulled me closer. "But I'm not always in danger, baby.

I'm okay. I'm careful and I'm good at what I do. You just have to trust that."

"I'm trying to trust that but it's hard, you know? By four in the morning, I was pretty hysterical with worry. You can't imagine what I was like."

"Yes, I can," he said sadly. "I went through this same thing with my ex-wife, Laura. She couldn't handle it, either."

Silence followed as I pulled away and looked up at him. "That's why Laura left?" I asked.

"Yeah." He leaned back and took a deep breath, but his normal enthusiasm for life was missing. "Laura said the lifestyle of a cop's wife was just too much for her. The nerve-racked, sleepless nights. Waiting for the phone to ring with news you don't want to hear. She said she'd lay awake for hours, praying no one would knock at the door to say, *'We hate to inform you, Ms. Bartholomew, but your husband won't be coming home again.'*"

Ice chilled my veins. "Did she just walk out?"

"She left after I got wounded that last time. It was only a minor knifing but, by then, apparently even that was too much for her. Her things were gone by the time I got dismissed from the E.R."

"I had no idea."

"That's why we never had any kids. She said she just couldn't bring a child into this world if they stood a chance of losing their dad. She knew I was a cop, but reality hit her when I would have to go out on a call. She worried herself sick most of the time."

"Oh, Sonny, I'm so sorry."

"I do know it's hard. It's a lot to ask of anybody. But it's what I do. This is the only career for me."

I sat there in silence, the old wooden swing creaking as we swayed back and forth. Suddenly, the crickets sounded louder and the silence between us began to suffocate me. I didn't know what to say. I needed to say something. I swallowed hard.

"Sonny, I'm not sure I can do it, either." There it was. Out there.

He cleared his throat and swallowed.

"Don't you believe in fate, Blake? I mean, if I lived my life so worried about every single second that I didn't know for absolute certain that you were safe, I would drive myself nuts. It works the same way for me, too."

"No, you know I'm not out there every minute chasing down murderers and criminals. I don't have to have a gun on me at all times." I felt the tears coming. I wanted to stop this conversation. I hated the direction we were going.

"Exactly. I do because I know how and when to use it. Technically, I'm safer than you." He was trying his best to reason here but I was just an emotional wreck. Reason wasn't about to make it into my already full head.

"Blake, listen to me. I am a big believer in fate. When it's my time, it will be my time. I can't live my life expecting to die. All I can do is live it to the fullest until my time is up. That's what being a policeman has taught me. You just never know when that time is. You could die from a heart attack, the flu, the bus that comes around a corner too fast. Or maybe you die in your nineties, next to the woman you loved your whole life—even if you were a cop."

"But you're pushing fate this way," I argued. "I was so worried that night. I was up pacing until you called. If I do that all the time I will go crazy from lack of sleep. And I'm... I'm..." I inhaled a deep breath. "I'm afraid I will do that every single time."

"If you do, it hinders me 'cause I'll be worried about you sitting home by the phone. I won't be safe 'cause my mind will be on you and thinking about when I can get to a safe place and call. It could put me in danger not to be focused on the job at hand." He stopped and looked deeply at me. "You gotta think about this, Blake. It's important and I've already been through it once before. It's not an easy life to live, the life of a cop's wife. Only you will know deep down if you can handle it."

"I want to. I promise, Sonny, I want to. But I need some time, okay? I need to figure out how I can do it. And I will figure it out. Nothing is more important to me than having you." I snuggled into his neck and closed my eyes.

Could I do it? If I ever worried, I couldn't tell him. Then that would worry him. Could I keep it all bottled up inside all the time for the rest of my life? I knew if I wanted a life with Sonny, this was part of the deal. Was it a deal I could make?

Tomorrow was Vivi's shower and we'd be celebrating her upcoming marriage and new life. I was so happy for her, but I was wrought with worry that I might wind up just like Kitty if I wasn't careful. Too many husbands.

34

I got up early the next day, dressed for the shower extrava-
ganza and headed straight over to Meridee's to wait for the
Fru Fru boys. The day was finally here, and I let the excitement soothe my soul. It had taken some extra makeup, but I
didn't think the ravages of my tears from the previous night
were noticeable anymore.

I plastered the biggest smile I could muster on my face and
went up the stairs at Meridee's. I entered the house, and its
peace enveloped me as always. Meridee gave me a big hug,
just a little longer than usual. "You okay, sugar?"

"I'm great, Nanny." I ducked my head. Maybe I needed to
pack on a few more layers of makeup protection around her.
No matter, she would be able to see right through it. "You
look beautiful today. Are the planners here yet?"

"Not yet." She kept scurrying around the kitchen, setting
out food as though a whole van full of goodies wasn't about
to arrive any minute.

"I hope everything's okay. The Fru Frus were s'posed to be here half an hour ago," I said, taking a cup of coffee from her. "They are always so prompt, too."

"I'm sure they'll be here soon."

I frowned. "Maybe I better give them a call. They have so much to do here to get this place ready for this afternoon. I mean, their decorations are amazing. That's why we hired them."

"Now, Blake, you know it will all work out," Meridee said.

I wasn't so sure. Maybe I was still feeling the effects of worrying about Sonny over the past few nights, but I felt like something was wrong.

I reached for my cell phone and punched in Jean-Pierre's number. No answer. I left a voice mail. "Hey, y'all, it's Blake. Just checking in to see where y'all are. It's about 10:45 and I am here waiting at Meridee's. Call me."

I hung up and sat still, thinking the worst. We had only about ten people coming today. Vivi's two cousins were coming in from Tennessee, and her one journalist friend from her days at the *Tuscaloosa News* years ago. She'd also invited a couple of old friends from our University of Alabama college days. I could come up with food in a pinch, but I sure wasn't the Fru Fru boys.

They had planned quite an elaborate event, several cakes, specifically created for Vivi. Then there was the fashion show with mother/child models, all the makeover artists and the over-the-top decorations, including a five-foot ice sculpture!

I started pacing. I called the number again. No answer.

"Blake, sit down, you're gonna wear yourself out before the party even starts," Meridee said as she washed the biscuit pan and stuck it in the dish rack.

I kept peering over the sink out the kitchen window, look-ing down the driveway. I dared not call Vivi. She would fly

into a major panic, and that meant superdrama. I wasn't up
to that this morning.

I fumbled around in my bag and found Coco's personal
card in an inside pocket. I dialed the number with my heart
thumping. No answer. I left another message, this one a little
more agitated. They were nearly an hour late and I couldn't
reach them. A Fru Fru Affair was *never* late. Ever.

I checked the clock, figuring if I could run over to Piggly
Wiggly and get a cake, then maybe I could throw together a
rush job bridal-baby-bash shower myself. I peered over the
window one more time when my cell phone rang. Oh, thank
God and all his angels, it was Jean-Pierre. I hit speakerphone.

"I have been a wreck, where are y'all?" I said, sounding
frantic I was sure.

"Well, we have had a little accident and we are at the emergency room."

"Oh, Lord!" Meridee looked over with worry on her face.

"Oh, honey, not the real emergency room, we're at the
hair salon."

"What!" I said, completely confused.

"Coco had a fight with the flatiron and it singed his hair
near completely off on one side. We raced him to Dedra and
she's having to give him a bi-level."

I had no idea how to react. I was so mad and so relieved.

"When will you get here? I have been a nervous wreck.
You didn't answer your phone," I said.

"Oh, sweetie, I am sorry, but Coco's hair was still smokin'
in the car. I think I ran every single red light to get him to
our surgeon here at the CHU—critical *hair* unit."

He laughed at himself, and I could hear poor Coco tell
him to stop with all the hospital and emergency room jokes.

"Listen, sweetheart, we will be there ASAP, I promise.
Dedra is a whiz and she is almost done. We have plenty of

time to get everything up and decorated. No worries, sugar. It'll give you wrinkles."

"Why was Coco straightening his hair today?" I had to ask. "He usually wears curls."

"Well, believe it or not, he wanted to look good for the mystic. He thinks she might get a vibration or something from him and he wanted to give off his best vibes. I tried to tell him today was not about him, but he insisted." Jean-Pierre gave an exaggerated sigh. "So Coco lost the battle with the hair appliance and a big ol' chunk of his beautiful hair lies on the bathroom floor, lookin' like a charcoaled rat."

I was sorry I asked. "Please, just hurry."

"On our way, sugar." And he hung up.

"I told you everything would be just fine," Meridee said.

I hoped there were no more surprises today, but with a visit to the psychic coming in a couple of hours, I doubted I'd get my wish.

The wedding planners arrived thirty minutes later and we had Meridee's house covered in pink from front to back at record speed. It looked a bit like a pink bomb had exploded, but in a surprisingly tasteful way. Baby pink tulle draped throughout the house, looking like whimsical pink clouds. The large dining table was set with a white tablecloth with rose-hued runners going side to side. An extra-tall centerpiece of blush-colored peonies and pale pink roses filled an elegant silver vase, greenery spilling softly over the sides.

All of the decorations were up. Even the clothesline of baby girl clothes and teeny pink socks were strung wall-to-wall behind the incredible cake.

The cake itself was a masterpiece. Eight cream-colored stands of various heights were linked together with pink staircases. Each stand, from the top tier to the lowest, held a different lettered baby-block-shaped cake, spelling out the baby's name, *Tallulah*. The tiers led the way down to the center cake, which was in the shape of a 1900s baby buggy. It was absolutely stunning to see, and I was glad I had allowed myself to trust Jean-Pierre with this surprise.

The ice sculpture arrived that afternoon and was set in the center of the living room and bustled with pink tulle. The ice was carved in the shape of a pregnant woman from the side, her hands on her baby bump and her hair piled on top of her head with a sculpted ribbon flowing down her side. I have to say, the Fru Fru boys had certainly lived up to their reputation.

Around two-fifteen, everyone started to arrive, all dressed up and ready for the shower. Vivi's two cousins from Tennessee were as funny as I had remembered. It had been so many years since I had seen them, but they both looked the same. Annabelle and Abigail were twins, a tad younger than Vivi, and they were both gorgeous.

"Oh, my Lord, this place looks like a dream!" Vivi said, walking in slow motion as she took in the transformation of Meridee's house. "I am livin' my fairy tale, y'all."

Everyone came in and took a seat in the large living room to have their makeovers and then watch the fashion show. It was grand, with all the models walking around the huge ice sculpture and songs like "Baby Love" coming from speakers under the tables.

Everything was going just as planned until we heard the air-conditioning pop off.

"Oh, no," Meridee said. "That damn AC is on the fritz again." She ran to the hall to check on it. "It's seriously dead," she shouted a few minutes later. "Guy can't get out here to fix it till tomorrow."

I locked panicked gazes with the Fru Fru boys. It was August in Alabama and we had a five-foot ice sculpture in the middle of the living room. Before we knew it, we were all perspiring and the ice sculpture was sweating big-time, transforming into a long, skinny blob before our eyes.

"What should we do?" Coco said to Jean-Pierre. "It's gonna overflow on these hardwood floors."

"I think we need to put it outside, but let's see if we can make it past the fashion show first."

The fashion show went on for a few more minutes but the ice was starting to melt fast. The boys grabbed both sides of the pan and tried to lift it themselves, but despite how much it had melted it still weighed a ton. Eventually half the guests at the party were balancing the slippery pan in their sweaty hands, moving at a snail's pace as they carried the darn thing out to the back porch.

By then, everyone's makeup was running down their cheeks from the heat, making us all look like we were of the raccoon persuasion, with our black mascara smudging dark circles under our eyes.

While the ladies refreshed themselves with cold drinks and the Fru Frus mopped up the wet living room, Vivi leaned over to me and whispered in my ear.

"Blake, what does that look like to you?"

The ice sculpture had taken on a new form. "Oh, my God, it's a penis! Maybe we should cover it before anyone else notices."

Bonita came over with bulging eyes. "Hey, y'all, does that thing look like a ginormous woody to you?"

Too late.

"Yep, it sure does," Vivi said. She turned to me and shook her head and all three of us burst out laughing. "We can't leave it out here like this."

"I don't know. I kinda like it," Coco said with a wicked grin.

"I think it's a little too bachelorette-style for this event.

There are too many kids around in the neighborhood," Bonita pointed out. "Somehow, I don't think it's the kind of calling card your grandmother would care to broadcast from her porch."

I went inside and found a fluffy pink bathrobe with a hood, and came back out onto the porch. "How about we cover it with this?"

"Well," said Coco, "it's pink, so it fits with the other decorations."

Still laughing, we all moved inside to the dining room, where Coco claimed the head of the table and took charge, clanging the side of a glass with a fork. "Lovely ladies, may I have your attention, please?" he began. "We are so happy y'all are having such a grand and glorious time, aside from nearly swimmin' in Lake Vivi. We'd like to let you know the surprise we have in store for you at this time."

Everyone set down their champagne flutes, which were filled with the cocktail of the hour, The Sassy Belle. Vivi and I had made this drink up years ago. It was our own peachy twist on a mint julep, with a little extra Tennessee Bourbon and a splash of peach schnapps. Vivi and I had ours sans alcohol, since she had the baby to think of, and I was happy to take on the role of designated driver this afternoon.

"We have the great privilege of taking you all to see the famous Tuscaloosa mystic, Myra Jean."

Jean-Pierre elbowed Coco and murmured, "Tuscaloosa psychic."

"Whatever. We will be taking a caravan down to the river now where we will all receive a little clue into our future."

All the guests turned to each other and mumbled in delight.

"Before we leave, I want to make a toast," Vivi said. "Thank you, Coco and Jean-Pierre, for organizing such a fabulous event that I will never forget. Meridee, thank you for the use of your home. It's one of the most special places on earth for me."

Vivi then turned to Bonita. "And to my sister in every way, Miss Bonita. Thank you so much and welcome to our group. I just love having you in the family and working with my Arthur. You make him so happy."

Then Vivi came and held my hands. "Blake, I love you and always have. You will forever be bonded to me and we will always be Sassy Belle sisters. I think back over my whole life, all made up of important moments, rough times and easy times. No matter what, whether we're up for a beauty pageant, graduating from high school or just breezin' around in the summertime, you are in every single memory, laughin' or holdin' my hand, tellin' me I could, or that everything would be okay. I'm so glad you're my friend. Thank you so much for this amazing shower."

Everyone clapped and Vivi took one final swig of her drink. "Now, ladies, we are heading down to the river. My psychic is waitin' on me!"

And before we knew it—as Coco had said—we were off to see the wizard.

We all made our way out to the screened porch and got in cars for the ride over to the river. Myra Jean lived in an old trailer park out there, where she had been ever since I was a little girl.

Vivi got in Kitty's car with Bonita. I was going to drive Meridee in her car. At least, I had planned to be the driver until Meridee slipped into the driver's seat ahead of me. All four feet ten of her. She had to sit on a cushion to see out the windshield, and reaching the pedals was a crapshoot if we needed brakes in a pinch.

"Nanny, let me drive. I know the way," I said, kinda nervous for my life but trying to sound nonchalant.

"No way, sugar. I love to drive and I don't get to do it enough anymore."

That was for a pretty good reason, but Meridee positioned herself on a seat of pillows behind the wheel and gave me a look that said she was not going to be argued with. I made the sign of the cross over my chest as I climbed into the old Buick. I could not believe I was willingly getting into a moving vehicle with a driver the size of an eight-year-old.

The car was a dark red 1970 Buick Electra 225 limited. Fancy. It was the last new car my grandfather bought her before he began to get sick. Meridee swore she'd never get another car to replace it, and she'd kept her promise. The only problem was that this car was the world's longest vehicle ever created. It was not just a boat. It was the whole entire ark— and that was a lotta car for anyone to drive, let alone a Lilliputian like Meridee.

I belted in. First stop, Sweetie-Pie's. Meridee promised to pick up her old dear friend and talented seamstress Sweetie-Pie Jones on our way to see the psychic. Sweetie-Pie was the one making Vivi's wedding dress—she'd made all our pageant dresses growing up, and we wouldn't have trusted the job to anyone else. Unfortunately, she'd missed the shower due to an emergency fitting for a pageant contestant, but she hadn't been out to see Myra Jean in ages and she wasn't about to miss an opportunity to try to speak with her deceased husband, Harold. She was waiting on the front porch when we arrived, with her big, yellow, flowery handbag hanging from her forearm.

"Land sakes, Meridee, you drivin' like a son of a gun. You ain't changed a bit!" Sweetie-Pie said with a laugh as she walked to the car. "Oh, Lordy, I am so happy to see you still driving this old thing. Sho' ain't nothing like this baby on the road no more."

I got out and went to sit in the backseat to let the two old friends visit. Sweetie-Pie wasn't much taller than Meridee. What a sight we must have been! A big old boat of a car coming down the dirt road with two little old ladies barely peeking over the dashboard.

I white-knuckled it all the way, the dust and dirt flying as we left the asphalt for the long drive down by the river to the trailer park. Myra Jean's mobile home was older than most of the others. She had been out here as long as I had known her.

Meridee came to a sudden screeching stop, sliding in front of Myra's double-wide sideway, like she was stealing a base.

"It's always so easy to park here." Meridee unclicked her seat belt and opened the door. "Must be the skid factor with the dirt."

Uh-huh. It took me a little longer to get out since I had to pry my fingers, one at a time, from the door handle.

Myra Jean came out from her home and stood on the make-shift porch, her long, brightly colored caftan billowing in the evening breeze coming off the river. "Oh, my God, would you look what the cat dragged up?" She clapped her hands, then held them out toward us. "It is so good to see y'all again. Get on over here and give me a hug."

Everyone else had already arrived and been seated in chairs scattered around the tiny living room inside the trailer.

Myra Jean was a very tall, willowy woman with bright red hair—from a Clairol bottle—piled high on top of her head. I had never seen it down, but I figured it must go to her waist, at least.

She wore a scarf around her forehead tied at the nape of her neck, and the ends streamed down over her right shoulder. She was from the sticks. No real education to speak of. She was schooled in the metaphysical—she just *knew* things.

As a child I remember being a little scared of her. Meridee would bring me here when she and Sweetie-Pie came on their monthly visits. Myra Jean would get out her cards and her incense. Sweetie-Pie would sometimes fall into a trance and say she saw her late husband, Harold. I'd look everywhere for the man, but I never saw him, even for a second. I had asked Meridee about that later, when we got back to her house.

"No, child," she'd explained to me right before bed, "you ain't gonna see Harold like you see me. He's a ghost."

I was about nine years old at the time and I had crawled straight under the quilt with her just in case Harold decided to visit us that night.

To my grandmother, there was nothing out of the ordinary about seeing a spirit. She was just like that, though. Nothing too out there for her. Ghosts, psychics, she happily believed in the unexplained. So long as there was no sufficient proof that they *didn't* exist, she saw it possible that they could.

Kitty would say when she left me at Meridee's house in the summers while she went to work, "Now look, you crazy old woman, don't be takin' Blake to see that nutty friend of yours."

Meridee would give Kitty a smile and take me anyway. Kitty had known, though, so I guess she hadn't really minded that much. On a few occasions, I even remember Kitty herself going out to Myra Jean's. She'd say, "Now, Blake, don't you tell your daddy…" Whichever daddy it was at the time. I have reconciled with the fact that I just come from a crop of crazies.

As we made our way up the steps, Myra Jean looked at me. "Well, I'll be damned! Is this little Blakey?"

I smiled.

"You have got to be kiddin' me. C'mere, baby girl, and let me get a look at you. Well, aren't you just about the purtiest thing I ever did see? Look at all that long dark hair and those big beautiful blue eyes. Oh, my, I get such a good feelin' 'bout you, baby. You got someone wonderful loving you in your life now for sure. I can feel it!" She hugged me and kept right on talking. "Y'all come on in and have a seat with the rest of these ladies. Want some sweet tea?"

We made our way into her little mobile home. She hadn't

done one thing to it since I was here about seventeen years ago. I was in my early years of high school when I stopped coming to see her with Meridee. Boys had taken over my interests by then.

Inside, we greeted all the girls from the shower, and I sat down on the couch next to Vivi. It was a tiny place. The olive-green rug was stained and threadbare, and the yellow couch just as faded. Oversized lamps with green glass bases sat on either side of the sofa on undersized TV trays, which were doubling as end tables. The lamps had colorful silk scarves draped over their tops, giving the room a nice rosy glow. An older model TV with rabbit ears sticking up from behind sat in the corner of the room near a sliding glass door. Sheer, ratty-looking curtains draped down from the ceiling and puddled on the floor over the doors to keep the glare out. The small kitchen was crowded and the countertops cluttered with trinkets and knickknacks.

Myra Jean sat in the brown velvet cloth recliner to the side of the room. "I am happier than fuzz on peaches to see y'all, you know that?" She was exuberant.

Coco and Jean-Pierre sat in kitchen chairs that had been squeezed into the tiny living room. Coco sat up straight, literally on the edge of his seat. He was smiling like a child about to see Santa. I could hear him mumbling, "Here we go. Here we go."

"You're lookin' good, Myra Jean," Miss Sweetie-Pie said.

"Yes, you never change a bit," Meridee agreed, reaching over and squeezing Miss Myra's hand. "I have really missed you."

"Me, too, honey," Myra Jean said. She looked over at Sweetie-Pie. "Seen Harold any lately?"

"No, I think he may have gone on by now," Sweetie-Pie said, her smile wistful.

"Well, I'll see if I can find him here today for you before you go." Myra Jean was a compassionate soul if a bit eccentric. I always did like her.

She reached over and grabbed Vivi's hands. "Look at you, momma. Aren't you just a vision? Having a girl, too. Congratulations. I am thrilled to be part of your shower. But, honey, I'm seeing your wedding right now and we need to have a little talk."

This was how Myra Jean did things. There wasn't any formal introduction or palm reading or incantations muttered over a crystal ball—she'd just be in your presence and start to feel things and see things and then blurt them right out without warning.

"Not good at all, baby girl. We need to talk. Your wedding is not on a lucky day. You got problems there."

Vivi's mouth dropped, and I tensed up. Myra Jean was for real, I was sure now. She knew about Tressa, among so many other things. She had a gift. Meridee smiled and nodded as the others in the room gasped.

"Don't say anything, let me see if I can get a clear picture," Miss Myra said, closing her eyes. "Oh, my." She stopped and opened her eyes, dropping Vivi's hand. "Another vision just popped in, and I'm not so sure I *wanna* see this. A certain somebody here, and I won't mention any names, needs to get themselves a room. You're too old to be hookin' up at your momma's house."

We all burst out laughing. All of us, except Kitty.

"Oh, Lord, y'all. I need a break for a sec." Myra Jean got up and took a deep breath, stretching her palms toward the ceiling.

Meridee went into the kitchen with her and got a tray of iced tea for everyone. Myra Jean put a package of saltines on a tray with a can of aerosol cheese. You had to love her, she was trying to serve her guests. Okay, so it was a bit *different* from the goodies at the first half of the shower, but it was still technically an hors d'oeuvre. I mean, who doesn't love cheese and crackers…even if it is spray cheese? Meridee and Myra Jean sat again, and the readings commenced.

"What's not good about my wedding day?" Vivi asked impatiently.

"The date." Myra Jean raised her eyebrows. "You got this weddin' date thing all wrong."

"What?" Vivi asked.

The Fru Fru boys both sat up straight and looked nervous. "But the date's all set."

"I know it's all set," Myra Jean said, looking at the planners. "Don't mean it's right."

Vivi turned to the boys and asked, "Have the invitations been sent yet?"

"No, the printer caught a mistake on them so they're running a bit late," Jean-Pierre said. "They'll go out next week. The wedding is at the end of September, about five weeks away."

"That's just not right," Myra Jean continued. "I have a date in mind, and it has a glow around it." She closed her eyes again. "Yes, I can see it in my head now, and this is the date you *must* get married on. It's the date the spirits are showing me."

"Well, for God's sake, Miss Myra, what is this magical date?" Jean-Pierre asked, with a mountain of anxiety all over his face.

"September first." She leaned back in her chair as if the announcement had taken a toll on her. "Your other date has a really bad aura."

"September first? Oh, honey, no way," Jean-Pierre said. "That's Bama's big football kickoff day. That's impossible. This

town will be crazy with traffic and tailgaters." He was rev-
ving up for a hissy fit. "All the restaurants and hotels will already be booked solid. Caterers, too. No, we just cannot do it."

Troubled, Vivi stood up and paced for a minute, then turned
back to us. "I know you're right, Miss Myra, but I just don't
see how in the world it's gonna work. The date we have now
is Bama's off day—no game, which means Lewis is free and
it was perfect."

"No, it's not perfect," Miss Myra said. "It's bad luck."

"But kickoff is the biggest day of the year for Lewis. He'll
be in the press box all day, and when he's not there, he'll be
at the new radio station. It's the inaugural broadcast! It's the
freakin' kickoff, for heaven's sakes!"

Coco had his phone out and was looking something up.
"Wait, wait, wait," he said. "I don't know about y'all but I
don't like messin' with spirits. We can work around this. Look,
the game is at noon on September first. The wedding is already planned for sunset, so timingwise, we wouldn't have to
change our schedule at all."

Jean-Pierre interrupted, "But what about all the restaurants
and hotels? Nothing is going to be available. We only have a
couple of weeks to try and find new caterers and everything
else. This will be an absolute mess."

"No," Coco insisted. "We're professionals. Everything will
just have to get worked out at warp speed."

Bonita had been quiet, but I could see the wheels in her
head turning. Suddenly, she broke the silence. "I have a great
idea," she said, standing up as though this were too important
an announcement to deliver from a sitting position. "Why
don't you let Arthur cater the whole thing? He would love to
do it for you, and I will help him pull it off."

She was smiling, an eager look on her face, awaiting a response from anyone. "Well, what do y'all think? All the Fru

Fru boys have to do is get the cakes and leave the rest of the food up to us. He's already hired some waiters, so they can help serve and refill glasses. It doesn't have to be all barbecue, either. Arthur is a whiz in the kitchen. I'll even bring my orange-pineapple ice cream, if you'd like. It's win-win for everyone, since this would be a fantastic way to promote the business for our big opening."

Vivi spoke up first. "I absolutely love this idea! No one but Arthur should be doing my wedding anyway, if he's willing. But I still need him to give me away at the altar. He can do both, right?"

"Absolutely. I'll make sure of it." Bonita smiled.

Somehow, Vivi and I knew that if Bonita was in charge of something, we'd have no cause to worry about this at all. It felt like a huge weight had been lifted.

Bonita sat back down, satisfied with herself. "When we get back tonight, we can start gettin' that menu together. Arthur will be so tickled."

"Whoa," Jean-Pierre jumped in. "Just a minute. Are we really changing the entire wedding day based on a prediction?" He looked a bit exasperated. "I don't mean any disrespect, Miss Myra, but we've already planned—"

"Yes, I do believe we are," Meridee interrupted, grinning. "Get used to it."

Kitty got up to get some more tea. Coco stood up and slinked over to Myra Jean, smoothing his hair, and sat down. He reached over and put his hand on hers.

"I believe we need to do exactly what you say. Do you think you can see anything for me?" Coco asked, scooching closer.

"You have got to be kidding me!" Jean-Pierre said, still clearly more upset than Coco was over the change of dates.

"Oh, sweetie, you have had yourself an accident recently—

somethin' smokin'.'" She was closing her eyes and shaking her head, lost in the vision.

"Yes, I burned my hair clean off this mornin' with the flatiron," he said, very excited. "Oh, my God, she is so for real." Coco was smiling. I snickered to myself—I didn't want to tell him that we could all still smell the singed hair from a mile away.

"You are going to do well in your business," Myra Jean continued. "You have a great attitude and that will take you far, my dear." She smiled and started to drop his hand when she looked suddenly overcome by another vision. "Wait," she said. "I see something else. Men."

"Okay, you've so got my attention." Coco popped his eyebrows up with excitement.

"Lots of men in tight, white, butt-hugging pants. Oh, my word, you are just surrounded by them."

"Hallelujah, my dreams *are* coming true!" He nearly skipped back to his seat.

Coco laughed, thrilled with his predictions, while Jean-Pierre sulked in the corner.

Myra Jean stood up and walked around the room, handing out visions like they were Halloween candy. "Oh, my, you ladies are some busy belles, I'll say."

The cousins would be moving. There was more baby magic in the air. On and on. Then she approached the couch where I sat. Myra Jean stood in front of me, shaking her head. "I see something I missed before. The flames of passion had been so bright that they hid it. Baby girl, you are in hot water. You better be careful, sugar. Somebody's out to be your undoin'."

"What do you mean by that, Miss Myra?" I was pretty sure she was referring to Dallas Dubois, but I wouldn't say no to any details she might be able to send my way.

"I don't know," Myra Jean said. "This happens sometimes. I'll see something one minute and the next, it's gone. Just be careful. You got some enemies." She turned back to her recliner.

Great, I thought. *Thanks for the sleepless nights I'm gonna have.*

Vivi leaned in to me and whispered, "Get everyone out and say goodbye so I can talk to her in private and ask her about the 'other woman.'"

I gathered everyone and they hugged Miss Myra Jean and walked outside into the evening air. I hung back so I could hear all about this other woman. The Tressa situation had me scared.

"Miss Myra, do you know anything more about that other woman we discussed a couple of weeks ago?" Vivi asked tentatively.

Miss Myra, though, wasn't known for her subtlety. "Oh, sweet thing, I do. Don't trust her. She's not who she seems. She's desperate and feeling cornered."

"What do you mean?"

"She'll stand and fight, and she's dangerous, like...some kind of spider. Tell that fiancé of yours to watch out, too. She's centered on him."

"Are we in danger?"

"You could very well be. That's what I'm sensing."

Vivi was getting more and more upset. This was not how I wanted her shower to end.

"Miss Myra, can you say anything about Vivi's baby?" I interrupted, trying to change the mood.

"Oh, yes, that baby is a doll," Myra Jean cooed. "I can see she has red hair, just like her momma."

Vivi smiled.

"Your little one is a pistol and cute as a button. She'll be a happy and healthy baby. Y'all ain't got nothin' to worry about in that department." Myra Jean leaned back in her chair. "As long as you watch out for the spider-woman...."

36

I docked Meridee's boat in her garage, locked up, then jumped into my own car. I had so much on my mind. Myra Jean's predictions bothered me. They'd been so spot-on for everybody. The spider-lady comments to Vivi were downright eerie, but her warning about my having enemies and someone being out to get me had me worried. After my conversation with Dallas about the videotape, I thought we'd passed the worst with her. I'd been sure we'd scared her off with threats of lawsuits, but if Myra Jean was right, she might still be lurking behind every corner, hoping to catch me and Sonny doing something wrong. Dallas would do anything now that her job was on the line.

The stress of getting caught, on top of everything else I was trying to deal with, was almost overwhelming. I felt compelled to tell Sonny that I needed to focus on the wedding now, especially since the date had been moved up. I couldn't focus on Vivi and her big day with the threat of Dallas and her cameras exposing everything under the sun. Also, the truth was, I just needed time to think. I knew for certain how much Sonny meant to me, and I loved how he made me feel, but I was only beginning to realize what it meant to be in a relationship with someone who had such a dangerous career. I wasn't sure yet that I was cut out to be a cop's wife. And I was still in the middle of breaking free from my role as politician's wife—did I really want to get involved in another relationship where my partner's career would take over my life?

I knew this was all too much for me to deal with alone. It was time to talk to Sonny about this, since he deserved to know what I'd been thinking. I called him and told him I was heading over to his place.

"Hey, gorgeous," Sonny said with just a touch of wariness when I walked into his house. He had no idea what I was about to hit him with, but he knew something was up. "How'd things go with Myra Jean? What'd the old psychic have to say?" He led the way into his living room, trying to keep things jovial as he motioned toward the couch. "Why don't you get comfy and tell me 'bout it."

"I can't stay, Sonny." I was fixin' to crush his world, but I had no choice. I had to do it, for both our sakes, at least for a little while. "I just wanted to tell you what happened, then I need to go."

"Well, that's a disappointment."

I swallowed hard, my mouth sticky and dry. "Myra Jean did have some things to say, and they were definitely warnings."

"Oh, baby, is somethin' she said botherin' that gorgeous head of yours? You know psychics just say what *might* happen. They don't know for sure. No one does."

"Exactly," I said. "And I am scared to death of what *might happen* if we keep going on like this. She pretty much warned me that Dallas was after me. That I had some serious enemies."

"Blake, you put Dallas in her place with that camera stunt she pulled," Sonny said. "Nothing ever hit the news. You've won. The worst is over."

"No, Sonny, I don't think it is. Myra Jean could tell there was still something out there to be worried about. Dallas has her ways… She can still do so much more to me and to the people I love. She's in control as long as she has that tape. She knows now that things are going on between Jane and Harry, and is all over us just waiting for us to make the wrong move. I don't think she'll stop till she gets some viable evidence she can use. Her job is on the line and you know as well as anyone what it's like to have a career you love that you don't want to let go. She'll stop at nothing. We can't take that risk anymore."

Sonny took in a deep breath. "I don't like the sound of where this is going. What are you thinking, baby?"

"That we really need to watch what we do for a while."

"What do you mean by *watch?*"

"Sonny, it makes me sick to say this, but I think we need to cool our relationship off until the election is over. We can't give Dallas any more fuel for her fire. She'll have the whole county burning if we let her."

"Blake, you're talkin' nearly three months. I can't last that long without you. God, baby, I just found you again. I can't lose you now." Sonny had moved closer to me, looking lost and shocked at what I was proposing.

"I'm so sorry, Sonny." I swallowed hard to keep the tears from falling. "But I know myself, and if I get too comfortable, like we were the other night, I'm gonna slip up. Next time, it might not be Dallas with those cameras. It might be some other reporter. Someone that I don't have any ammunition to stop. I can't let everything fall apart because of me.

We could all be ruined in town. I can't do that to Harry, to my friends and family, but most of all, to you. You're the most innocent in all of this. You're single, and you're just trying to love somebody. If Dallas turns what we have into something ugly and dirty, I could never forgive myself."

I felt the tears spill over and run down my cheeks.

"Blake, you're running scared. Is this really about Dallas, or does it have something to do with what we talked about the other night?"

I hesitated, not sure if I was ready to admit the other side of this. "Sonny, I just need more time to think, that's all."

"Damn, Blake. C'mon. What we have is so much bigger than all this B.S. You'll get used to my job. I won't take any unnecessary chances and I'll prove to you that you don't have to worry all the time. I just can't lose you." He was getting upset and I could see all of his emotions welling up inside him.

"Right now, I can't make any promises. Everything is too much to take in. I'm feeling overwhelmed, Sonny. When the election is finished and Vivi is married—and Tressa and Dwayne are locked up—we can put the focus back on us and figure how to make this work. But I can't even begin to think about how to move forward with you while I've got all the rest of that weighing down on me."

"Blake, I can't stand the thought of not having you in my arms or being able to kiss you. I waited so long to finally get you back. We don't have to do this. The last time I had to let you go for three months, I lost you to Harry. I can't risk that again."

Sadness welled so full in my throat. I couldn't swallow anymore. "That was different. You weren't willing to even give a long-distance relationship a shot. You didn't lose me then, you let me go. Now I'm not saying I'm walking away from this forever. I just need to get things sorted in my life so that there's space to make this work. We need to have some time apart. I'm sorry."

"Does this mean I can't even come out to Vivi's?" he asked softly. "I was lovin' bein' out there with everybody...." His lips were quivering, sadness overtaking him. I was breaking his heart.

I hated doing this to him. I hated it. But I remained silent, no longer knowing what to say.

"I don't know how I'm gonna make it without you," he finally said.

"I don't know how I'm gonna do it, either," I said, embracing him, feeling his warm kisses on my tear-filled face. He pulled me close. I heard his tortured breath and a sad, slow song playing from the stereo, and I started sobbing. I wanted the music to stop, but Sonny pulled me up and into him close and sweet, caressing his big hand up and down my back.

"Dance with me, Blake," Sonny whispered against my hair. "Just let me hold you a little longer before you leave me."

We slow-danced in the quiet stillness of his living room. He held my hand out to the side, like a gentleman, kissing my fingers, one by one, then eventually tucking my hand in his and holding it between us, like he'd never let go.

He closed his eyes, swaying gently, rocking me back and forth in his arms. Sonny was always taking charge and making me feel better, even when he was hurting, too.

"I love you, Blake," he murmured. "And I am never going to stop loving you. I have never been more certain of anything in my life. So if taking a break is what you think we have to do, I'll do it. I can't stand the thought of it. I will ache for you every single day until after the election, when we can go out in public and it won't matter. I'll be here waiting because I want to keep you. I wanna be seen with you on my arm, so ever'body can look at me and say, how'd that lucky fool get a babe like that?"

We smiled though our tears.

"I love you so much, Sonny. I am so sorry."

Sonny put his index finger to my lips. "Shh," he soothed. "No apologies. This is only a break for now. *Not a breakup.* I will not lose you, Blake. Not ever again."

I tried to smile. "We've only just gotten to the place that I've longed for, Sonny. I need you so badly, but I know we have to do this."

Sonny kissed me goodbye and opened the front door. He smiled at me, but it didn't reach his eyes. I left his driveway, watching him in my rearview mirror. He stood on his porch, leaning against the side post, his hands in his pockets. I turned out on the little dirt road and he faded from sight. If this break was supposed to make things better, why did I feel like everything had just gotten so much worse?

37

Two miserable days later, I was at the office on the phone with Wynona Aaron when Wanda Jo popped in and slipped a message under my nose that read, "Call Sonny ASAP. They've got news."

"I'm sorry, Ms. Aaron, but something has come up and I need to run. I'll talk to you next week or sooner if I have anything new to share."

I hung up and dialed Sonny. I felt a pit in my stomach take root after the talk we had the other night. It felt wrong not to be able to see him and run to him.

"Blake, I'm glad you called. We've had a new development in the Aaron case. How soon can you get here to discuss it?" He sounded so formal and businesslike. This emotional distance was killing me.

"I'll be there in a minute." I hung up, my hand lingering on the phone. I let out a deep breath. At least I'd get to see him.

I called down the hall to Wanda Jo to let her know that I'd

be at the police station, then raced across the street—just like I did that night during the thunderstorm in May, when Sonny gave me his white shirt that I never returned. I ran under the old clock and across the side street, crossing just in front of the Warrior River Bridge and rushing into Sonny's office, my feet pitching fits. I felt I deserved an award for running across two city streets in my Jimmy Choos. Even in a crisis, shoes are what it's all about. Just ask Cinderella or Dorothy.

"Hey, Sonny, what's going on?"

Sonny stood up and got me a chair. "We got some partial fingerprints from the boat. Better still—they match the ones on the can Dwayne dumped outside his club. Tressa's prints, which we pulled from that fast-food bag and Lewis's watch, haven't shown up anywhere else."

"Can you arrest Dwayne?"

"Not yet," Bonita said as she walked in and pulled up a chair. "Placing him on the boat doesn't prove that he killed Walter, it just proves that at some point he was on that boat. But I think our suspicions of this guy were right."

"We think Dwayne was posing as a day worker and that he was the one who pushed Walter off the boat. I'm willing to bet it was his idea for Tamlyn to marry Walter—someone rather lonely who didn't talk to his family much. Maybe they thought he'd be an easy target, and once they'd killed him, he and Tressa could get all of the insurance money. If we can prove that T/Tressa was using her sister's identity to marry Walter and pull off this scheme, then we can put a case together against her, too," Sonny said. "Unfortunately, a lot of this is still circumstantial. We either need a confession or someone who can officially ID Dwayne as being the worker on the boat with Walter when he died. Blake, you saw the artist's sketch, so we're pretty sure we've got the right guy. But we need a crew member to confirm it. If it *was* Dwayne, he'd be the last one who had contact with Walter, making him a prime suspect. Based on that, we'd definitely be able to bring him in for questioning."

"Cal called this morning," Bonita said. "There's an unsolved murder in Tennessee where the benefactor is one Tamlyn M. Hartman. So we have us a pattern."

Sonny added, "Maybe that department's investigative team has some information or photos we can use to nail Tressa."

"Isn't it enough to charge her based on bigamy and forged documents?" I asked.

"I don't want to miss out on charging the two of them with murder, if I can prove it."

Bonita said, "We believe Tressa is being forced into this by Dwayne, which is why we think she's trying to get so much cash from Lewis to sign the annulment. She's hoping she can take the money and disappear, escaping Dwayne in the process."

Sonny nodded, his gaze lingering on me just a bit too long.

"We really need those annulment papers signed by this Friday," I said. "That's the final deadline. I talked to the probate judge and he said as long as we get all the paperwork in by then, the wedding license can be issued."

"I know. Our plan is to get two birds with one stone. I need you to try and contact Tressa and ask her to come back here Friday to the grand opening of the Brooks Mansion to get the money from Lewis and to sign the papers. If we're right about Dwayne, he'll likely follow her out here to see what she's up to, since he keeps such a tight leash on her. We'll be there to catch her taking money from Lewis, and we can bring her in on extortion charges once she's signed the papers," Sonny said.

Bonita got up and pushed her chair back. "Meanwhile, we'll get the tugboat captain down there to get a look at Dwayne, too, and make a confirmation that he's the day worker who was with Walter when he died. Once we get that, we can bring him in, as well."

"We will set up everything we can for Friday," Sonny said. "Everybody and their brother will be at the grand opening so we can keep the captain's surveillance and this whole sting hidden in plain sight," Sonny said. "Though Dwayne may very well come in another disguise."

"Okay, this sounds like a viable plan. Let's work it." Bonita walked out of his office and headed down the hall.

Sonny got up and gently closed the door behind Bonita. I tensed as he came closer and closer.

"I know what you said, but when we have to see each other like this, the rules feel blurry." He leaned down and kissed me gently, softly, slowly.

I pulled away, though it was the last thing I wanted to do.

"Blake," he said. "This hurts."

"I know. It hurts me, too." I picked up my purse. "I'll call you, okay?"

"I love you," he said, looking like he wasn't sure when he'd see me again.

I had to admit I wasn't so sure, either. Right now, we had the excuse of this case, but after that... Not seeing him, even weekly, would feel like a death. My heart couldn't take much more, but I couldn't afford a mistake.

"I love you, too, Sonny," I said. I blew him a kiss and walked out and closed the door. I slipped into the bathroom down the hall, amazed I was still holding it together. As I stared at the sad woman in the mirror, all I could think of was *How am I going to stay away from my cop?*

38

Late August hit us like opening the door of a dishwasher midcycle. The heat and humidity were so claustrophobic that even taking a deep breath felt impossible. The rest of the workweek had passed, and I had stayed away from Sonny unless it was business. It was sheer agony most of the time.

I'd managed to get Tressa on the phone and she'd agreed to meet us at three o'clock for the grand opening of the station. She'd sounded desperate to make this happen, but midconversation I heard Dwayne barge in on her and yell in the background. She'd hung up right away, and I hoped he hadn't hurt her. The plus side was that he was clearly suspicious of Tressa and I was certain he'd follow her out here when she came for the money.

The drop date for the sting was today, and I was hoping with everything I had that Tressa would follow through. She could technically go on like this forever, marrying rich men, Dwayne killing them off and then taking their money and setting up in a different part of the country. In fact, if she hadn't made that little mistake of marrying Lewis in a college prank all those years ago, bringing her to our attention, who knows how many more rich, lonely men would be dead? I wanted this to end here—we all did. The question was, did Tressa?

My main concern, though, was for Vivi and Lewis. We were cutting the deadline for their paperwork too close. If we didn't have the annulment papers filed for her wedding license by midnight tonight, everything could fall apart and we faced the possibility of having to postpone the wedding. And even worse—this might be our only chance at getting the papers signed, period. If we failed, Vivi and Lewis would never be able to get properly married. We were really under the gun.

That morning I went downstairs to find Vivi standing at the sink. She had a cup of coffee and looked racked with nerves.

"Hey, little momma, are you okay this morning?"

"I'm just a little jittery," she said as she sipped her mocha.

"Honey, the cure for jitters is not coffee. Here, I'll take that." I took the mug from her and handed her some OJ. "What's going on under all that red hair this morning?"

"Today's the day. If we don't get that signature, I can't get married. I mean, not really married, what with bigamy being illegal and all. It's just too close now. I don't handle this last-minute stuff so well." She took a sip of juice.

"You don't?" I said in mock amazement. "Let me call Dallas and get that on the news." I reached over and patted her hand. "Look, Vivi, Bonita and Sonny have it all planned out. Lewis will lure Tressa into the office at the mansion and we'll get the money transaction on tape. Bonita and Sonny will deal with her while the other officers are handling Dwayne, who we're hoping the tugboat captain will be able to ID. We're gonna do more than get those papers signed, honey. We're gonna get a couple of criminals behind bars."

★ ★ ★

We arrived at the Brooks Mansion just before 10:00 a.m. The big celebration had just started, but the crowd was thick, despite the already suffocating temperature.

The mansion looked amazing with its new coat of paint, repaired front porch and restored windows and shutters. Lewis had ordered all the carpets, period bannisters and crown moldings before the restoration began. The old mansion had stood still as time wore her down, but the face-lift and renovations and the crowds outside seemed to infuse her with new life. She was experiencing a revival, in every sense of the word. She was so lucky Lewis had saved her and loved her so much. Everything just glistened.

I stopped for a minute after I got out of my car just to look at her. Lewis bought her, with Meridee's help, but we'd all worked together. I'd held off the people who'd tried to purchase the place and have it mowed down and turned into a shopping center. My fight had lasted just long enough for Lewis to slip in and buy the place up. Meridee always said that things always worked out like they were supposed to. I hoped today would be no different.

"Gosh, the mansion sure is beautiful. I'm so proud of my Lewis," Vivi whispered.

We made our way to the front porch and the oval cream-colored plaque with crimson writing that read simply The Brooks Mansion, Circa 1837. The letters over the door were painted in crimson and read: WCTR Radio, Alabama Crimson Tide Network. It was perfect.

We went inside and walked through the front foyer where large vases of massive magnolia and hydrangea arrangements sat on huge round mahogany tables. Passing immaculate parlors with shiny wood floors and tapestry carpets running up the center of the curving staircase, we found Lewis's office.

"Hey, baby, this place is spectacular." Vivi leaned into Lewis and hugged him, tippy-toeing up and kissing him on the cheek. "I just adore all the final touches. So 1800s. You did a wonderful job, honey."

"Red, you look fantastic." He kissed Vivi back, both of them literally flushing with excitement. "Today is gonna be big."

"Hey, Blake," Lewis said as he hugged me. "This is amazing, huh? We'll get that woman in here to sign, and then we're gonna get us a license and have a wedding. It's all worked out."

I didn't want to ruin the moment, so I kept my worries to myself. When we got Tressa's signature on that annulment form and all the papers were filed, *then* I'd have a mint julep on the porch and take it all in. Until then, I'd be biting my nails—figuratively, of course. I'd never *really* ruin my manicure.

39

Vivi and I went outside after Lewis gave us the grand
tour. Meanwhile, coeds from the school of communi-
cation were conducting tours in the home for the townspeo-
ple that had arrived for the celebrations. On the grounds out
front, a petting zoo had been set up just to the right of the
main house. To my surprise, Dallas had set herself up atop
the lone mule and was talking happily about the festivities to
the camera pointed at her from below. Never would I have
thought she'd go so close to an animal with such a stink, but
I guess I shouldn't be surprised that she'd do anything for a
good screen shot.

Meanwhile, a small merry-go-round already had a line.
Fire trucks and police cars were on display—it truly was a
community event.

A line of young women made their way to a table where
a little job fair was taking place. The interviews were for the
spot of station receptionist. All of the young ladies were done

up like they were on their way to a pageant. All that was missing were the tiaras. Many of them were already in fits because the humidity was melting their makeup.

Harry arrived with Dan and set up a little area for some quick hand-shaking and campaign speaking. Bullhorn McGraw was there, of course, in his green pickup truck, sitting on the lawn chairs in the back of it right alongside his wife and hollerin' into his megaphone.

Hot dog stands, cotton candy and popcorn shacks were set up in the center of the quad. Students at the university were just coming back from summer break, and Lewis had the Alabama cheerleaders and some members of the Million Dollar Band, Alabama's marching band, there to entertain the crowds.

It was festive, to say the least. Kitty and Meridee were over at the mayor's tent, drinking iced tea. When I hugged them, I could smell that their iced tea was already spiked with Jack, even though it was still morning. I decided to bite my tongue—I mean, it *was* a celebration, after all. And more than that, it was Lewis's coming-out party, showing the entire town exactly who he really was. I was so happy for him and for Vivi, too. Today was a day of new beginnings. Now we just had to sweep out the old—the old wife, I mean.

The citywide party seemed to be going pretty well and, since it was hotter than all of hell, we had huge numbers of volunteers for the dunking booth.

I should have known, though, that things couldn't go smoothly for long. Harry had his shirtsleeves rolled up and was shaking hands with the crowd, so of course, Bullhorn thought he needed to compete. Bullhorn had his driver pull the truck up near the little goats in the petting zoo and then stood up to speak. However, there is a rule that, if you grow up down South, you just know. *Don't startle the mules.*

Bullhorn must not have been thinking, 'cause certainly he

knew the rule by heart. He bellowed into that megaphone and the lone mule with Dallas perched on top went nuts, breaking through the fence and running at turbo charge straight toward the media tents.

Dallas grabbed the mule's neck for dear life, screaming and wailing as it charged past.

I saw Dan leave Harry and run after her, the mule keepers running right behind him. It was actually the most fun for Vivi and me as we watched her grip the mule's neck, losing a sparkly high heel as they galloped right past us, followed by all the people chasing her.

As they all ran past, I toasted with Vivi. "To Dallas, as she chases her dreams," I said, raising my iced tea to Vivi's. We both burst out laughing, but her cameraman just kept right on rolling. Dallas actually did achieve one of her dreams that day—she'd been the lead for the six o'clock news!

The festival coordinator brought up the rear of the impromptu parade, hightailing it over to the now-collapsed media tents with her clipboard. "That damn Bullhorn! We told him to stay in his area. *Everyone* was assigned an area!" We all could not stop laughing. It was perfect—just what we needed in the moment.

I have no idea where the mule stopped but eventually Dallas came wobbling back, her bottle-blond hair in a fit full of snarls, grass and twigs. The mule and a few of the goats trotted straight on by, the zookeepers trying to rope them. It looked more like a rodeo than a city festival. And now the chickens were loose, flapping up onto the bed of Bullhorn's truck. I saw Harry double over laughing.

"Oh, my God, I am fixin' to wet my pants," Vivi said, toasting with me again.

Eventually three o'clock came and we headed inside the Brooks Mansion to meet Sonny and Bonita. I hadn't heard from Tressa, but I knew how bad she wanted out and away from Dwayne, so I was certain she'd show up.

The anxious minutes ticked by. Sonny pretty much had to stay out of sight because of running into Dwayne that night at the club. They had set up their monitoring equipment in a little closet off of Lewis's office. Bonita was making some calls and chatting with me and Vivi. Vivi was mostly pacing, with her hands on the back of her hips.

We were all inside Lewis's new office, a gorgeous chandelier hanging overhead from the twelve-foot ceilings, and we could hear the construction workers walking around finishing up the last-minute renovations upstairs.

"Where in the world could they be?" I asked aloud. "I mean, this is nuts. I've called Tressa three times and she doesn't answer."

"I know. I am just a wreck. The courthouse is gonna close at five o'clock. Then what'll we do?" Vivi despaired.

"Okay, y'all don't get too upset just yet. People like them don't just disappear when there's money on the line," Bonita promised.

"But what if Dwayne figured something out?" Vivi said, looking out the front window at the ensuing carnival. She turned to Bonita. "He won't care about the money if he finds out Tressa was gonna take off on him. Maybe he's taken Tressa and skipped town? If those two wreck my wedding, I'm gonna hunt them down like it was the very first day of deer season— for the rest of their lives." With that, Vivi headed into meltdown mode.

I decided to take Vivi for a walk outside and look around. I carried my cell phone in my hand, gripping it as if it carried the president's nuclear codes, my eyes scanning the grounds for Tressa. The mayor was in the dunking booth and Kitty and Meridee were in line to throw the ball at the target. We

waved to them as we passed. Dallas had finally pulled herself back together after her ride on Secretariat and hovered
around Dan and Harry for interviews. The live truck from
WTAL was all set up for the six o'clock news near the front
of the house. No sign of Tressa.

I could see Vivi was getting more and more jittery. I had
to admit, it didn't look good. We were both standing out in
the middle of the grounds, when my phone rang.

"Hello?" I said, trying not to sound desperate.

"It's me, Tressa. My phone's been dead and I was running
late trying to get Dwayne off my tail. Hopefully y'all will
still be there. I gotta go." She sounded desperate and it made
me nervous for her. I knew she was trying to get here and get
Dwayne out of her life.

"Let's get back to the office quick so I can tell the guys," I
said to Vivi, spiking my heels back across the grounds.

Vivi was walking at a clip to keep up, her feet wet and her
sandals getting muddy. I updated the boys once we all sat in
Lewis's office, my watch saying it was now six o'clock. And
we were still without a signature.

Vivi had almost worn a hole in the brand-new carpet. She
never sat, just paced back and forth, biting her nails. Soon it
was pushing seven o'clock. I knew no one was gonna stay at
that courthouse waiting late for us to get this annulment filed
before midnight.

I decided to call for backup. I needed a political favor, and
Harry wasn't the only one who knew a few people in high
places. Kitty had been great friends with the probate judge
of Tuscaloosa County for years. Harlan McIntosh had been
a friend of my daddy's, too, all the way back to high school.
He would have to be my superhero for tonight.

I gave him a call and told him the basics of what was going
on. He agreed to come out and wait with us so that once we

got Tressa's signature, he could sign his authorization before the midnight deadline. He said they were on their way over anyway to bring his grandkids to the petting zoo. *This is why I know I can never leave Tuscaloosa,* I thought. I had a history here, reaching back to before I was even born. I had a whole entourage of superheroes. It seemed like I always needed them, too.

All we had to do now was pray that Tressa and Dwayne would show before midnight.

40

The clock struck eleven, and we all sat motionless in Lewis's office. We were becoming numb with fatigue and grief. Again, Tressa was not calling—or answering. Bonita and the tugboat captain had been walking the grounds all evening, but with no sightings of Dwayne so far. Vivi stood at the window with Lewis right behind her, rubbing her shoulders.

"You know, it's not even the time thing," Vivi said. "It's the fact that legally you are married to that criminal, and she could decide to come after you again anytime. If she doesn't show, we might never be able to get legally married. She is your legal wife and Tallulah and I will have nothing." Vivi had taken all she could, her nerves and worry getting the best of her.

We all watched out the window as the petting zoo packed up the animals and pulled away and the carnival people broke down the merry-go-round and the dunking booth. Then my cell rang and everyone jumped. *Tressa.*

"We are right here in the office, Tressa. But if you don't get here in the next few minutes, this deal is off." I tried to sound demanding and in control. I wanted to throw her into a panic and get her here so the judge could have it in his hands by midnight. The stress was getting the better of all of us.

It was 11:45 p.m. when Tressa drove into the side yard. Her headlights bounced off the walls of the mansion. Everyone was in place. Sonny and Bonita were in the little closet with the listening devices. The judge went down the hall into another room. Sonny had signaled the other officers outside, a couple of them undercover and standing nearby with the captain of the tugboat, ready to ID Dwayne if he showed himself.

Vivi, Lewis and I sat in Lewis's office alone, my heart pounding out of my chest. Lewis had put a briefcase with fake hundred-dollar bills banded together open and on his desk so Tressa could see it as soon as she entered.

Suddenly, the ceiling gave a loud creak. We all looked up, wondering if someone was still upstairs. It creaked again. The chandelier above Lewis's desk was swinging, slowly. Another loud crack reverberated through the room, and the plaster around the base of the chain began to crumble to the desk below. Lewis grabbed Vivi and shoved her into the hallway as I ran out next to her, literally diving over her to the floor. Lewis leaped backward and pinned himself up against the wall just as the huge chandelier crashed down, a million pieces shattering all over the desk and floor below.

Lewis scuttled around the mess, trying to get out of the way in case anything else came crashing down from the second floor. I fell to the floor and Vivi ran into the wall in the hallway. Lewis was pushed up against her, covering her body with his. The chandelier glass had exploded over everything in sight.

Sonny came running in from the other room.

"Oh, my God," he shouted, falling to his knees and bending over me. "Are y'all okay?"

Vivi was crying and holding her stomach.

"Vivi! Vivi! Baby, are you okay?" Lewis was in protector mode.

"I am, I think. What the hell?" Vivi asked. She was scared and rubbing her belly.

"Those damn construction workers. I had an inspection the other day and everything checked out. I don't understand," Lewis shouted. He held Vivi's head in his big hands, looking at her, to see for himself if she was okay.

I found my head in Sonny's lap as he knelt down beside me. I was scared to death, but decided here was as good a place as any to figure out what happened. So I stayed still.

"Blake, are you okay?"

"Yes," I said. "Just scared, I think."

Bonita appeared in the doorway from the side door to the outside, two undercover officers at her side. "Y'all expecting these two by any chance?" She had Tressa and Dwayne both in cuffs, each with an officer.

"What the hell?" Sonny said.

Sonny helped me up and we both brushed ourselves off.

"They were outside, planning on racing in here, grabbing the money when y'all were all knocked out, maybe even killed, by the falling light fixture," she said. "But I saw them start running just as the lamp started swinging and radioed to the officers outside. They ran them down and cuffed them. They had found Dwayne dressed like a construction worker running from the building. Our tugboat officer took one look at him and confirmed that he was, in fact, the guy working out with Walter Aaron when he was murdered. Turns out, Dwayne set a small explosive up on the second floor to bring

down the chandelier. I brought them inside—I thought you
might like to do the honors, Officer Bartholomew."

"Dwayne Martin, you are under arrest for suspected murder
of Walter Aaron, and the attempted murder of Lewis Heart,
Vivi McFadden and Blake O'Hara Heart. You have the right
to remain silent..."

My mind wandered off as he spoke. I loved watching him
work. He was wonderful in his element. Tough and strong
and serious and with me, he was soft and tender and funny. I
fell more in love with him with each word he spoke. I was so
proud of him. His job was so important and few cops loved it
as much as he did, or had as much ingrained integrity. Sonny
Bartholomew was simply a good man. A really good man.

And I realized right then I would be a fool to let him go.
Being with him in this moment made me certain I could learn
to be a cop's wife. I belonged with him. In fact, I could watch
him do his thing all day. Bringing down the bad guys and
helping the innocent was what drove him. Protecting people.
He was one of those cops who was in it for all the right rea-
sons and that made me respect him in a way I had never felt
for someone before.

"I guess we read Tressa all wrong," Bonita said to me. "Here
we thought she was trying to escape Dwayne, when really
she'd had him involved all along. Goes to show you can't judge
a book by its cover."

"I guess not. Take 'em down and lock 'em up. I'm on my
way. Fantastic job, Bonita."

"What about the annulment paper?" Vivi asked Bonita with
a prayer in her eyes.

We looked at the clock: 11:58 p.m.

"Oh, have your stupid husband." Tressa sighed as Bonita
handed her a pen and the paper from Vivi's hands. "He's no

good to me now, anyway." She scrawled a messy signature on the dotted line, then handed it back to Bonita.

At 11:59 p.m. exactly, the paper was handed to Judge Harlan McIntosh. He signed it that minute and turned to leave for the courthouse directly. We had made it—just barely, but we made it.

"Oh, Bonita, thank you." Vivi ran over and threw her arms around her neck.

"Hey, baby, how's about we get hitched?" Lewis said, looking at Vivi like he could eat her up. He kissed her like he would never let her go.

Sonny hugged me as Bonita and the two officers left with Tressa and Dwayne. As soon as they were outta sight, he held me up against him and squeezed me gently.

"I was so scared," he whispered. "I thought you were hurt when I found you on the floor. Blake, I swear I don't know what I would do if something ever happened to you."

"I'm not going anywhere, baby, I promise. And…I need to tell you something."

"What, baby?"

"I was wrong. I can't wait," I whispered in his ear. "We'll have to be careful, Sonny, but I have never been so sure of who I am and what I want as I am right this minute."

"And just what is it that you want?" He grinned.

"You, Officer, just you." He kissed me, long and slow.

There we stood, Vivi and me in the arms of the loves of our lives.

41

E vents at the station took forever, what with all the reports to be filed and information recorded. I stuck around for all of it, though, since I knew that afterward I'd get Sonny alone again for the first time in what had felt like forever.

To avoid suspicion, Sonny took off before me and I followed in my car soon after. I couldn't wait to spend an entire night with him uninterrupted. The break we'd taken had been hard, but I realized now that the separation had been good for me, forced me to think. Nearly dying under that chandelier tonight, but for the grace of a few inches, had taken all of those thoughts to a whole new level.

Sonny was right, I'd realized. There was no way to predict how much time we had on earth, so we'd better use it wisely— and that included being with the people who meant the most to us. We would be careful not to flaunt what we were doing in front of everyone and his brother, but we would be together.

My relationship with Sonny, including the self-imposed

break we took, made things crystal clear to me for the first time in my life.

I *could* shine next to him. I *could* be strong—and independent—and, unlike Harry, Sonny wouldn't feel threatened by that. Now I could go into this relationship with a stronger heart than I'd ever had before. I *could* ask Sonny to love me, and give him everything I have in return, and neither of us would be weakened by that. Rather, we would become stronger together.

And I also wasn't running anymore. I was no longer even worried about Dallas. She had calmed down since I'd threatened her with that privacy act and she knew she'd have to break the law to get anything on any of us. And she certainly couldn't afford that with her job on the line. It was time to stop focusing on all the things that could go wrong, and turn my attention instead to what I could make right.

I smiled as I turned into Sonny's long dirt drive. Before we'd left the station he'd whispered that I was in for "A night like you have never experienced."

I couldn't drive fast enough.

When I made it to the house, I found that Sonny had packed a picnic of snacks in a basket and grabbed a blanket to sit on. We took it out to a really secluded spot in his backyard. It was so fragrant in the summer night air. His beautiful German shepherd, Bryant, was already asleep in the little doghouse Sonny had built him.

Sonny pulled out a couple of bottles of cold Budweisers, and we sat down on the grass. "I'm so glad you're here," Sonny said. He had that playful look in his eyes that I had always loved, and the moonlight was dancing across his shoulders.

He laid me back on the blanket, the sweet scent of magnolias drifting overhead as he settled his face next to mine. His hands wrapped underneath me, pulling me up toward him. Nothing relaxed me like being with him. Nothing ever had.

"I love being here. It's so intoxicating," I said, as his lips traveled over my neck.

"Are you sure that's not the beer that's got ahold of you?" he mumbled while he continued tasting me.

"No, it's you. All you," I said, rolling my head back so he could get a better bite.

Sonny rose to his knees, scooped me up in his arms and carried me inside to his bed. Standing over me, he began unbuttoning his shirt. I lay watching him for a moment, then reached up and unzipped his pants.

He slowly undressed me, almost as if this magical night had made time stand still for us. He gently slid his body on top of mine.

I was entangled by him, seduced by his way, his smell, his bare chest. I was powerless against him. We stretched out and then wrapped ourselves around each other. I let Sonny lead. I wanted him to be in control and to just take me along for the ride.

"Now, about that little surprise I mentioned," he said, reaching under his pillow and taking out a bottle of coconut massage oil. He had it wrapped in a heating pad to make it warm.

"I do believe I can assist you in relaxing all those muscles you banged up tonight." He smiled at me as he removed the cap. I turned over to let him start on my back.

Straddling me from behind, he began working the warm liquid into my skin.

"Oh, baby, this is heaven." I exhaled and stretched out my legs.

"Just be still and I will have you feeling good in no time." His deep voice caressed me as much as the oil.

He slid his strong fingers around my shoulders, working on every muscle like he had a map to my body. His hands slipped down, gently stroking the side of my breasts, pushing slowly underneath my ribs, then around to my lower back. He worked his way lower, past my hips, pressing firmly but slowly.

Finally, I turned over and smiled up at him lazily. "You missed a spot," I whispered. "Maybe even more than one."

"I would never want to neglect my favorite parts." He grinned.

I raised my arm over my head and rested the back of my hand on the pillows above me, exposing more of me to him. He stopped just long enough to pour some more of the deliciously hot oil into his palm. His long fingers slid gently from the side of my breast to my wrist, my skin tingling as he dragged his hand down my abdomen to my thigh, then slipped underneath to give me a gentle squeeze. Wherever he traveled, he worked his magic.

I don't know why, but this time felt different with him, as though we were really an official couple. Not sneaking around, though technically we still were. Not the hot, wild passion that we had that day in my office. We shared a rhythm tonight that felt as if we belonged to each other.

Maybe the difference was in me. I felt free.

"Blake, you are so beautiful. I have never loved anyone like I love you," he said as he kissed my wrist, then the crook of my arm, making his way to the top of my shoulder, up to the hollows of my collarbone, rolling his mouth under my jaw and then pressing his lips to mine. I opened my mouth and let him in, kissing him deeply and slowly.

If I never put my clothes on again, and could just lie next to Sonny's muscled, tanned body pressing into me, I would be happy, satisfied and complete.

"I love you, too, Sonny. The kind of love people live for.

The kind of love we die for. I have found all of that with you. I just want to lie here in your arms forever."

"You just say the word, and I'll make it happen. Forever."

Sonny was delicious and sexy, sweet and precious all at the same time. How could I leave? I couldn't. I was here for the night, although by this time there wasn't much of it left. I doubted, with the capture of Dwayne and Tressa lighting up the news, that Dallas would be lurking outside Sonny's tonight. We were not the top story anymore.

I wrapped my bare legs around him, dragging my calves along his bare backside. I kissed his chest, nibbling him, then looked up at him and smiled.

Both of my hands now over my head, he pushed his hands up my arms until he reached my palms. Clasping his fingers through mine, he made love to me with an emotion and a connection that we both had never felt. There was an awareness of what we were doing. It wasn't as if I was falling into something uncontrollably. I was choosing this. *We* were choosing this. and we were *us* now. One. Nothing in my life had ever felt this right.

Eventually, he lay still on top of me, breathing in my skin and kissing my neck. "I know one thing now for sure," he whispered against my skin. "I am never gonna let you go again."

I placed my hands, fingers splayed, over his back and pulled him into me. We kissed in the slow morning light that was now streaming through the bay window of his bedroom, and then fell asleep wrapped in the comfort and security of each other's arms.

It was the single best night of my life.

42

The day of the wedding came at last. I'm not sure any of us could really believe it was finally happening.

"Y'all come on down for breakfast," Arthur called from the kitchen. "Gonna be a big day round here."

I had already been awake for a few minutes when I heard Arthur announce breakfast. The bacon had reached my nose long before his sweet voice reached my ears. Sunlight danced across the wood floor and reached across my cream-colored duvet. I turned over, stretching, and saw Vivi at my bedside, hands on hips, poofs of red hair bouncing under the whir of the ceiling fan.

"Well, well," she said. "Mornin', Miss Priss. We gonna sleep all day?"

I smiled and sat up. "Good morning, yourself. Are you ready to become Mrs. Heart?" The irony stuck in my throat— she'd be celebrating her new name, while I would soon be giving up that moniker.

"Blake, honey, I've been ready for years." Vivi held her hand out and pulled me from the bed. I grabbed my satin baby-blue robe, and Vivi and I headed downstairs, giggling like a couple of giddy, love-struck teenagers. "Mornin', Arthur," we chirped.

"Mornin', you two. We have us a big day ahead, and we best getta goin'."

"Not before we eat some of this breakfast. Smells fantastic!" Vivi said. "Probably better than Waffle House."

"Ain't no probably to it," Arthur shot back with a grin. "Come on now, eat up. I got me a weddin' bash to cook for."

"Arthur, oh, my, you have totally outdone yourself," I said. "Biscuits 'n gravy, bacon 'n eggs, hash browns 'n waffles. Vivi, you better be careful or we won't be able to zip you up."

"Now, now. Don't you get her worried about all that, Blake. Today is all about celebratin', and the best way to do that is with some good ol' food," Arthur said as he kept the feast coming. "Plus," he added with a wink, "I took all the calories out 'fore I put the spread on the table."

Arthur knew how to make you feel good. He set the cast-iron skillet between us. It was full of scrumptious cinnamon rolls, the icing still sizzling and melting into a spoonable goo on the bottom.

"Now, y'all be careful you don't go a-touchin' that while it's hot," Arthur said, taking care of us as usual.

"Lord have mercy, Arthur, it's just me and Vivi," I said. "You could feed an army with all this."

"I'm gonna sit right down with you here directly and I'm not the only one," he said, laughing. "Miss Kitty done called. She and Miss Meridee are on their way right now." He was smiling and running around the kitchen. Excitement was thick in the air.

The wedding ceremony was planned for that evening at

sunset, but today was also the big season kickoff game—the beginning of the new Crimson Tide quest for the national championship.

Everyone knew exactly where they would be at game time: either at the game or in front of a radio or television. Game time was one o'clock, but would last at least four hours once you included playing time, extra time for broadcasting with commercials, and the inevitable time-outs. This meant that everything football-wise should be finished just about 5:00 p.m. The Fru Fru boys had set the ceremony to begin at precisely 6:30 p.m. That still gave Lewis an hour and a half to leave the game, get ready and be waiting for Vivi at the altar right on time.

A knock on the door had Arthur walking around the kitchen table to hold the screen door open. "Well, well, y'all come on in here, beautiful ladies."

"Smells absolutely divine, Arthur." Kitty leaned in and kissed his cheek, her oversized charm bracelets jangling.

"Y'all have a seat. We have plenty of food, so help yourself to whatever strikes your fancy."

Both Kitty and Meridee moved around the table to the empty chairs and slid in—Meridee next to me and Kitty next to Vivi—and began passing the grits and gravy.

Arthur, having finally gotten it all on the table, including fresh orange juice and peach preserves, took his seat at the end. He had lots of help down at his restaurant for the wedding feast, so he was at his leisure to sit and enjoy this moment with us.

I held this precious moment in my heart. In a few hours, things would change—for the better, of course, but change just the same. I loved the idea of Vivi getting married and, in these minutes of prewedding, early-morning laughter and good food with people I loved, I felt safe and happy, on the precipice of something exciting.

Once breakfast was finished, the table was cleared and everyone pitched in to clean up the feast. With hugs goodbye and the promise of the evening's big event on our minds, we all went our separate ways to get ready.

"Talk to you in a few, daaaahlin'," Vivi said, mimicking an old movie star. "I must get in my beauty soak before I see my prince. Ta-ta." She shut the bathroom door.

A thrill went through me as I realized I would be dancing with my own prince tonight. Sonny was my prince and Vivi had her own, even if he wasn't arriving by stagecoach this evening...unless somehow that might get him through the game traffic any faster.

43

"Come on, Vivi, we're gonna be late!" I yelled from the bottom of the stairs. "We need to give Miss Sweetie-Pie some time to work with the dress in case it doesn't fit right." The final fitting for the dress was in a couple of hours—everything dress-related had to be last-minute, since Vivi's pregnancy meant her size was changing all the time. We wanted that dress to fit perfectly, which meant Vivi had to try it on now, just in case baby Tallulah had decided to grow some more at the last minute.

"I'm looking for my tweezers!"

I rolled my eyes. "Oh, my heavens. Are we having an eyebrow emergency?"

"Actually...I am," Vivi said nervously, almost tripping down the stairs. Why in the world she already had her sunglasses on in the house was beyond me—till she pulled them off to reveal a nearly missing eyebrow.

"Well…let's not panic," I began, knowing this was about to turn into a full-scale catastrophe if I didn't manage it right.

Her eyes teared up and I could tell she was about to pitch a bridal hissy fit—which is much worse than your average hissy fit, almost indistinguishable from a full-on conniption. "I was trying to even out my brows for tonight and I guess my nerves took over and I was thinking about all the stuff I have to get through today and, before I knew it, I plucked out the entire thing."

"First of all I don't think we need to find those tweezers. I think you've plucked enough for now."

"I wanted to see if you could try to even them up for me."

"Sugar, I hate to be the bearer of bad news, but that left brow would need to be almost completely removed if we're gonna even things up."

I should've known better. That pricked the dam and she began sobbing.

"I look like an idiot," she said, crying. "Blake, I am so stupid. Why was I allowed to have tweezers, today of all days?"

I held Vivi and gave her a minute to let out the anxiety. I knew she really wasn't thinking if she thought everyone would be staring at her eyebrows instead of her six-month baby bump. But I just held her and never said a word about it.

"You will be beautiful, honey. I know you will. You always are. Every minute of every day, you are beautiful." I smiled in encouragement. "Besides, I am a cosmetic queen's granddaughter and the official queen herself will be here tonight. We will get you all fixed up and you will sparkle like the star you are."

"Blake, what would I do without you?" Vivi said with a sniffle. "You are too good. I just don't want to look perpetually surprised in all my wedding photos, you know?"

"I understand. Now dry up those tears, so we can get over
to Sweetie's. She's got your dress waitin'.'"

Vivi dried her eyes with a tissue from her purse and blew her
nose as we walked through the kitchen and out the screened
door. We stopped on the back porch to glance over at the rose
gardens. Arthur was out there directing the traffic and the
hubbub of the prewedding activities. He was handling things
till the Fru Frus got there.

We were awestruck.

The tents were beautiful, with a swish of blush-pink over-
laying everything in sight. Little fairy lights twinkled from
tree limb to tree limb to the wraparound front porch. Pink
lights were even underneath the yards of pink tulle, sweep-
ing over everything, giving a magical feel to the entire yard.
The flowers looked like poofs of cotton candy, and the cream-
colored tablecloths reflected the rosy hues.

The side yard under the magnolias was a blur of organized
chaos, everyone moving in a frenzy, all seeming to have a job
to do. More white tents were going up on the side yard just
past the rose gardens, under the ancient pecan trees. Stargazer
lilies and baby pink hydrangeas were being delivered in creamy
white ceramic pitchers and placed in the center of each table.
Musicians had set up their stands and violins made their way
out of the leather cases. Everything looked soft, warm and inviting. Come evening, the little lights would cast a rosy glow
over the yard and magnify the colors of the sunset.

We stood still, admiring the incredible work that A Fru
Fru Affair had done.

Vivi smiled. "Would you look at that? It's really happening. Today is my wedding day and it's as magical as I ever
dreamed."

"Yes, sweetie, it is, and I cannot tell you how special it is
for me to be here with you."

She reached for my hand and gave it a squeeze. We both breathed in the intoxicating fragrance of hundreds of stargazer lilies, then I helped the little mother down the back steps and into her powder-blue convertible. We were off to get *the dress*.

44

Sweetie-Pie was waiting on the front porch, and inside was the much-anticipated, one-of-a-kind, Sweetie-Pie Jones's original wedding gown.

Sweetie-Pie was an original, herself. She designed prom and pageant dresses for every girl in the county and became so well-known that she was even creating the gowns for the Miss Alabama contestants to Miss America! She did the dresses, while Meridee did the makeup. Sweetie was a few years younger than my grandmother, but they graduated from the same high school. Since Miss Sweetie-Pie was always at Meridee's house, the command center during pageants, they spent a lot of time together. That's how they became such good friends. All the fittings and makeup for local events were done at Meridee's, with Miss Sweetie-Pie there to make sure the dresses were perfect. I have known Sweetie-Pie my whole life. She even designed my wedding dress when I married Harry. Today, it was Vivi's turn.

"Hey there, you two gorgeous girls, get on over here and give us a hug," she called from the porch.

"You look beautiful as ever, Miss Sweetie-Pie," Vivi said.

"Thank you, sugar. I'm fighting back the wrinkles with that special—" Miss Sweetie stopped midthought. "Where the hell is your other eyebrow, Miss Vivi? It's plumb near disappeared." She looked up at Vivi, squinting.

I stood there violently shaking my head no, trying to let Miss Sweetie-Pie know she shouldn't say any more.

"Vivi had a slight mishap with the tweezers this mornin'," I said, trying to put off a new hissy fit. "Miss Meridee's gonna fix her right up in just a few."

"Oh, well of course she is! You couldn't be in better hands than Miss Meridee's, and I know that for a fact. Now, y'all ready to see this creation? I hope you love it, Miss Vivi. You should feel like a princess on your special day."

Sweetie-Pie guided us inside, then slipped to her studio in the side room and reappeared with a cloud of layers and layers of tulle in white, cream and a hint of blush. Sequins and pearls shimmered and sparkled in the light.

Oh, the gown was a thing of fairy tales. The bodice, in white taffeta, fitted to an empire waist, leaving plenty of room for baby. A thick blush-pink satin sash ran just above her belly and tied in a long bow at the back, the ribbon flowing all the way to the floor. The strapless neckline was in a sweetheart design that would show off her strand of pearls and new ample cleavage just perfectly.

Vivi started to tear up, moving in slow motion, arm outstretched gently, as if she might ruin it with one touch or dispel the ethereal vision into mist. "Sweetie, you are a genius. This is the most beautiful thing I have ever seen."

"Now, don't you go a-cryin', Vivi McFadden, or your eyes will be all puffy and that will throw off the lines of my dress."

We all laughed.

"Now go try it on and let's see if I guessed right about how big that baby of yours was gonna be."

Vivi took the dress in her arms, a look of unexpected joy on her face, like she had just won the pageant and couldn't believe it. We all walked into the studio, Vivi shaking her head in amazement.

"I can't believe I will be wearing this tonight." She laid the dress on the bed. "I never even thought I would be having a wedding, much less wearing white."

We both burst out laughing. "White is fine, Vivi. You can wear any damn thing you want. It's your wedding, last I checked."

The dress was perfect for her. *Yep, I'm a pregnant bride* and *I'm wearing white, so there.* It was just so Vivi.

"C'mon, honey. Let's get you in it," I said, smiling and excited.

Vivi put her purse down on a table and began to undress. She had on a creamy lace strapless bra and matching panties. Her burgeoning tummy was a spectacular thing of beauty. She took lacy flats out of her bag.

"No heels. I have enough trouble balancing right now as it is," Vivi explained at Miss Sweetie's look of surprise. That woman lived for glamorous dresses and stilettos, so this was close to blasphemy as far as her fashion sense was concerned. "I've always been more of a barefoot girl anyway." Sweetie knew better than to argue with the bride on her wedding day, so she smiled and stepped out of the room while I helped Vivi into her dress.

"You look stunning, Vivi, and you're not even dressed. Now, Sweetie-Pie said she made this an easy one zip, in case she needs to let it out a bit," I said.

I steadied Vivi as she stepped in and pulled up the dress. Her frizzy red hair was poofed out in crazy curls, not having been tamed for the day yet. She looked like an ice cream cone with a vibrant cherry on top. I zipped her in and she turned around.

"How do I look?" she asked.

My mouthed dropped. She was perfect. A vision of a princess—granted, an extremely pregnant one, but still very much a princess.

"Well?" she begged. "C'mon now. I need to hear the truth."

"Vivi, the truth is that I have never, ever seen you more beautiful than right this second. Not in a pageant dress, not as my maid of honor, not ever. You're just perfect."

I couldn't hold back the tears. I clutched my fists to my heart, staring at my dearest friend in the world, in her wedding dress. It was a moment for sure.

About that time, Miss Sweetie knocked and came on in. "Miss Vivi, you look fabulous, if I do say so myself. How's it feel?"

Vivi turned to face the full-length wooden mirror in the corner of the room. At the first glance of herself, she just stood there motionless, speechless.

"I can't believe that's me," she whispered. "The dress feels wonderful, Sweetie. No pullin' or tuggin'. It's easy to move in, too, so I can dance the night away with Lewis," Vivi said.

With that, she spun around to give her skirt a twirl, and knocked over the table that held her purse and shoes. A lamp hit the floor and a vase of fresh gardenias from Sweetie's garden crashed to the floor, leaving a puddle of water and petals on the carpet.

"Land sakes, Miss Vivi, you gone take out my house." Sweetie and I hurriedly cleaned up the vase before Vivi could pirouette backward and cut her heel. Next thing you'd know, we'd be at the E.R. and she'd miss her own wedding. "If you hold on a minute, I'll show you how to turn it into a dancin' dress."

"A dancin' dress?" Vivi asked.

Once we'd collected the last shards, Miss Sweetie made her way back to Vivi. "Yeah, looka here, you just unzip this, and the whole skirt comes off. You got ya'self a little cotton eyelet skirt attached to that beautiful bodice. See?"

Sweetie zipped off the tulle and revealed the pretty skirt underneath. Eyelet hearts cut into stark white, tea-length fabric. The skirt was very classy.

"That's amazing, Miss Sweetie!" Vivi was happy. "I love it!"

"Okay, let's get you outta this so Meridee can get you all made up. Tell her no skimpin'. She needs to do justice to my dress."

We all laughed.

"Thank you so much," Vivi said, then smiled. "You really are a genius. You made me a beauty, too, and that's no easy feat."

Miss Sweetie laughed. "Go on, girl, you always been purty. You're the best kind of purty, too—the kind that don't know it."

Vivi kissed Miss Sweetie on the cheek, then shut the door behind her. I heard her talking in the other room, probably to Harold. I had set the lamp upright along with the table, and picked up Vivi's purse and shoes, now wet with vase water. Meanwhile, Vivi was a bull in a china shop with all of her excitement.

I thought we were done with the accidents, but then she began trying to unzip the bodice down the side, but the zipper wouldn't budge. She tugged and pulled at it but her belly was in the way.

"Here, sugar, let me get that. You have a baby between you and freedom."

I bent toward her and began working on the zipper. It really wouldn't budge. I had my head under her armpit so I could see what the problem was when suddenly the zipper gave a quick jolt and moved just enough to catch my bangs.

I let out a holler as I felt my scalp being yanked.

"Oh, honey, are you okay?"

"My bangs are caught!" I screeched. "Don't move an inch. You're gonna snatch me bald-headed."

But Vivi turned before she heard my answer and my hair pulled even tighter into the zipper. Good and stuck now, I was bent over with my head trapped in Vivi's armpit. One thing was for sure, we could *not* go down the aisle this way.

"Help, Sweetie-Pie!" I yelled until she came running in.

"Oh, my Lord, what in hell have y'all gone and done now?" Sweetie ran over to us and pulled my hair back to reveal my bangs trapped in the dress. "We gonna have to cut you right on outta there, baby girl."

"No! My beautiful dress!" Vivi screamed.

"Not you," Sweetie-Pie said. "I ain't 'bout to go and ruin *my* masterpiece. I mean you, Blake, baby. We gonna have to cut your hair outta this here zipper. Now stay right here, don't y'all move. I'm gonna reach over here and grab my scissors."

"No! That's my hair we're talking about," I cried, feeling slightly wild. "I cut my bangs just for the wedding. You can't chop them now!"

The way I saw it, it was between my ruined hair or Vivi's… slightly damaged wedding dress. From my point of view, the creator of the dress was right there to fix any dress emergencies, but it would take several weeks to grow my bangs back. No question, the dress was the loser. But Sweetie didn't see it quite my way.

"Please, Miss Sweetie, can't we do anything else?" I begged.

"Let's see." She thought for a second. "Nope!" And she

snipped my bangs right off, Vivi bouncing over a few steps and me falling backward.

Standing straight again, I couldn't help but laugh. Vivi looked like she had forgotten to shave her pits for about a year with my bangs hanging out from under her arm. Miss Sweetie worked the zipper feverishly, shredding my leftover bangs into sawdust until Vivi was freed.

"Oh, thank you, Miss Sweetie, you're a lifesaver," Vivi said.

"Yes, and quite a hairstylist, might I add," I offered sarcastically.

"Oh, Blake, I am so sorry. And you had already done your hair. We need to even *you* up now," Vivi said, giggling.

Yes, we would be a sight at the wedding—if we made it there in one piece. We hugged Miss Sweetie-Pie goodbye, and then she put the dress in a garment bag and said she would see us around four-thirty or so to make sure Vivi was in the dress and didn't need anything else.

"Now, y'all take good care of this here dress now, okay? I can't make us up another in an hour." She laughed and patted Vivi's behind. "Go on now and have a happy weddin' day. I'll see y'all directly. I gotta go get beautiful myself."

Lord, help us, I prayed, *let there be no more mishaps.* My maid of honor tiara was already barely hanging by the last hairs on my head.

45

The drive back to Vivi's was a flurry of excited conversation. Now that we knew her dress was perfect, it felt like a heavy weight had lifted from our shoulders. I mean, really—once you've got the right dress, everything else just falls into place.

We put the top down, since my hair was a goner now anyway. Vivi, meanwhile, put a gorgeous Calvin Klein scarf over her hair, looking like a 1950s movie star, riding in her little powder-blue Thunderbird convertible.

Meridee would arrive at the plantation soon to do our makeup, and we had to check in with Arthur and the Fru Fru boys—then salvage my hair and Vivi's anemic eyebrow.

Lewis was broadcasting the kickoff, so the guests would all be listening to a radio or watching a TV until it was over. We turned into the gravel drive at the plantation's front gates under the shade oaks and magnolias. Little white whisps were floating above our heads and catching in the branches. It looked like hundreds of dandelions.

"Lord have mercy, are those...feathers?" Vivi asked as we drove in.

"I do believe they are." My heart sank.

"What in the name of God are feathers doing floating all over my wedding yard?"

As we drove past the fountain, I swore I heard the sound of a rooster. Just then, Arthur dodged in front of the car with a huge net and we came to a skidding stop amid spitting gravel. He didn't even notice us, since he was too busy chasing a cluster of chickens running wild across the lawn. Vivi jumped out and ran over to Arthur as he lunged at the chickens with his net, leaping over the rooster as he went.

"What the hell is Arthur doin' chasin' all those chickens? They're not on today's menu! And why, in the name of sweet baby Jesus, do I have a rooster runnin' around, crowin' all over the place?" She was growing more livid by the second.

"Miss Vivi! Miss Vivi!" Jean-Pierre came running, his iPad under his arm. "Oh, my God, I am *sooooo* sorry. We asked the petting zoo for ten swans, but I guess our order was mixed up with another and instead they delivered a dozen chickens and a rooster!"

"Don't worry, Miss Vivi," Arthur said, as he and his hired waiters chased down more chickens. "We're gettin' 'em all."

"Well, there better not be a damn llama on the way. Tell them to unmix us. Right now," I ordered, getting into matron of honor mode.

"I can't have chickens here today! They'll leave little poop piles from here to campus by the time I walk down the aisle. Where are my swans?" She was upset, hot and pregnant. And a bride. This was not a combination to be messin' with.

"Swans? Where is your eyebrow? That is the real question," Coco said as he ran up to all the chicken commotion. He never was one for tact.

"Not now, Coco," I warned. I looked at Vivi and she covered her face with her hands.

Then Coco turned to me, his eyes wide. "Look at your hair. We could almost be twins! We may start ourselves a whole new trend of uneven cuts." He smiled as if pleased to think I was copying him.

I didn't scream at him, but it was tough. I pointed to my hair. "*This* was a mistake. I'm getting extension hair in an hour."

"I don't know if I'd bother," Coco said, tilting his head. "I kinda like it."

"Just get rid of the chickens," Vivi snapped, and we turned to walk inside.

Vivi took a deep breath. "How much time before Meridee and Kitty get here?"

"Any minute," I reassured her. "Now, don't worry. You will be ready in plenty of time for the big walk down the aisle, so just relax."

"You know me. I don't feel quite right if my nerves aren't on fire about somethin'."

We both laughed.

I glanced at the clock as we passed it. Three-thirty. Three more interminable hours and counting. Surely, nothing else could go wrong....

Vivi called Lewis. "Hey, handsome, how's the game goin'?... Our time still lookin' good?" Her face suddenly changed. "You're kiddin' me, right? The score is that close?...No damn way!" Even on her wedding day, a Tuscaloosa bride would still be worried about football.

She plunked down on her bed. "Lewis, please make sure

you are here by five-thirty...I know. I know you'll do everything in your power. I just sorta can't wait to get married to you." She laughed. "At least history is on our side. In my whole life the kickoff game has never been forced into overtime with Alabama. So I'm not too worried."

She listened again then smiled. "I love you, too, baby. Now get on over here and make me an honest woman...Okay. Bye."

"What's going on in the press box?" I asked.

"The score is within a field goal, Blake! Good God, what the hell, Bama? Don't those boys know I got a weddin' to get to?"

"Everything will work out," I soothed. "Lewis will be on his way before we know it. Bryant-Denny Stadium is only fifteen minutes from here. After the game ends, he'll have an hour and a half to drive it. That's plenty of leeway—even if it does go into overtime."

"Why did Myra Jean say the wedding had to switch to today?" Vivi wailed. "This is crazy. Missing eyebrow, your bangs all chopped up, missing swans and chickens runnin' wild through my yard... If *this* is the good day, what the hell would have happened on the bad one?"

"Well, honey, she said today's date had a glow around it."

"Yeah, probably 'cause the house will catch on fire, the way things are goin'."

"Look," I said. "Lewis is gonna get here and you are gonna be stunning. Now, let's go wash your face and get your hair set. Twyla Jamison's coming to do our hair."

"Twyla? That's great!" Vivi exclaimed, perking up. "Twyla is wonderful, and she's worked on all those beauty pageants. She'll be able to do something with this mop." Vivi gestured to her red, wiry mess.

"Well, I hope she's bringing hair extensions cause there is

no way she's gonna cut my hair to even up this butcher job," I said, fluffing my short, stubby bangs.

"I don't remember your wedding being this crazy and desperate," Vivi said.

"Not till *long* after the ceremony, sugar. C'mon, let's get ready."

Just then, Kitty, Meridee and Twyla came in through the kitchen, talking and laughing.

"Hellooooo," Kitty trilled. "Where is everybody?"

"Up here, Mother," I called down the stairs. I heard the trampling of high heels shuffling up the curved wooden staircase.

"In here." I directed them to Vivi's enormous retreat.

"Hey, honey, how are you two doin'?" Kitty came in first and distributed hugs. Meridee followed with her huge case of magic tricks. Twyla was right behind.

"We're good, Mother, but we had a couple of little accidents today," I said.

"Good God Almighty, Vivi, did you run into a lawn mower? Where the hell is your eyebrow?" Meridee was nothing if not blunt.

Kitty looked at my shorn hair. "You two weren't playin' beauty shop like y'all used to, were y'all? Not today?"

I sighed. "No, Mother, it's a long story that we don't have time for now."

"Kitty, we got more to do than I thought. We'd best get a move on," Meridee said, looking concerned. "We may need more miracles than I got in this case of mine. You shoulda told me to bring my magic hat!"

Miss Sweetie made her way up the stairs. "Where's the party?"

"In here, Sweetie-Pie." Meridee looked excited to see her old friend and partner. After another round of hugs and hellos, we focused on business. The whole beauty team shifted into high gear, and it was good for them to all come together again, especially for Vivi.

"Okay, ladies, let's get gorgeous," Meridee announced.

Vivi and I sat on matching tapestry vanity stools in her spalike powder room. The peach-colored walls, heated floor, marble counters and sconce amber lighting on the walls on either side of the deep jetted tub created a soft, romantic feeling. The big lights around the mirror looked like something out of a Broadway dressing room. Vivi would finally be getting ready for her spotlight. Moisturizers and foundation applied, blush, eye shadow, black eyeliner applied '50s style, with little cat corners, false eyelashes out to there, and then came the eyebrow.

"Okay. Sugar, I'm gonna build you some eyebrows to match and no one will ever know," Meridee assured her.

"Thank goodness, Miss Meridee. I knew I could count on you."

"I've seen worse than this. Take Blake's hair, for instance. That's gonna be a challenge."

"Thanks, Nanny. I wasn't quite nervous enough," I said with a smirk.

"Love you, baby." Meridee winked. "Twyla's gonna get to you in a jiffy."

This was an official girl-fest. It reminded me of our pageant days. Hot rollers plugged in, lipstick expertly applied. Twyla took over with the big paddle brushes, jacking our hair straight up to Jesus. We were enveloped in a fog of Aqua Net, the official hairspray of the pageant world. All that was left was the perfume and the jewelry. Twyla clipped in a series of long brunette hair extensions and slipped a rhinestone headband on me to hide the chopped pieces and the clips. Not that comfy, but I could take some Motrin if it started hurting too much. Beauty trumped pain in my world any day.

As Meridee was finishing up, she stopped and pulled a black velvet bag from her case. "Vivi, I want you to have this with you when you marry Lewis." She pulled out an unusual brooch. "All the women in the family have worn this on their wedding day, and you are my family, as much as anybody."

I immediately recognized the jeweled brooch given to Meridee's great-grandmother over a hundred years ago that I had worn at my wedding. It was *the* family heirloom, handed down to all the women on their wedding day. The jewelry always went back to Meridee, and would until her passing, at which time it would go to Kitty, then me. Meridee was loaning it to Vivi and officially extending our family.

"It will work as something old and something borrowed," Meridee said, taking it from Vivi and helping her pin it to her bra. "It's worn for luck and longevity, although in recent years, the *longevity factor* seems to be wearin' off a bit." Meridee scowled at Kitty, then me.

"Touché, Mother," Kitty remarked.

"Oh, Meridee, the brooch is stunning. I am honored."

"Pretty laaadieees," Coco sang, appearing in the doorway of the bathroom beauty shop. "How y'all doin' in here? We are about an hour or so out from the big event."

After Coco oohed and aahed over our transformations, he said to Vivi, "We have a place downstairs set up for the bridesmaids as they arrive. Your cousins Abigail and Annabelle just called to say they're almost here. Your two sorority sisters, Mary Elizabeth and Patricia Catherine, are already downstairs and getting dressed in a room off the front parlor."

He went over to the window and pulled the drape back with a flourish. "And there is not a chicken, rooster or feather in sight, unless I put them there. The swans are swimming peacefully in their fountain pond, and Jean-Pierre is finishing up the cake tables now. This wedding is gonna be stunning."

We all rushed to the window. I'd never been so thankful to have hired the Fru Fru boys.

Vivi sighed in relief. "It all looks so wonderful."

"Okay, my job here is done. Y'all are up to date. Ta-ta." He left and sashayed down the stairs.

Vivi began to fiddle with the brooch again. "This means a lot to me, Meridee."

"It's been passed down from our ancestors, but I have never found out who or which ones. Maybe the luck of the Irish is blessed into it. Take good care of it and give it back to me later," Meridee said. "Okay, sugar, apply your perfume, and then where are your pearls?"

Vivi spritzed on her signature Chloé scent, then touched the small, navy blue velvet pouch. She gently untied the black silk drawstring and pulled the baby pearls from the bag. "Daddy gave me these when I was just a child. He told me I would wear them on my wedding day." She smiled with tears in her eyes. "I wish he could be here."

"I'm sure he is with you right now," I said. "He is so proud of you." I placed the pearls around Vivi's neck and fixed the clasp.

We all were looking into the big, lighted mirror at Vivi. Twyla put Vivi's hair loosely up in a chignon at the nape of her neck, with tendrils hanging down and tiny pearl pins stuck throughout her auburn locks. Her lips were a simple blush pink to match the tulle in her dress. It actually looked like we were going to pull this wedding off without another hitch.

Then the screen door slammed downstairs and we heard Sonny yell out, "Where is everybody?"

"Up here!" I called.

Sonny arrived at the bathroom door, breathless. "Didn't know if y'all have heard, but Bama just went into overtime."

Well, shit.

46

Vivi was on the phone with Lewis and she was about to go to pieces. "But you have to get here, baby, and the traffic's gonna be a nightmare. What are you gonna do?" She listened, but still revved higher. "Please just come as fast as you can. I'll be waiting at the altar." Vivi hung up. "What the hell? We got a hundred and fifty people on their way and the game's in overtime," Vivi said, her eyes filled with worry. "I was such a fool to plan this wedding for today."

"Now listen to me, Vivi." Kitty broke up the panic. "Your Lewis will get here, and we're all gonna be ready. There's plenty of good food, drink and company to keep folks occupied if we have to wait. No more tears. Meridee's gonna run outta makeup if you keep this up. Now, who needs a margarita? I know I do." She locked arms with Sonny. "Take me to the open bar, dear. Momma needs some sauce, and my man Charlie ought to be here any minute."

Sonny leaned over to kiss my cheek on his way out, and

nobody said a thing. I could hear Kitty's jangling bracelets and chatting all the way down the stairs.

Meridee and Sweetie were heading downstairs, too. Twyla packed up her things while talking on her cell phone, then headed down after them. They'd all be close at hand should a hair, dress or makeup emergency arrive, but for now, Vivi and I were the only ones left in the bathroom.

She looked over to me. "Kitty's right. I need to just go with the flow. Everyone will find something to do in case he's late."

I got up and walked over to the large window that looked down over the grove. More people were starting to arrive. "No one looks stir-crazy yet."

Sonny had hooked up the radio through the speakers in the trees and the game was on for everybody to hear. We had about an hour till showtime.

Vivi looked at herself in the mirror and smiled, still amazed by the reflection.

"Time to get you in your dress, don't you think?" I asked persuasively. It was past five-thirty now. We turned off the big Hollywood lights and left the fog of Aqua Net behind. *Here we go,* I thought, *groom or not.*

47

We walked into Vivi's boudoir and eyed the dress lying across the bed, its tiny, iridescent sequins catching the last flickering streams of sunlight. It had a life all its own. Like it was breathing. The *dress*. It held magical powers and would soon turn Vivi into a real-life princess.

"It's beautiful, isn't it?" she asked without expecting an answer. She stepped into the strapless ball gown and slipped it up over her lacy thigh-high silk stockings. The tulle took up most of the room and the train was attached at the top of the back, which hit her just below the shoulder blades. It flowed across the floor and fell in a long puddle of silk and satin like a royal cape. It was a masterpiece. I zipped her up, making very sure my hair was nowhere near.

I took the tiara from her mahogany dresser and placed it on her head, securing it with about twenty bobby pins. The tulle veil fell gently to her bare freckled shoulders. She looked at me through the mesh, her green eyes glistening, and smiled.

"Do I look okay?" Vivi asked in a nervous voice.

"Oh, sweetheart, I have never seen anything more beautiful," I answered with tears welling up.

"I sure hope I still look like this when Lewis finally gets here." Suddenly, real tears welled in her eyes, too. "What am I gonna do, Blake?"

"About what?" I asked.

"The game's in overtime. Lewis will never get through all that traffic."

"He arranged for a police escort through security at the university. That will speed things up."

"Even the police escort won't be enough. Everyone's gonna think I'm a complete fool standing by myself—pregnant—at the altar." She let out a small cry of sadness. "I'm gonna look like a big ol' pregnant fool in a big ol' hypocritical white dress."

"Listen, honey. No one is gonna think any such thing. Everyone here knows Lewis is hung up for a little while longer. Sonny is downstairs listenin' to the game and we're gonna know the very minute it's over. After that, Lewis will be on his way. We'll just wait for him."

"But we're gonna miss the sunset. It won't be the same after," she wailed. "What we need is a helicopter to swoop in and bring him to me."

"I wish."

Feeling more depressed with every minute, Vivi and I walked down the curved staircase and into the kitchen. We looked out the window over the sink and could see the makeshift tailgate party set up under the old pecan trees.

A few groomsmen were sitting in lawn chairs, along with a couple of the bridesmaids. Everybody was yelling at the big screen that one of the groomsmen plugged in with a long orange outdoor cord strung from the back porch. The plus side was that nobody seemed to notice the delay in the wedding plans, since everyone was too swept up in the excitement of the game.

"Only in Alabama," Jean-Pierre said, stepping in from the back door. "Vivi, your nutcase of a dog is out there humping everybody from here to Mississippi."

"He reminds me of you," Coco teased, coming into the kitchen right after him.

Jean-Pierre rolled his eyes. "Well, everything was going as planned, but as we wait, people are drinking more and more, cheering for Alabama. This place is getting rowdy, and it's gonna get worse the later it gets."

"Great. My beautiful, elegant wedding has become one big-ass tailgatin' party." Vivi eyed the wedding party sitting in the lawn chairs, toasting each other and throwing some back.

Lewis's voice was booming over the radio Sonny had set up. "Bama's got the ball on the twenty yard line."

Everyone leaned forward, listening hard and looking at the silent TV. This was typical in Alabama. Fans will mute the TV to listen to the play-by-play from the Voice of the Crimson Tide. It just seems more exciting that way. Kinda like you're there at the game.

"I predict it's gonna be touchdown Bama in just a second," I told Vivi. "Just hang tight. It's almost over."

"Bama's got the ball on the twenty and there's the snap, it's in the air, Johnson catches and goes..." Lewis was screaming the plays. "He's going, going, he's gone to the ten, *TOUCH-DOWN ALABAMA!*"

Everyone erupted into cheers. I grabbed Vivi's shoulders and we jumped up and down, clouds of tulle and all.

Lewis sounded euphoric. "The Crimson Tide has clinched the heart-stopper! In over a hundred years of this rivalry, Alabama has only lost seven times. This was not to be number eight. I am handing over the mic to my copilot here in the booth, Ted Roxby, because I am on my way to a very important event. To celebrate this fantastic victory, *I am getting married tonight!* Hang on, Red! I'll meet you at the altar, baby. I'm coming!" And he signed off.

Vivi and I were still standing and dancing in the kitchen. Everyone was goin' wild out there under the pecan trees. They were cheering, standing up, jumping up and down, hugging each other and generally whoopin' it up to the max. This was an Alabama football wedding now. Lewis would be proud.

Sonny made his way to the house. "See there, Red," Sonny said, winking at her love name. "Lewis is on his way."

Vivi was smiling ear to ear and blushing. She was bouncing on her tippy-toes, clutching her hands to her chest. "Oh, my God, I'm so nervous all of a sudden."

Kitty walked in from the porch with Mayor Charlie, and seeing them gave me a brilliant idea. I pulled my mother aside. "Does Mayor Charlie still use his chopper?"

"Yes, in fact, it's over at the game right now," Kitty answered. "He was supposed to be in it himself, but he had his driver bring him here in case we wanted to leave early. You know, in case we want to do a little celebratin' in private."

"TMI, Mother," I said. "Waaaay too much, as a matter of fact. Now listen, will you ask Mayor Charlie if he could call his pilot and see if we can get Lewis on that chopper, so he'll make it in time?"

"Fabulous idea, darlin'! Let's ask." Kitty turned to Mayor Charlie, who was now talking to Sonny. They had stepped out on the back porch and lit celebratory cigars. That was a sight. My lover and my mother's lover in conversation as the sun began taking on the first hues of sunset.

"Hurry, Mother."

After a quick conversation, the mayor took out his phone and called the pilot. It was 6:10 p.m. and the guests were still being seated. Arthur was greeting people and glancing over at Bonita, who was helping out the Fru Fru boys.

Mayor Charlie said, "Get Lewis on the phone, Vivi, and tell him to go straight to my helicopter. It's where it usually is, and the pilot is waiting for him."

"Oh, my God, Mayor Charlie, you're a lifesaver!" Vivi grabbed her cell from the kitchen table and called Lewis, blurting out the message in an excited rush. "Yes, the mayor's helicopter. That's what I said. Run, baby, run! We gonna have us a sunset weddin', after all." Vivi hung up, beaming. "He's gonna make it, y'all. Do you believe it?" Vivi would have her prince arrive by stagecoach, after all. And an airborne one at that!

Arthur had heard the news and he came up the back steps to hug the mayor, then Sonny, doling out man-style back slaps and handshakes. "Thank you, Mayor. How ya doin', Sonny?"

"Just fine," Sonny said. "I hear you're the lucky son of a gun giving away our Miss Red tonight."

"I am that for sho'," Arthur answered proudly, and laughed. "Always loved that child like she was my own. She is something extra special. Hey, anybody see a big beautiful girl come through here?"

"You lookin' for Bonita?" Sonny asked.

"The one and only."

About that time, Bonita emerged from the powder room and gave Arthur the once-over. "My, my, sugar, you are lookin' mighty dapper in that tux."

"You are quite stunning yourself," he said appreciatively.

"You compliment me like that, and I'm gonna have to keep you around," she said, winking at him, then kissing him on the cheek.

Bonita looked like something out of a slick fashion magazine. Her bouncy shoulder-length hair was cut in long layers with light bangs hanging just over her right brow. She had on a pink silk suit with a skirt, and carried a cream-colored evening bag encrusted with little crystals and pearls. Her pink satin peep-toe sling-backs were dyed to match her outfit. She was a vision that would stop traffic, and Arthur always lit up like a streetlight at the sight of her.

Arthur had precooked almost everything and the two of them had enough hired help to keep everything afloat till after the wedding. Then they planned on running the reception start to finish themselves.

"Well, you gonna see me to my seat, handsome?" she asked Arthur.

He offered her his arm. "Would be my pleasure and my honor," he answered. They descended the back porch steps, and then off they went.

We all moved out onto the porch, when Coco came running up to the group. "It's almost showtime! I need to round everyone up and get you in your places."

It was 6:20 now. Ten more minutes for Lewis to arrive. The little orchestra was playing classical music, and the seats were filling with wedding guests, talking and laughing in anticipation.

Cal, Lewis's best friend and the computer guru whose tracking down Tressa made this wedding possible, was one of the groomsmen. He was meandering around in his tux, looking pretty sharp.

Back in college, no one ever thought he or Lewis would ever get married. They'd been perpetual players. Now Cal would be the last of the single guys from the frat days. He still looked like a college boy. It made me want to fix him up with a nice girl, but I barely knew any besides Vivi and me, and we were taken. *Maybe one of Vivi's cousins,* I thought.

I noticed Dallas in the side yard, watching Cal like a hungry feline looking for dinner. I shuddered. She'd had a major

crush on Cal during high school, but she was so full of herself and starved for attention that he never took her seriously.
Nor did he look at her now, even though she was there as a
seasoned reporter amid her media peers. I would definitely
not hook him up with Dallas. Dan The Man stood by her
side, but she paid him little attention. I guess she didn't need
him anymore.

Harry was there, of course, being best man, but he wasn't
in his seat. He was running all over, stumping as much as he
could, making the rounds and patting everyone on the back.
Judge Jane hung back from him, but I could see her watching him with a little smile.

We were all waiting on the helicopter, when we heard a
raucous cheerful sound in the distance. It was horns—and
drums...*and* flutes. No one could believe their eyes—or ears—
as members of Alabama's Million Dollar Band came marching
up the gravel road. They were playing the wedding march, alternating with "Yea, Alabama," the Crimson Tide fight song.
Cal must have arranged this. He had a nephew in the band.

I couldn't help but laugh. "Vivi, this is perfect!" I squealed.

"I love it, too! Lewis will be so tickled. What a fantastic
surprise!"

Jean-Pierre came running over, looking less than pleased.
"Blake, may I talk to you for a second? *Alone?*"

I stepped out of earshot of the rest of the bridesmaids and
wedding party.

"What in the name of sweet Jesus is this?" he demanded. "I
have a miniorchestra up there at the gazebo playing "Canon"
and these...these...*horn blowers* are crashin' my classy wedding!"

Coco ran up beside us, breathless with excitement. "Oh,
my God! Y'all aren't gonna believe this."

"What now?" I said, my exasperation hitting a new high.

"Football players," Coco gushed. "Uniformed football players, in tight white pants, are getting out at the front gate. The band is playing them in. Miss Myra Jean is for real!"

"Oh, my Lord, this has taken a turn for the worse," Jean-Pierre said.

"No, don't you see? Everything is gonna work out great. Miss Myra told me I was fixin' to be surrounded by men in tight white pants, remember? It's happening just like she said." Coco bounced up and down with joy. "If she were here I would totally kiss her!"

Jean-Pierre was upset as he folded his arms in a huff. "This is not how this was supposed to go, Coco. If you like this idea so much better, why didn't you just plan it this way yourself?"

"Lighten up, Jean-Pierre," Coco said. "Whose wedding is this, again? Yours or Vivi's? Now you take a look at that blushing bride and you'll see that this is exactly how it's all supposed to go. Miss Myra assured us this wedding would be great. And, really, how can you have a problem with sexy football players in uniform!"

"Lewis is gonna love this," Vivi said as she made her way over to all of us. "Y'all gave me the magic I wanted. We'll just count this as a bit for him."

"C'mon," Coco said, pulling Jean-Pierre's chin up from his chest. "Don't be upset. This wedding is gonna be talked about forever."

Jean-Pierre gave a reluctant smile. "I guess you're right. Lewis needs a bit of his own magic, too, and we did do an amazing job on the rest."

"Sho' 'nuff, sugar. I never could have done all this without you," Coco said. "Look at me. You are what make us, *us*. You're the *Dolce* in Dolce & Gabbana, and the *Ver* in Versace."

Jean-Pierre smiled for real this time. "Let's get this show on the road. One three-ring circus coming up!"

48

The band marched into the courtyard where the fountain splashed. They began the fight song and in ran the football players, just like they did at all the games. The team bus had arrived with a police escort, but I knew it had to be some of the second and third string since they had made it here so fast. First string was probably still hittin' the showers.

Coco had gone down to help "organize things" so he'd been in the middle of all the players. Deliriously happy that his prediction had come true, he now positioned himself for a perfect view of the football players lined up along the gravel drive.

It was 6:25 now and the sun was just about at magic hour, lighting the evening sky in a wash of pastels. Lewis knew how important it was to Vivi to get married at the magic hour, in the glow of the sherbet-and-turquoise sunset, and she was going to get her wish. Suddenly, we heard a roar overhead. The helicopter would be arriving in seconds.

Vivi and I hurriedly took our places at the end of the pecan grove with Arthur, Harry and the rest of the wedding party. The helicopter was loud now. Coco and Jean-Pierre rushed everyone to their seats. "Hurry," Coco called out to the guests. "Miss Vivi wanted a sunset wedding, and we are gonna give her one."

Jean-Pierre was scurrying to and fro, shouting, "Someone hold the quartet, please, till Mr. Heart makes it to the gazebo."

No one could hear him for the Million Dollar Band and the helicopter.

Nor had anyone given any thought about telling the pilot that there was no place to land. Well, no place close to the altar, anyway. The chopper overhead started a breeze in the garden. The little tree lights flickered, then started shaking wildly. Tablecloths were blowing and the tents suddenly leaned to the right.

The pilot, seeing all the waving arms, yanked the helicopter back up.

Arthur sprang into action like a superhero, running in his tux out onto the open field on the other side of the house. Jumping up and down and waving madly, his tuxedo tails flying, he managed to get the chopper to hover over the grassy area halfway down the gravel road near the plantation gates. Then he ran out of the way and watched.

The groom was landing like he was the President on Marine One. You could feel the relief fall over the entire venue. The missing groom had finally arrived. Lewis was in the field, getting out of the helicopter, his hair and tux blowing askew. He saluted the pilot and bent over at the waist to make his way under the still-turning blades.

I leaned over to Vivi and shouted, "See, sweetie? Lewis is here, and you're fixin' to be Mrs. Vivi Heart."

"It's about damn time." Vivi leaned over to me and gave

my shoulder a bump, smiling. "We got about three rays of light left. That man does like drama."

"Good thing." I winked and bumped her back.

Arthur ran back to take his place next to Vivi.

The familiar wedding march began with the little orchestra even though Jean-Pierre was trying valiantly to stop them. He gave them the cut sign, wiping his fingertips across his throat and violently shaking his head, to no avail.

It wasn't time, but the wedding march was the cue for the bridesmaids and groomsmen to start heading toward the altar, so they took off down the aisle in time to the music.

"Okay, Vivi," I said, not knowing what to do. "Here we go, ready or not."

Vivi looked at me with her eyes bugging out, "We can't go yet. Lewis isn't here," she yelled. "Stop this!"

"I can't. No one can hear me!"

The helicopter lifted up into the evening sky to head for home. Fortunately, Lewis had changed clothes before he left the press box and, as he made his way toward the rose gardens, he finally heard the orchestra—and the marching band. Panicked, he broke into a run.

Harry hadn't heard the command to wait, so he started dragging me with him as he headed down the aisle, leaving Vivi standing behind us, arm in arm with Arthur.

All of the rest of the wedding party was already waiting at the gazebo.

I yanked on my arm a little to slow him down. "Damn it, Harry," I snapped under my breath. "We were supposed to wait."

He smiled like he was doing the right thing and tugged me harder. "You mustn't have been paying attention when they told us to go when we heard the wedding march. Everybody else is already at the altar."

The music continued, and Harry and I arrived at the rose-and-azalea-covered gazebo. I realized Vivi and Arthur were still standing still at the end of the grove. There was no one to signal the musicians to play "Here Comes the Bride."

I spotted Lewis to my far right, running down the gravel road, dust flying behind. In a way, it was really romantic, the way he was running to his bride to be there as promised, at the altar, at sunset. If he didn't have a heart attack, he'd make it for the sun's last dying gasp.

Coco flagged the musicians, signaling them to wait for a minute. Instead, the orchestra announced the bride and started her entrance song.

Wide-eyed, Vivi began her walk toward the flower-bedecked matrimonial altar, minus her groom.

The Million Dollar Band pumped up the volume on their version of the same song as Lewis dashed up the road. He ran under a makeshift tunnel of cheering football players lining the sides of the drive and began his sprint toward the gazebo, trying to beat the music and make sure Vivi would not be standing at the altar alone, waiting on him.

Lewis was running hard and fast, his fists clenched, head up high, his dress shoes kicking up dirt and rocks everywhere. Vivi was taking the tiniest baby steps she could in order to wait for the groom to get there first, but, even so, she was almost to the priest.

Lewis breezed by me and dashed to his place under the tiny blush lights of the gazebo. The sunset glistened through the trees. Twilight was upon us. Vivi had arrived at the altar, right on time.

Lewis was huffing and puffing, watching Vivi take her last baby step.

"Red, you take my breath away," he blurted to Vivi as she arrived.

Everyone laughed. Lewis was so lovable.

"Dearly Beloved," said the priest from St. Catherine's as everyone took their seats.

"Who gives this woman in holy matrimony?" he continued.

"I do," Arthur answered proudly. He lifted her veil to kiss her cheek and smiled. Then he turned to walk back and settle in next to Bonita.

The vows began. Harry stood next to Lewis, and I was beside my best friend since third grade.

Lewis went first. "Vivi Anne McFadden, I cannot remember a day when I didn't love you. For as long as I can remember, you have been my source of laughter and joy—my soft place to fall. I give you *me,* all of me, till I am gone from this world. I have wanted to make you my bride forever. But I wouldn't do it until I could give you everything." He gestured to her blossoming tummy. "Seems like I have."

Everyone giggled.

"Now I can be the man you deserve." He rested his hand gently on her baby bulge. "And I promise to be the best daddy to this here little cheerleader. I promise to make you proud. I promise to make you happy. The same way you have always made me feel. You, Vivi, are my smile, every single day. I promise to love you and respect you and make you my partner in life. As long as I live, your happiness is my daily priority. Without you, life would be empty. I promise to fill you up with love and happy times in sickness and in health, for the rest of my life."

I looked around Lewis and saw that tears were glistening on Cal's cheeks. Even Harry seemed moved. My face was definitely wet, too. Thank God for waterproof mascara.

Vivi shook as she began reading her vows to Lewis. "Lewis William Heart, I have loved you for as long as I can remember. As a teenager, I dreamed of this day, and there has never been anyone else for me but you. You are my missing piece."

Lewis kissed her hand.

"Lewis, I promise to be here for you for the rest of my life. To support you and all of your hopes and dreams and plans. To believe in you and root for you and cheer for you. To always be on your side. To be your wife, your lifelong partner, your lover and mother to any children the good Lord gives us. I promise to be a happy football wife, knowing you are doing what you love in that press box. And I promise, on a football Saturday, never to nag you to hurry your ass home. Well, except maybe on your wedding day."

Everyone broke out with laughter.

She continued, "You are, and have always been, everything to me. You are my laughter, my joy…you are my heart…my Heart. I promise to love you and care for you in sickness and in health for all the days of my life."

At that moment, Jean-Pierre sent Harry The Humper down the aisle with the rings tied to his collar in a blush-pink satin drawstring bag. He had almost made it all the way when suddenly he stopped and looked up at Judge Shamblin, who was sitting oblivious in an aisle seat. Without any warning, he began a hyperhumping of her leg.

Harry the human was standing up front and couldn't do a thing. I giggled and Harry glared at me to stop. The judge slung off the poor dog, and Lewis got his attention and lured him to the altar.

"Come on, here, boy. You can do it."

The dog barked with joy at seeing his buddy Lewis. Everyone was chuckling under their collective breath as Harry The Humper trotted to the altar.

"Thanks, buddy," Lewis said, as he untied the little pink sack from the dog's collar.

Vivi turned and handed me the bouquet of soft pink peonies and baby pink tulips. The sun had set and the garden was awash in blush-pink twinkling lights.

Lewis slipped the platinum and diamond band on her shaking hand. She slipped her daddy's ring on his.

"Now, Mr. Heart, you may kiss your bride."

Lewis stood still, trembling, his piercing blue eyes staring into Vivi's with obvious wonder that she was actually his. He slowly lifted the tulle from her face.

Taking her cheeks into his big hands, he said, "I love you, Mrs. Heart." He kissed her softly at first, then pulled her in closer, taking her with the urgency of a man who'd waited for this moment for a very long time. He finally released her and smiled, still holding her face and looking into her eyes.

She laughed. "I love you right back, Mr. Heart, especially when you kiss me like that," she said, kissing him again.

When they finally broke apart, the priest said, "May I present to you, Mr. and Mrs. Lewis Heart." Media cameras rolled and flashes of cameras went off in the twilight. Amid whoops and hollers, Lewis and Vivi faced the guests. The Million Dollar Band played them out right along with the orchestra.

The football players had lined the sides of the aisle and formed the tunnel for Vivi and Lewis to run through. The photographer got a great shot of them as they made their way to the end. Harry and I followed at a quick pace to keep up with them.

As soon as they were at the end of the grove, everyone began getting up and running after them, tossing confetti in the air as they went.

This was just like the fairy-tale wedding Vivi had dreamed of. Okay, a tunnel of big ol' football players weren't exactly knights with swords, but they were pretty close. And from the radiant look on Vivi's face, it worked for her just perfectly.

Epilogue

I lay down in my bed at Meridee's house and took a deep breath to settle my stomach. A cold cloth draped my forehead. God, I hated being sick. I didn't have time for this. It had been about a month since the wedding, and things were just starting to calm down for everyone. My goal was to get my life back in order, starting with recovering from this bug. I knew I was just exhausted. We *did* have quite the exciting summer.

Unfortunately, Sonny and I had been so busy that we were not seeing each other as much as we would have wanted. Stumping with Harry was taking a toll on me. I was barely home most of the time, and all the fast food and fast-talking was not agreeing with me. I was running all over the state with my soon-to-be ex, and I was just pure worn down.

Whenever I was home, Vivi and I were like shopping fools, getting ready for Tallulah's birth, which was not too far away now. I admit that I was having a bit of baby envy. How could you not with all those cute little ruffled dresses we were buying, or the little Bama cheerleader outfit Lewis had brought home? Tiny shoes, tiny hats... It was all baby, all the time.

But, right about now, all I really wanted was sleep, perhaps some vitamins and *definitely* a vacation—preferably with Sonny.

Maybe after the election ended.

My cell phone rang. Speakin' of Sonny, his sexy baritone came through the phone. "Hey, princess, I have a proposition for you."

"Oh, my, sir. Your propositions always land me in a heap of trouble. Let me think." I paused a moment. "Why, yes! I would *love* to hear your proposition. Does it involve you getting naked?" Despite my feeling awful, nothing could make me not want Sonny.

"Me, naked?" Sonny laughed. "I think I could be talked into it, sugar."

"Then I'm in. What do you have in mind?"

"Well," he said, turning serious. "A college buddy of mine has me watching his cabin out near Tannehill for the weekend. I guess there were a few break-ins in the area recently, and he's worried 'cause he's gotta be out of town."

"And the potentially naked part?" I urged.

"Well, baby, the cabin is far away and very secluded. I hoped you might wanna meet me there. I don't think anybody would see us. I can text you an address for the GPS, so you can head over as soon as you're packed."

Relief and anticipation swept through me. "Sonny, I feel better already."

I jumped up and, in short order, packed my floral tapestry weekend bag and told Meridee what I was doing. She just smiled and didn't even tell me to be careful. I kissed her goodbye and drove off into the twilight, my excitement building with every mile. I flipped the music on, rolled my windows down and reveled in the evening air blowing through my hair.

He was sitting on the porch as I drove in and his face just

lit up when he saw me. He always made me feel so special. I loved seeing that grin on his face.

Sonny got up and walked down to me.

"Hey, handsome, you still got clothes on," I teased, reaching in the backseat and grabbing my bag.

He laughed and took my satchel. "I'll remedy that problem really soon." He gave me a kiss, then held me close. "You are a sight for sore eyes, Blake."

"I intend to be great for your other parts, too," I said, resurrecting my best bad-girl smile.

Sonny shook his head, but his eyes were twinklin'. "This is gonna be quite the weekend."

I gave him a playful hip bump. "Don't you know it, sugar." The fresh air must be doing wonders for my stomach bug because I felt wonderful and ready to take him straight to bed.

He squeezed me around the waist, and we walked together up the steps and into the cabin. He had opened the windows and the cool night breeze floated inside. October was in the air and the scorching temps from August were just a memory.

"I have missed you, beautiful," Sonny said, kissing me passionately in the quaint living room. He had made a fire in the fireplace and even brought apple cider. I could smell the delicious aroma of it, mulling with spices on the stove. We made ourselves comfortable on the blankets and pillows he had thrown on the floor. He sat down next to me, kissing me, touching me like it had been an eternity since we had last been together.

Eventually Sonny went back to the kitchen to pour the cider into mugs, and while he was busy my cell phone rang. I hoped it wouldn't be Harry again, ready to fill me in on my next duty as senatorial candidate's wife. But it wasn't Harry, it was my doctor. I had seen her only a few hours before because this bug had been lingering for longer than I'd liked. My heart skipped. A doctor calling on a Friday night couldn't be good news. I almost didn't want to answer. I didn't want anything to ruin the perfect weekend that Sonny had set up for us.

"I'm running to the powder room," I called to Sonny as I bolted to the bathroom with my cell phone in my hand. "Hello?" I whispered, as I closed the door.

"Blake, is that you? I can hardly hear your voice."

I turned on the water and spoke a little louder into the phone. "Yes, it's me. Is something wrong, Doctor?"

"Sorry to call so late, but some tests came back that I thought you should know about immediately."

"Okay," I answered, my heart racing.

"I ran a pregnancy test, and it's *positive*. You're having a baby."

I stared at myself in the bathroom mirror, clutching the phone to my chest.

"Hello? Blake, you still there?"

"I…uh, yes, sorry. I'm just…"

"Baby, is everything okay in there?" Sonny shouted from the kitchen.

"Sure, honey," I called back. *Just peachy.* I dropped my hand to my still-flat tummy and pressed, both shocked and amazed by the news.

"Thanks, Doctor." I hung up, still looking at myself, and exhaled. Nerves grew in the pit of my stomach. I knew it was Sonny's. I had been with only *him* since last May. But we had never talked seriously about starting a family. Hell, we hadn't even had a chance to be a couple out in public yet. I stared at myself in the mirror a bit longer. Was I ready? Was he?

Well, I thought to myself, *I guess we're about to find out.*

★ ★ ★ ★ ★

Acknowledgments

While writing this novel, one of my Sassy Belle sisters and closest lifelong friends, my "sister" Susan, was diagnosed with stage three ovarian cancer. The sadness and crying took over the writing at least for a while. It took a village of people to push me over the finish line. I am so grateful to:

Ted, my husband, and Brooks, my wonderful son, for being there for me every single second as I dealt with Susan's illness and my deadline. Brooks, I am so proud of the man you have become, quick to offer me your shoulder and always telling me you love me. Ted, I could have never finished without you and your love. Having the two of you is my ultimate blessing.

Susan's children and family, who kept me afloat during her crisis.

My mother, you are, as always, my strength and the wind beneath my wings. I love you more than any words could say. I can do anything because you have always told me I could.

My mother-in-law, Dr. Margaret Ishler Bosse, you were

priceless in the writing of this book. I kept your numbered questions beside me constantly in the final revisions.

My Sassy Belle sister Lynn Watts Zegarelli, you are the sane voice in my head. Thank you for talking me down out of the tree so many times.

My fairy godmother/agent/friend Elizabeth Pomada, in the wee hours before turning this manuscript in, I had your voice in my head and your edits laid out in front of me. What would I have done without you? You mean so much to me.

Clare Cavanaugh, you have been a fantastic writing coach and editor. I will never forget all of your hard work helping me whip this manuscript into shape with gentle pushes, working with me in the wee hours of the night, over Christmas, with the flu.

The rest of my family, Bruce and Janelle Albright, for always cheering me on. Corey Albright, my oldest nephew and my "other son" for the constant love. Always remember, you were supposed to be mine! Christopher Albright, for always giving me so much love! Joyce Albright, my other Sassy Belle sister, for all the delicious food and laughter! My aunt, Patsy Bruce, for always believing I would be a writer; one that actually got paid. My other in-laws, Dr. Richard Ishler, Dr. Ann Ishler and Dr. Richard Bosse, for all the support, always. My favorite teacher of all time, Dr. David Thompson. To say you changed my life doesn't even cover it. Julianne Ishler and Jake Ishler, my artistic niece and nephew, are you sure y'all aren't really MY children?

My fantastic family at Harlequin MIRA, Michael Rehder and Quinn Banting and the design team for the loveliest of covers. Beautiful and oh so sassy and Southern, I just love it! The terrific marketing and PR team of Sheree Yoon and Michelle Renaud, thank you! My favorite assistant editor on earth, Michelle Venditti. Your insightful guidance is purely magical. You hold my hand like no one else. My lovely editor, Valerie Gray, I am so thankful to you for continuing to believe in me and push me to be better.

And as always, to the place I will forever call home, Tuscaloosa, and my friends and family there, I love you like no place else on earth and hope I make y'all proud.

The Sassy Belles

SOUTHERN RECIPE SAMPLER

ARTHUR'S SWEET-SPICY BBQ SAUCE

INGREDIENTS:

1 cup ketchup
½ cup molasses
½ cup apple-cider vinegar
½ cup Worcestershire sauce
1 teaspoon onion powder
1 teaspoon garlic powder
1 teaspoon cayenne pepper
1 teaspoon chili powder
1 teaspoon ground mustard
½ teaspoon ground black pepper

DIRECTIONS:

1. Combine all ingredients in saucepan. Bring to a boil on
   stovetop and reduce to desired consistency.

—Florence Bruce

ARTHUR'S SAVORY RIBS

INGREDIENTS:

1 rack of baby back ribs
Arthur's Dry Rub
Arthur's Sweet-Spicy BBQ Sauce

DIRECTIONS:

1. Rinse and pat ribs dry. Remove thin membrane from back of ribs by slicing into it with a knife and then pulling. (This will make ribs more tender and allow meat to absorb smoke and rub.)

2. Coat meat generously with Arthur's Dry Rub, massaging it into the meat. (For Arthur's Dry Rub, combine all dry ingredients from the Sweet-Spicy BBQ Sauce and rub generously over ribs before cooking.)

3. Wrap ribs tightly with plastic wrap and chill for 8 hours.

4. Prepare a hot fire by piling charcoal on only one side of the grill, leaving the other side empty. (For gas grills, light only one side.) Always cook ribs on low setting and let cook through for tenderness. Place cooking grate on grill. Arrange ribs over unlit side.

5. Grill ribs, lid closed, for two hours, adding 5 to 7 charcoal pieces every 45 minutes to 1 hour, and keeping temperature between 225°F and 250°F. Add a handful of hickory chips to the charcoal every 20 to 30 minutes. Spritz ribs

with apple juice from a squeeze-trigger sprayer each time you add wood chips.

6. Grill 2 more hours, rotating rib slabs occasionally, adding hickory chips and coals as needed to maintain the low temperature.

7. Remove ribs from grill and place on heavy-duty aluminum foil. Spritz ribs generously with apple juice and tightly seal. Place foil-wrapped ribs back on the grill; cook 2 more hours.

8. Remove ribs from foil, place flat on grill, and baste generously with Sweet-Spicy BBQ Sauce. Grill 20 more minutes. Remove from grill, and let stand 10 minutes. Cut ribs into 3-rib sections, slicing between bones.

—Betty Albright Spavins

BONITA'S SOUTHERN FRIED CHICKEN

INGREDIENTS:

1 whole chicken cut into 8 pieces—2 breasts, 2 legs, 2 wings, 2 thighs (I do not fry the back)
¾ to 1 cup all-purpose flour
1 to 1 ½ teaspoons freshly ground black pepper
1 to 1 ½ teaspoons salt (can use seasoned salt)
Vegetable oil (use enough in skillet to come up the pieces about halfway, or substitute with Crisco shortening)

DIRECTIONS:

1. In big bowl, soak chicken in enough salt water to cover the pieces and refrigerate overnight. (Add about 1 tablespoon of salt per cup of water.)

2. Drain chicken, but do not pat it dry.

3. In a wide, shallow bowl or plate, mix together flour, pepper and salt. Roll chicken in flour mixture to coat. Refrigerate for 20 to 30 minutes, then coat again. (This step turns a good crust into a great crust.)

4. Put oil in pan, heat on medium-high heat until very hot. Place the coated chicken pieces in the oil, being sure not to crowd the pan. Cover the pan and turn down the heat to medium.

5. After 12 to 15 minutes, the bottoms of the pieces will be brown. Turn over and cover, continue cooking until brown on all sides. Adjust the temperature if chicken seems to be browning too fast.

6. Remove the breasts after 12 to 15 minutes, depending on their size. The dark meat takes a little longer.

7. All the chicken will be ready in about a half hour. Remove from pan, drain off fat onto thick layers of paper towel, and serve with mashed potatoes and gravy.

—Lynn Watts Zegarelli

VIVI'S SOUTHERN DEVILED EGGS

INGREDIENTS:

6 eggs
Salt and pepper to taste
1 tablespoon sweet relish
1 teaspoon mayonnaise
2 tablespoons milk

DIRECTIONS:

1. Bring eggs to a boil in a medium-sized pot, then reduce heat to low and allow eggs to simmer for at least 9 minutes.
2. Remove eggs and allow them to cool. (For faster cooling time, place eggs under cool running water.)
3. Peel eggs, then cut in half, collecting yokes in bowl together and cooked whites on a platter to be stuffed.
4. Take a fork and crush yokes until there aren't any lumps. Add salt and pepper, relish and mayo. Mixture should not be really thick, so add milk to thin and fluff. If mixture is still too thick, add more milk in tablespoon increments. Once mixture is the consistency you like, stuff platter of eggs and serve.

—Joyce Miller Albright

BLAKE'S FRIED GREEN TOMATOES

INGREDIENTS:

3-4 large green tomatoes, sliced
1 cup cornmeal
¼ cup flour
Salt and pepper to taste
1 cup milk
½ cup canola oil

DIRECTIONS:

1. Mix cornmeal and flour together with a fork until well blended.
2. Sprinkle tomato slices with salt and pepper and dip in milk, then coat slices in the flour and cornmeal mixture.
3. Pour canola oil into a large saucepan (should cover the bottom of pan but not the tomatoes). When oil is hot, add the tomatoes, but don't put too many slices in pan at one time. They should never overlap or touch each other.
4. Fry tomatoes over medium to high heat until golden brown. Remove and place on paper towel to drain. Serve hot.

—Joyce Miller Albright

MERIDEE'S FRIED OKRA

INGREDIENTS:

Oil or Crisco shortening, enough to come halfway up the side of your pan

2 pounds fresh okra, sliced ½-inch thick. (Thinner than this and it burns all up into nothing. Okra must be fresh. If you don't cook it when you get it home, it will get too hard in the fridge.)

½ cup cornmeal

½ cup buttermilk

1 cup flour

2 teaspoons seasoned salt or plain salt

¼ teaspoon cayenne (or black pepper if you don't like spicy foods)

DIRECTIONS:

1. Heat oil in a large, heavy skillet (cast-iron is best) to 350°F.

2. In a separate bowl, mix cornmeal, flour, salt and pepper.

3. Dip okra in buttermilk and then in meal-flour mixture. Add to oil and cook until golden brown.

4. Remove and drain on paper towels. Serve hot, with hot pickled pepper sauce on the side.

—Lynn Watts Zegarelli

KITTY'S SOUTHERN COLESLAW

INGREDIENTS:

1 small fresh cabbage, grated coarsely
Salt and pepper to taste
½ onion, finely chopped
1 ½ tablespoons of dill pickle relish (or chop up whole dill pickles)
1 large tablespoon mayonnaise

DIRECTIONS:

1. Place grated cabbage in large bowl and lightly sprinkle top with salt and pepper.
2. Add onions, dill pickle relish and mayo, adjusting to your preference. (If you use whole dill pickles chopped, also add a little of the pickle juice.)
3. Mix well and serve cold.

—Joyce Miller Albright

SOUTHERN BISCUITS

INGREDIENTS:

2 cups self-rising flour
¼ cup Crisco shortening
Buttermilk
Butter

DIRECTIONS:

1. Preheat oven to 450°F.
2. Put flour in a bowl and make a well at the center with hands. Add shortening into the well, then begin cutting it into the flour.
3. Add buttermilk until the mixture is sticky, then roll the mixture into flour on the sides of bowl until it forms a stiff dough.
4. Roll small balls of dough (should be about 2 inches round) in your hands and place onto a greased cast-iron pan. Press with fingers to form a biscuit shape. Continue until all dough is gone.
5. Add a pat of butter on top of each biscuit and bake until golden brown. Butter insides of biscuits immediately after removing from oven.

—Connie Hunnicutt Stringer

SONNY'S POUND CAKE

INGREDIENTS:

1 cup butter
½ cup shortening
2 cups white sugar
3 eggs
3 cups all-purpose flour
1 teaspoon vanilla extract
1 teaspoon lemon extract
7 fluid ounces lemon-lime flavored carbonated beverage

DIRECTIONS:

1. Preheat oven to 325°F. Grease and flour a 10-inch Bundt pan.

2. In a large bowl, cream together the butter, shortening and sugar until light and fluffy.

3. Beat in the eggs one at a time, then stir in the vanilla and lemon extracts. Beat in the flour alternately with the lemon-lime soda, mixing until just incorporated.

4. Pour batter into prepared pan. Bake in the preheated oven for 70 minutes, or until a toothpick inserted into the center of the cake comes out clean. Allow to cool on a cake rack for 30 minutes before removing from the pan.

—Florence Bruce

MERIDEE'S SOUTHERN PEACH COBBLER

INGREDIENTS:

1 cup of flour
1 cup of sugar
1 cup of milk (can be 1%, 2% or whole milk)
½ teaspoon vanilla flavoring
1 stick butter
1 large can of peaches (drained)

DIRECTIONS:

1. Mix sugar, flour, milk and vanilla in a large bowl.
2. Melt butter in serving dish. Pour mixture into the dish over the butter and add peaches on top.
3. Bake at 400°F for 30 to 40 minutes.

—Joyce Miller Albright

ALABAMA PECAN PIE

INGREDIENTS:

1 cup granulated sugar
1 cup dark brown sugar
1 stick butter or margarine (softened)
3 eggs
2 tablespoons flour
2 tablespoons milk
1 cup chopped pecans
1 9-inch pie shell

DIRECTIONS:

1. Mix all ingredients together and bake in a 9-inch pie shell for 50 minutes to 1 hour until browned and set.

—Connie Hunnicutt Stringer

KITTY'S APPLE BUNDLES

INGREDIENTS:

2 Granny Smith apples (peel and cut each apple into sixteen equal pieces)
2 tubes of store-bought crescent rolls
2 sticks margarine
1 ½ cups sugar
1 teaspoon cinnamon
1 can (10 oz.) Mountain Dew soft drink

DIRECTIONS:

1. Preheat oven to 350°F.
2. Roll two pieces of apple in a crescent roll and place in a 9x13-inch greased baking dish. Repeat until all apples are rolled.
3. Melt margarine and mix with sugar and cinnamon. Pour over apple bundles.
4. Pour Mountain Dew over bundles, and bake for approximately 45 minutes. (Yield: 16 bundles.)

—Nikki Neighbors Perez

THE FRU FRUS' STRAWBERRY BRIDE'S CAKE

INGREDIENTS: (SERVES 12)

1 package strawberry cake mix
1 container frozen strawberries in sugar (thawed)
2 8-oz. containers of Cool Whip (thawed)
1 can sweetened condensed milk

DIRECTIONS:

1. Bake cake according to directions and cool.

2. In large punch bowl, crumble half of cake into bottom layer.

3. In a separate bowl, combine one container of Cool Whip, sweetened condensed milk and strawberries. Pour a layer of this strawberry mixture over crumbled cake. Repeat to create layers.

4. Top the final cake layer with remaining container of Cool Whip. Garnish with fresh strawberries. Refrigerate 2 hours before serving. (Cake must remain refrigerated.)

—Janie Wallace

THE FRU FRUS' RED VELVET GROOM'S CAKE

CAKE INGREDIENTS:

1 stick softened butter
1 ½ cups sugar
2 eggs
2 ounces red food coloring
1 cup buttermilk
2 heaping tablespoons cocoa
2 ¼ cups cake flour (don't use all-purpose)
1 teaspoon vanilla extract
1 teaspoon baking soda

DIRECTIONS:

1. Preheat oven to 350°F.

2. Cream together butter and sugar. Add eggs one at a time, beating after each one.

3. In small bowl, mix red food coloring and cocoa until cocoa is completely dissolved. Add to the creamed sugar/butter.

4. With electric mixer on low speed, add buttermilk and flour in alternating fashion, beginning and ending with flour. Mix well, but do not overbeat (which will make cake too dense).

5. Add vanilla and mix well, then mix baking soda into batter.

6. Pour into two floured and greased 9-inch round pans. Bake in preheated oven for 25 to 30 minutes. Cool and frost.

ICING

ICING INGREDIENTS:

1 pound softened cream cheese (soften by setting out—do not microwave)
4 cups confectioner's sugar (10x), sifted
2 sticks softened unsalted butter (soften by setting out—do not microwave
1 teaspoon vanilla extract

DIRECTIONS:

1. In a stand mixer with the paddle, or with a hand-held mixer in a big bowl, mix cream cheese, sugar and butter on low speed until well combined.
2. Turn to high and mix until frosting is light and fluffy, about 4 to 5 minutes. During the mixing, scrape sides of bowl with a spatula a few times to catch everything.
3. Frost cake!

—Lynn Watts Zegarelli

BONITA'S GOLDEN PUNCH

INGREDIENTS:

1 large carton of orange juice
1 can of frozen lemonade
1 large can of pineapple juice
1 ½ cups of sugar
6 cups of water
7 bananas
2-litre bottle of 7-Up (or ginger ale)

DIRECTIONS:

1. Puree bananas in a blender with some of the juice. Pour into a large container with all remaining ingredients and mix well.
2. Fill three gallon-size Ziploc bags with 8-9 cups in each and freeze overnight.
3. When ready to serve, empty one bag of the frozen punch into a punch bowl and scrape it so it becomes slushy. Use about ¾ of the bottle of 7-Up (or ginger ale) per gallon bag.

—Veronica Dawson